[redacted] THE &

RITA AWAR

"[Grant writes] hig ad-ventures about aviatrix heroines."

—Chris Gilson, author of *Crazy for Cornelia*

THE STAR PRINCESS

"Titillating love scenes . . . Readers who like their romances sprinkled with sci-fi elements will embrace this book."

—*Publishers Weekly*

"Sexy humor and playfulness make this tale of romance and political intrigue a hot buy! Grant gets better with each book, making *The Star Princess* her best to date."

—*Romantic Times*

"A fascinating storyworld. . . . I strongly recommend *The Star Princess* as a thoroughly enjoyable experience."

—*Romance Reviews Today*

"Witty dialogue, well-developed characters, and insightful explorations . . . abound in this funny, sexy story."

—*Library Journal*

CONTACT

RITA, P.E.A.R.L., and Sapphire Award Winner
Best Alternative Reality Romance—
All About Romance Annual Readers' Poll

"Susan Grant's splendid visual imagery, natural dialogue, and superb characterization . . . will wring your emotions, touch your heart, and leave you breathless."

—*Romance Reviews Today*

"Susan Grant continues her stratospheric ascent with her latest, combining action and romance in a gripping, thought-provoking package."

—*The Romance Reader*

MORE PRAISE FOR *NEW YORK TIMES* BESTSELLING AUTHOR SUSAN GRANT!

THE STAR PRINCE

Winner of the Dorothy Parker Award for Excellence
Romantic Times Reviewers' Choice Nominee

"Political intrigue, deadly intentions, and power struggles give the plot of *The Star Prince* the depth and passion that is fast becoming Susan Grant's trademark."

—*The Midwest Book Review*

Winner of the 2002 Colorado Award of Excellence

"Susan Grant [takes] readers on an exotic, exhilarating adventure . . . and proves she has a true gift for storytelling."

—*Romantic Times*

THE STAR KING

P.E.A.R.L. Award Winner
RITA, Sapphire, and Write-Touch Readers' Award Finalist

"Drop everything and read this book!"

—Susan Wiggs

"Excitement, action, adventure and wonderful romance!"

—*Romantic Times*

"Evocative and exciting!"

—Mrs. Giggles from Everything Romantic

ONCE A PIRATE

The Francis Award Winner (Best Time-Travel)
Two-time RWA Golden Heart Finalist

"Grant's background . . . brings authenticity to her heroine."

—*Publishers Weekly*

"The best romance I read this year!"

—*The Romance Reader*

"A delightful, sexy story [that] you won't want to put down. A real winner!"

—*Affaire de Coeur*

"*Once a Pirate* is a fast and rollicking adventure. Following [Grant's] career as she hones her craft will be a pleasure!"

—*The Romance Journal*

TAKING FIRE

The missile looked as if it would miss, fooled by countermeasures and some amazing evasive flying. But then it came around, its plume of white vapor sweeping in a graceful arc. Bree stared in horror as it followed her wingman. "Razor-two, reverse left—reverse left!" Sweat stung her eyes. "Missile on your six, closing fast." *Come on, Scarlet, come on.*

The SAM was a half-mile behind. And then a quarter-mile. Dread tightened her throat. "*Harder left!*"

Bree jerked, startled as smoke and debris made sudden daytime fireworks. *Cam!*

Ah, God. There couldn't be a worse thing to witness than watching your best friend take a direct hit.

A warning alarm trilled in her headset. Bree wrenched her attention back inside. Lights in the cockpit flashed at her. A stoic computer-generated voice urged: *"Counter, counter."*

The other missile was locked on her.

Other *Love Spell* books by Susan Grant:

THE STAR PRINCESS
THE ONLY ONE (anthology)
CONTACT
A MOTHER'S WAY ROMANCE ANTHOLOGY
THE STAR PRINCE
THE STAR KING
ONCE A PIRATE

THE LEGEND OF BANZAI MAGUIRE

SUSAN GRANT

LOVE SPELL NEW YORK CITY

For my parents: Davis and Isabel

LOVE SPELL®

April 2004

Published by

Dorchester Publishing Co., Inc.
200 Madison Avenue
New York, NY 10016

ISBN 0-505-52542-9

Printed in the United States of America.

Visit us on the web at www.dorchesterpub.com.

THE LEGEND OF
Banzai Maguire

Prologue

If you have the chance to live life to the fullest, do it. Don't hold back, don't be afraid, take the absolutely biggest bite out of this existence that you can. The rewards are immeasurable, the eventual fulfillment soul-deep. I know. I guess you could say that I'm an expert on the subject. I've lived two lives, both of them to the hilt.

My name is Maguire, Bree Maguire. But you know me as Banzai, even now, after years of accumulated titles, honors, and a marriage have lengthened my legal name to the point where I can't help sighing long and silently at official events attended by those who expect and actually enjoy that sort of pomp, pageantry those closest to me know I'd rather avoid—the same people who know I never would.

Ceremony is a small sacrifice to make, you see. Once, I gave up everything that is important to a person. But, I would have died for my country, if asked. Instead, I was reborn into something better, something stronger. The United States was, too.

My quest took me to places I never imagined—not only geographical, but of the heart. It was how I first met the man who would be everything to me.

Now that I'm one hundred years into this winding path called life, my children tell me that I should record my memoirs before I pass on and leave the chore to the official biographers, who'll no doubt use the opportunity to make me into more of a legend than I already am—to my dismay, because the men and women I consider the true heroes went on with their lives after their deeds were done, some quite humbly and certainly without the idolization directed toward me and my husband. They are the ones who deserve our remembrance, those men and women. And now, here in this record of what happened, they will receive recognition.

You may wonder if our pasts were as colorful as they seem, if our adventures were truly as fantastic and wild as you learned in school. Why, yes, they were. They were all that, and more. . . .

2006

Chapter One

A can of Coke fell out of the soda machine and into Captain Bree Maguire's hand. She popped the lid and took a drink before rejoining the three other F-16 pilots in the hallway outside the squadron briefing rooms. It was a quick break before they made the trek over to life support to dress for their missions. "Cajun" Coley and his wingman were off to the practice range, but Bree and her wingman, Cam "Scarlet" Tucker, were headed out for the real thing: a patrol sortie over North Korea.

She delicately muffled a burp with the back of her hand. "Excuse me."

Cajun watched her with amused eyes. "You're sucking that puppy down, Banzai."

"I've got a low-caffeine warning begging to be extinguished." She took another greedy drink of her Coke.

"I thought you only did unleaded."

Bree wrinkled her nose. "Not at breakfast. Have you ever tasted a Milky Way washed down with Diet Coke?" She tore open the wrapper of her candy bar and took a bite. "Mmm. That's better."

"You're the only one I know who can make a Coke and a candy bar a two-course gourmet meal," Cam commented in her Georgian accent.

"Double the sugar-high, double the fun." Bree dug in her pocket for change. "Pick your poison, guys. I'm buying."

Cajun rubbed his stomach. "No, thanks. I already ate."

"Let me guess. Corned beef hash and eggs. Enlisted Mess."

"Yup."

Every officer at Kunsan Air Base knew that was where you got the best chow. If only she could quit slapping the snooze button on her alarm clock a half dozen times or more, she might work in a real meal before a morning flight. But sleep always seemed to win out over food. She grabbed eight hours whenever she could get them.

And Cajun wore the extra protein better than she ever could, she reasoned, noting his physique in a casual, red-blooded-American-girl-who-appreciated-hard-bodies sort of way. Cajun lifted weights—all the pilots did, including Bree and Cam, the squadron's only women. Building muscle increased the body's tolerance to high g-forces, which were fundamental to aerial combat. But Cajun must have stepped up his workout lately. Sweet. She ought to thank him for the effort. Stretched deliciously taut over his chest, the green fire-retardant fabric called nomex never looked so fine.

Bree glanced at her watch. "Ten past seven, Cam," she said. "We're outta here." She crumpled her candy bar wrapper and threw it in the trash, took a few more stinging swallows of Coke, and did the same with the can. "See you later, sweet thing," she told Cajun.

She pushed open a door that led toward the life support side of the building. In all his tight-bod glory, Cajun stared after her.

Laughing, Cam followed. "Ooh, he's not going to let that go, Bree."

"I wouldn't expect him to." Bree's mouth tipped in a lopsided grin others said matched her sardonic sense of humor, a humor that certain high-level brass didn't always appreciate. But Bree always considered herself a "fast burner," an up-and-coming flight officer with a bright future. No way would she risk her career for a laugh. True, her love of mischief lured her into throwing an occasional wrench into the system, just to see what happened, but deep down she was the kind of person who appreciated and admired the workings of a good machine. She supposed that was why she'd dedicated her life to keeping the one called the "US of A" well oiled and running fine.

Following in their six o'clock and rejoining fast, Cajun looked downright rattled. "Hey, Banzai!" His voice was familiar as a brother's and spiked expectedly with indignation, disbelief, and a good dose of challenge. "What'd you call me?"

"Sweet thing," Bree drawled over her shoulder.

"*Sweet* . . . thing?"

"Well, you are."

"Sweet, that is," Cam finished for her.

Bree nodded. "From an objective, female point of view, of course."

"Shee-at," he muttered.

"Check him out," Cam said. "He doesn't know whether to squirm or preen." Her southern accent always gave her banter an incongruous coating of graciousness.

"Is Scarlet right?" Bree smirked over her shoulder. "Are you blushing, Cajun?"

The pilot muttered something undoubtedly graphic. Bree grinned. She liked throwing Cajun off balance. When it came to teasing, no one in the squadron got a break. You had to be able to take the heat—on the ground and in the air. And the women gave back as good as they got, especially with men like Cajun, who'd come into the squadron certain that he was one hot stick, certain he could outfly everyone there—Bree, especially, because she was "only a female." Ah, but he'd learned humility. At her hands. He'd once told her that not only did she live up to her call sign, "Banzai," she deserved it. He was probably right. Japanese ancestry may have won her the nickname, but her flying was the reason it stuck. People could debate all they wanted about the fine line between insane and fearless, but her, she laughed at danger; she loved the rush. As an F-16 driver she pushed the limits, skated on the edge. The more risk involved, the more eager she was to tackle the mission. She was everything she wasn't in her personal life, where she preferred to proceed with caution, yellow warning lights flashing.

But even though she liked pushing the envelope, she never allowed herself to forget that being a good fighter pilot took work, hard work. Without discipline, focus, and an unquenchable passion for excellence, she'd likely wind up in the center of a smoking hole. She was twenty-eight; she hadn't given destiny a whole lot of thought, but one thing she did know was that she didn't want it to be *that*.

The hallway ended in the squadron life support shop, which was adjacent to a locker room where the pilots dressed for their missions.

"So, what about Cajun?" Cam asked Bree when the men were out of earshot.

"Cajun? What about him?"

"I think you ought to invite him over to your place tonight."

Bree gave her an incredulous look. "I don't think so."

"Why not? There's a spark there. I saw it."

"Spark? That was just my libido when I looked at his butt."

"See? You have so much in common. He *has* a cute ass, and you *like* them. Asses, that is. Male ones."

Bree laughed. "Shut up and get dressed."

Grinning, her friend reached around behind her neck and took off a pearl on a chain that the flight surgeon she was dating had given her. She placed the necklace in a basket in her locker. "There's nothing wrong with seeing if there's more, you know."

"There's not more."

"If you don't take the risk, you'll never find out."

Bree groaned. "Hello? We're talking about Cajun Coley."

"Admit it, Maguire. You're afraid," Cam teased. "Afraid to let a man get too close. It's a cliché but . . ." She turned away, that familiar prove-me-wrong expression on her face.

What could Bree say? She liked to keep her distance, and Cam knew it. Yeah, she'd suffered through her share of crushes, had fallen in lust a number of times, but she'd never been in love. Not really. She figured she'd know when it happened. It wasn't that she was looking for love; she was waiting for it to find her.

Frowning, she twisted off her U.S. Air Force Academy class ring and stored it in the locker. Of course, there was always the option of having a hot little fling with Cajun and be none the worse for it. But if that were the case, why did the whole idea feel so . . . so *unappealing?* There was nothing wrong with casual relationships. In fact, most of her recent relationships would fit neatly in that category. But she'd reached a point in her life where she'd grown out of quickie affairs, and yet hadn't found a man with whom she desired more. Lately, the only action she saw anymore was in her F-16.

But for now, the between-girlfriends conversation was over. Both women turned serious as they readied for the mission. If you didn't pay attention when you dressed for a sortie, you might leave something behind that could cost you your life.

Bree ripped off all the squadron patches from her flight suit and jacket with a loud hiss of Velcro before stowing the patches in her locker. Now, her flight suit was a blank slate except for her rank. It wouldn't do to have the enemy find out who paid for the fuel in her jet. Name, rank, service number, and date of birth: That's all they had the right to know.

Over her stripped uniform went a g-suit—"fast-pants," trousers with built-in air bladders that filled with the onset of g-forces, helping keep blood in the upper part of the body, especially the head, where its loss could cause a blackout with fatal consequences. Next on were her survival vest and a knife. She'd gone through this routine many times, but it never became rote. She thought about each and every step, making sure she did it right, especially when it was time to sign out a 9mm semiautomatic with one clip loaded and the other to stow in her right-leg pocket. That pocket was full of valuables, in fact: a weather-coated evasion map rimmed with handy-dandy basic survival information, a spare pocketknife, and her blood chit, a note written in fifteen languages promising gratitude—and a wad of cash to back it up—to anyone who helped her out if she was shot down.

The pistol went in a holster against her ribs and under her left arm. Then she removed her helmet from its storage peg and dropped it in the green cloth bag she would use to carry it to the airplane.

She met Cam's eyes. "Packed and ready." Cam nodded, and together they turned on their heels, as if already flying in formation, and walked outside to the flight line. Cajun and his wingman followed.

It was still dark, late winter in northern Asia. The air was so dry and cold that it hurt going down. To the east, a steel gray glow promised sunrise. In her head, Bree reviewed the mission to come. "This will be a U.N.–sanctioned patrol sortie," she'd briefed Cam earlier. "It'll be the usual drill, a flyover of the North Korea's side of the border during the first half, and over the South's for the second. Our mission is to provide a presence—and only that," she'd emphasized, more than once, although she knew Cam was well aware why they'd spend the next few hours carving racetrack patterns in the sky over the demilitarized zone, a no-man's land in effect since the 1950s between the two Koreas. The sorties were but one aspect of a broad, multinational plan to dissuade the two countries from starting a shooting war and keep them in the peace process that had dragged on for months now. As flight lead of the pair of F-16s, a position Bree had earned through rank and experience, she'd oversee the overall handling of the mission, tactics, navigation, communication, refueling, and weather, which in early February on the Korean Peninsula was butt-freezing cold. Fine weather for flying; bad news if you had to eject. Not that she planned to add that particular event to her schedule today, but she always briefed the what-ifs, all the same. Your number came up when you least expected it.

Cajun chucked Bree on her upper arm. He towered over her. "When you get back, I'm buying."

"I'm up for that," Bree said lightly. "I'll have a Diet. Maybe a bag of Cheese Nips. Ask me when we land."

"I meant beer. At the club. I want to hear more about my new nickname before I agree to it."

Bree looked down her nose at him. "Since when is 'agreeing' part of the process?" She turned to Cam. "Right, Scarlet?"

"Too right, Banzai."

Cajun winced, his expression one of inevitability. Just because he'd come into the squadron with a nickname didn't mean he was out of danger of a new one, and he knew it. Bree and Cam had been around awhile, but Cajun was the "new kid on the block" at Kunsan. The squadron's various initiation rites would be fresh in his mind.

"So how did you become Banzai?" he demanded.

"On Pedigree Night." Although it had been a year and a half since that night, she remembered every detail. Forced to buy—and drink—rounds of beer at the squadron's favorite local dive, she had the mission as the new pilot that night to maintain enough wits to offer up a relative worthy of the honor "badass ancestor." Squadron lore said that unless you could come up with a kick-ass relative, you couldn't prove your fighter pilot pedigree. From then on, you were a mixed-breed, affectionately known in the squadron as a pound puppy. But Bree hadn't even broken a sweat. She had Great-grandmother Michiko.

"She was four foot eleven, but she put the fear of God in every man in my family, and all of them were over six feet tall," Bree told Cajun. "The whole family owes our patriotism to her. She drilled it into us from birth." Bree threw her hand over her vest. "You'd better stand when they played 'The Star-spangled Banner,' and put your hand over your heart when you sang it or, oh, boy, Great-grandmother would be all over you. She loved her country. Her motto was 'don't be afraid of death; be afraid of the unlived life.' Well, she lived hers. She would have gone off to fight in World War Two if they'd let her. Instead, she spent the war in a Japanese internment camp, even though she was born and raised in Omaha. It tested her patriotism, she said, but didn't erode it. She got out, married a burly Roman Catholic Italian from the Bronx, and sent three sons off to serve in the marines."

One of them was Bree's grandfather, Sergeant Lou Vitale, a Medal of Valor winner who said his only surrender came after trying to produce a son to carry on the family's military tradition. He fathered seven daughters, none of whom had the remotest interest in the armed services. Then Bree came along.

She was the product of the second-youngest of those prim daughters and an auto mechanic of Irish descent. Her mother would buy her Barbie dolls, but she'd give each one a proper military haircut before sticking it in the cockpit of her plastic GI-Joe jet fighter. Grandpa Vitale would watch her play, a cigarette clasped in his callused fingers, his eyes shining with delight. He'd told her that she got her sass from her great-grandmother. Sass, Bree later learned, was what his generation called guts in a female. She wished he'd lived to see her accept an appointment to the U.S. Air Force Academy.

Bree zipped her jacket higher against the chill, and to ward off the weird sensation that swelled in the space around her heart. She missed the old man. "So, Cajun, to answer your question, when the squadron elected my great-grandmother, I toasted her victory, and someone shouted *banzai!* Then they all started yelling it. Ever since, that's what everyone's called me." She winked mischievously at Cajun. "Sweet thing."

"I told you," he said. "If you're going to call me that, you're going to explain it to me later."

"There's always the risk you'll learn more than you want to know."

"We'll see about that, Banzai-baby." He cuffed her again before they separated, headed for their individual aircraft.

"See you up there, Bree," Cam said, and walked off, too. Bree watched her go. Even dressed in a flight suit and combat boots, her wingman moved with bred-in feminine grace.

Cam's mother was a southern belle from a wealthy Georgia family and her father was an army general. Cam was supposed to have gone straight from charm school to hosting soirees for a West Point–grad husband. Instead, she'd pursued an appointment to the Air Force Academy. Tall, willowy, and blond, she defied expectations every step of the way, graduating at the top of her undergraduate pilot training class and kicking butt all the way through fighter lead-in training. She was Chuck Yeager crossed with Scarlet O'Hara, a top gun soaked with southern charm. Despite enormously different upbringings, Bree and Cam had become close friends.

But the strangest feeling swept over Bree as she watched Cam walk away. What was it? Something like affection mixed with regret, a sense of loss. A chill spun up her spine and she frowned. *Stupid*. Nothing was going to happen to Cam. But she shook her head as if it would clear her thoughts. Bad karma. She didn't like it.

Just be extra careful out there, she told herself.

Bree dropped her helmet bag by the front nose tire so she could inspect the sleek, gunmetal-gray F-16 that was hers for the next few hours. To her, the fighter was breathtaking, like a piece of modern art, all smooth lines and sharp turns—beautiful in a deadly way, like a bird of prey.

She walked around the perimeter of the F-16, checking for general airworthiness, and for signs of possible trouble that could take the form of puddles of fluid on the tarmac below the jet as well as stains on the fuselage itself. But today everything seemed to be in order, as usual.

Finishing up, she waved to the arriving crew chief, the airman who would guide her through the engine-start and taxi-out, and then climbed up a ladder into the cockpit, high above the ground. It wrapped around her snugly, that cockpit, as if the jet were custom-made for her.

Inside, she connected her g-suit to an air hose. Then, with an assortment of clips and straps, she attached herself to a seat that contained everything she needed for survival in the unlikely event of ejection: more survival kits, a radio, a GPS unit, a life raft, and, of course, her parachute. After her seat belt clicked closed, she donned her helmet, leaving the mask loose for the moment.

She poked her gloved thumb in the air, telling the crew chief that she was ready to start her engine. As soon as he acknowledged her hand signal, Bree lowered the clear, rounded canopy. It sealed her inside. She ran through her checklists, read from the booklet she'd strapped to her thigh. Everything not bolted, glued, or strapped to something was destined to fly around the cockpit. No pilot wanted that. You had enough to hold your attention *outside* the jet; you didn't need to create threats on the inside.

With a flick of her finger, the powerful engine rumbled to life. She checked her instruments for the engine's health, then put her hands up and in plain sight so the base weapons folks could remove the safeties on her guns. They wouldn't have touched her aircraft otherwise. She couldn't blame them; it must be disconcerting enough looking down the muzzle of a loaded gun without having to sweat the pilot's finger resting on the trigger.

Then it was time to leave. Bree taxied out, Cam behind her. She always looked over her wingman's aircraft, but she stared at Cam's a little longer than usual as the feeling of foreboding made a return appearance. Cam was fine, she told herself. Everything would be fine. It was a routine sortie. Bree forced her eyes to the runway ahead of her. The sky was turning from gray to blue, clear and cloudless. *You were born for this, remember?* Born to fly. Bree's spirits lifted with the rising sun. Nothing was going to happen to Scarlet. They were off for a little patrol duty and then would call it a day. That was all. "Razor flight's ready," she told the control tower.

"Razor flight cleared for takeoff."

The tower controller's voice came through her helmet headset. "Roger," she replied. "Razor flight cleared for takeoff."

"Two." Cam's response told her that she'd heard and understood the tower's instructions. Clearance for their "flight" meant clearance for them both. Cam would be rolling down the runway within seconds of Bree's liftoff.

Bree pushed the throttle up. The engine didn't rumble to life; it exploded—a multimegaton kick in the pants. Acceleration slammed her shoulder blades into the seat, and within seconds she was above a hundred knots and heading for twice that. The sheer force of the fighter never failed to awe her. All that power, in her control.

At rotation speed, Bree wrapped a gloved hand around the control stick of her F-16 and pulled back gently, sending the jet skyward. A glance over her shoulder told her that Cam was airborne, too.

Soon, Cam fell back to a tactical position a mile and a half behind her. Together, they headed to the airspace high above the DMZ between North Korea and South Korea, which they'd parallel from sea to shining sea—in other words, they'd race from the Yellow Sea in the west all the way across to the Sea of Japan, a body of water known as the Eastern Sea to the Koreans.

Bree leveled off at twenty thousand feet, relatively low, as cruise altitudes went, but where she'd been ordered to fly. Speeds and altitudes scrolled over the HUD—her heads-up display. The threads of data on a clear canopy showed her everything she needed to know. Down below, a few bomb craters were sooty footprints in the snow, evidence of a conflict that had people across an entire planet sitting on the edges of their seats. Bree got comfortable in hers and began what she hoped would be just another day in the office.

Somewhere high above her jet a modified 747 airliner bristling with radar and intelligence personnel eavesdropped on her radio calls to Cam. *Iris* could relay warning to the fighters, speaking to them directly, all while coordinating with the region's military commanders—and Washington, if needed. The integrated battlefield.

Ahead, the Yellow Sea gleamed like a sheet of stainless steel littered with cotton ball clouds. No threats, good weather. So far, so good. Bree thought of the bad vibes she'd felt before takeoff, and blamed them on too much sugar for breakfast. Sweet Thing might be buying the beers at the Officers Club after they landed, but Bree would get Scarlet a drink. It was the least she could do, after having spent the better part of the last hour fretting like a mother hen about the woman's safety. Cam wouldn't appreciate the solicitousness. Most of the time,

Bree was better at dampening her predisposition to be overprotective, to manipulate the parameters of her life so that no one got hurt. She was aware that the root cause was a psychological scar from killing her little brother.

Okay, technically, she hadn't killed him, but she'd been responsible: Brendan died while in her protection, and that was almost the same in her mind. The child therapists hired by her parents to help her through the tragedy had anticipated that reaction, and had used everything in their psychological bag of tricks to eradicate it from her six-year-old psyche after she took her brother and the family canoe for a joyride in the local stream. It wasn't the first stunt she'd pulled as a kid, and it wasn't the last, but never again would she have Brendan to take along with her. Spring rains had made the water faster and the canoe harder to control than she'd expected. She'd lost control. The canoe overturned and jammed between river boulders with her trapped beneath it. It was so dark and noisy she didn't realize at first that she was alone. But by then, Brendan had drowned, swept downstream where a neighbor found his body.

It had messed her up for a while, as a kid. Even now, most of what she'd consider her quirks stemmed from that day. She was an overprotective control freak who was afraid of the dark. Not that anyone would guess that about her. She could be such a "guy" when it came to sharing private doubts and feelings. It was one reason why she was better at flying than long-term relationships. Not that she was complaining; she liked being single. She liked having fun.

A burst of random radio static yanked Bree's mind back where it belonged: in the here and now, where she didn't have the luxury of letting her thoughts wander. She rolled up on a wing and turned back to the shore. Here, the landscape was very rugged and remote. The forest came almost to the beach, what there was of one: a narrow and rocky strip of sand, decorated she'd bet with mines and barbed wire instead of Pepsi bottles and empty containers of Coppertone. Another burst of static caught her attention as the coastline rolled under the belly of her jet.

Cam shouted: "Razor-two, Radar, RAW, hits bearing two-two-zero!"

Bree's pulse jumped with a surge of adrenaline. RAW was shorthand for radar alert warning. Cam's threat warning system had gone off. A radar site on the ground had turned on to take a look, telling them that somewhere down there a North Korean surface-to-air missile operator was tracking Cam as a cat stalked a mouse. It might want to pounce . . . or it might simply want to play. You never knew. But you had to treat every blip as a potential threat.

Bree answered quickly so Cam would know that her own jet hadn't picked up anything. "Razor-one is negative." She hated surprises like this. She'd read the intelligence briefing that morning, and it had been clean. Then she remembered a recent report on the North's shoulder-launched missiles. It was impossible to keep track of those. They could be loaded in a car and driven anywhere. Worse, an actual visual sighting of an aircraft wasn't necessary, as it had been in the old days. All anyone needed to complete the deal was a cooperative radar operator to help find a target. Then everyone with a personal missile launcher could fire away.

"*Iris,* what have you got for Razor flight?" The surveillance plane would have heard Cam's radio call.

"Stand by. We're checking it out."

"Checking it out," she muttered to herself. They could afford to sound that laid-back; they were sitting in a safer place than her wingman. But Bree tried to be patient. The intelligence gatherers were good, very good, and they'd saved her butt plenty of times, but they weren't perfect. They couldn't possibly keep track of every stray missile battery in North Korea.

Bree's threat warning system light illuminated. A swell of adrenaline froze her concentration into absolute focus. Her voice was calmer than she felt. "Razor-one has RAW. Nine o'clock."

"Two!"

She glanced from the warning light to her HUD, and then to the sky. It had been only seconds since Cam had reported her warning. Now someone was looking at Bree, also. But radar alone didn't pose a threat. Every fighter pilot knew it. The guys on the ground could aim all they wanted, but unless they were close enough, anything they lobbed over would fall short—and Bree was going to take care of that right now.

She accelerated, climbing to a higher altitude, anxious to put distance between her and the unknown threat before it became more than that. Cam followed, a half mile behind her. She'd rather go south than farther north, and she hoped Cam realized that, but the people on the ground checking them out were in that direction, keeping them on the northern side of the border. It almost smelled like a setup. But what could the North hope to gain by shooting aircraft engaged in operation Keep the Peace? With tensions as high as they were, it didn't make sense.

A loud alarm filled Bree's headset. She warned, using the radio, "Missiles!"

"Tallyho!" Cam shouted back.

Bree looked over her shoulder, craning her neck. There! Telltale white plumes of launched SAMs.

The ice in her veins surged like an arctic dam breaking. "*Counter, counter,*" Bree's threat warning system suggested in a female voice. But Bree was already releasing chaff and flying evasive maneuvers. Missiles came at you at supersonic speed. Confusing the little buggers was the only way out.

"*Counter, counter.*"

Bree gripped the control stick, wrenching it sideways, and pulled. Her vision narrowed. The sudden onset of g's was almost too much for her suit and body to fight. She tightened her leg and stomach muscles to squeeze the blood pooling in her lower body back up to where she needed it most—in her head. Her oxygen mask slid down her sweaty face. Harsh breaths roared in her ears as she sucked air into her squashed lungs.

Radio chatter filled her headset. Bree realized belatedly

that *Iris* was transmitting something about confirmed reports of SAMs in the air. Well, duh. *Sorry, no time to chew the fat. Gotta get rid of this missile on my ass.*

The aerial battle exerted tremendous forces on her body, alternating between the bone-crushing force of gravity and negative g's that propelled her insides upward and out. The missile streaked past. Woo hoo! It had missed! *Thank you, God.* But the missile passed her by only to lock on to Cam.

Bree's mood changed instantly. She was in a position to have a good visual on both of them. "Razor-two—missile at eight o'clock, low!" But Cam wouldn't have a visual. The SAM was in her blind spot: underneath and slightly behind. "Break right," Bree directed. "Break right!"

Cam flipped over on her right wingtip. The missile followed.

On Bree's HUD, Cam's jet was one of many shapes, whirling in a dizzying video-game battle. With her naked eye, she saw two birds of prey, one guided by mindless, mechanical technology, the other by human hands.

The missile looked as if it would miss, fooled by countermeasures and some amazing evasive flying. But then it came around, its plume of white vapor sweeping in a graceful arc. Bree stared in horror. "Razor-two, reverse left—reverse left!" Sweat stung her eyes. "Missile in your six, closing fast." *Come on, Scarlet, come on.*

The SAM was a half mile behind. And then a quarter mile. Dread tightened her throat. "*Harder* left!"

Bree jerked, startled as smoke and debris made sudden daytime fireworks. *Cam!*

Ah, God. There couldn't be a worse thing to witness than watching your best friend take a direct hit.

In the seconds that followed, Bree searched the smoky sky, fighting the emotion that if let loose would shatter her concentration. Then she saw it, an open parachute, and it was the most beautiful sight in the world. Even better was the glimpse of Cam's long legs dangling beneath the silk. Her wingman plunged down toward hills bordered by a U-shaped swatch of darker trees, a crescent of green in a vast sea of gray-blue conifers. At the speed of light, Bree committed the sight to memory.

A warning alarm trilled in her headset. She wrenched her attention back inside. Lights in the cockpit flashed at her. A stoic computer-generated voice urged: "*Counter, counter.*"

The other missile was locked on her!

Cam's ejection had sidetracked Bree—for only a few dozen heartbeats. But that distracted fraction of a minute might have been a fatal mistake. She gritted her teeth and hauled back on the control stick to bank away from the threat. Massive forces crammed her into her seat. *Not enough. Need more.* After what she saw happen to Cam, she knew it'd take every countermeasure, everything in her bag of tricks to escape.

Bree shoved the stick the opposite way and forward. Her seat belt and shoulder harnesses kept her bottom pressed firmly on the seat cushion, but negative g's thrust her insides upward, as if she'd just crested the highest hill on the world's biggest roller coaster. But her tactics weren't working. She'd have to reverse course, fly into the missile, and then hope her angle and speed would be enough to throw it off her tail.

Her threat warning alarm blared. She flew wildly. Ground became sky and the sky ground. Then, a painfully intense flash of light half blinded her. For one infinitesimal slice of a tick of the clock, Bree thought that the missile had missed, and that she was watching its flamboyant suicidal finale from the front row. But when something unimaginably powerful slammed her jet from underneath and threw her forward into her shoulder harnesses, she knew better.

The second missile had found its target.

Chapter Two

Transverse g-forces shoved Bree sideways. Her helmet clanged against the side of the canopy. Streamers of fuel gushed out of her left wing. The HUD gave almost too much information for her rattled brain to process. And then it blanked, giving her none at all. She hoped her mind wouldn't do the same.

Bree fought to keep control of the jet. A vibration in the fuselage swelled from a background buzz into a teeth-jarring rumble. Something screeched like the brakes of a freight train. It sounded as if the F-16 was coming apart. She'd have to bail out, she realized.

"If you're thinking of ejecting, you probably should have done it already." One of her instructors at basic fighter training school at Holloman AFB had told her that, and made her repeat it back to him. "Too many pilots die because they stay with their jet too long," he'd explained.

"If you're ever in that situation, lose the pride—don't let your ego kill you. Get out while the going's good and live to fly another day."

But had her instructor ever lost a wingman? Had he ever watched a friend fall into enemy territory? Surely, she had a few more seconds to pinpoint Cam's location, to ensure her rescue. The best chance at finding Cam would come from landing as close to her as she could. With their radios, they could communicate. Using global positioning units contained in their survival kits, they could locate each other. And then, together, they'd stay out of enemy hands until U.S. search-and-rescue forces caught up with them.

Bree's jet shook. Smoke began filling the cockpit. Then her engine shuddered and finally quit. Time attenuated, stretched out—a false impression. It was as if she had all the time in the world . . . and yet none at all. In that eerie in-between, she spotted a U-shaped patch of forest. There! It was the landmark she needed. She was outta there.

Bree took aim, grasping blindly for a handle between her legs. It was yellow with three simple words printed in bold lettering: PULL TO EJECT. Her gloved fingers closed over the handle and she pulled.

The canopy blew. Her seat rocketed up and out of the jet—with her strapped into it. The upward acceleration squished her like a bug. She seemed to hang in the air a few heartbeats. Then the earth called her back and she plunged out of the sky, still attached to the seat.

Wind beat at her exposed skin like icy paddles. She sucked in great gulps of dry air from her face mask until her throat was raw. She sensed rather than saw the ground rushing up to meet her. It was a sight she couldn't bear to watch. Luckily, she didn't have to for long.

She separated from the seat. The automatic parachute release worked as advertised. Silk boiled out of her backpack, jerking her up with ruthless force. Her hands clutched the risers, instinctively, hanging to the rough straps at her chest. Heart pumping, breaths ragged, she tipped her head back, examining the parachute above for rips and tears even though she felt more like blowing kisses of gratitude at the multicolored fabric outlined crisply in winter sunshine.

Then, her relief fizzled as the truth sank in. *You've been shot down, Banzai-baby. Over enemy territory.* What could the North be thinking, shooting down a peacekeeping patrol? They'd been making headway at the peace table over the past week. And now this: out of the blue, a reckless, hostile act. The Koreans needed peace, not more war. The act reeked of bad judgment.

As she drifted down, she knew that at that very moment in Paris an international tribunal was listening to testimony about the North's brutal treatment of South Korean soldiers captured a few months back and then released. She remembered the news photos of the survivors, and felt ill.

What waited for her down there? Beatings. Rape, surely. Bree shook her head. She couldn't think of that now. She was a soldier, all she'd ever wanted to be her entire life. Now it was time to step up to the plate and prove she deserved the title. From this moment on, her mission was to evade and survive. And to get her wingman home safely, a boggling responsibility that she couldn't allow fear to erode. So, she swallowed her nausea; puking seemed extraordinarily self-indulgent, under the circumstances.

Bree's gaze tracked downward to where a vast forest waited to swallow her. Trees, and more trees, as far as the eye could see. Landing in them would be like trying to hop across a bed of nails barefoot without getting stuck—or in this case, impaled on a branch. But there was something she could do to help her situation. She could try to steer. A pair of red lanyards hung behind her head, one on each side, designed for that purpose. By pulling on them, she detached four lines that released unneeded panels in the parachute, allowing her to maneuver. She liked being a driver a whole lot better than being a passenger, but the new configuration also made her fall faster. Buffeted by the wind, she plummeted toward the pointy treetops.

The ride rapidly neared its end. It was no longer a forest that she observed, but a series of trees that she skimmed. The trip would have been memorable in its beauty if only for the terrifying circumstances. Desperately, Bree tried to clear the tallest trees, but hundreds of shorter ones looked just as dangerous. Her boots began hitting branches and made a terrible scratching sound.

The collisions multiplied, slowing her and pulling her down into the green obstacle course.

Branches scraped across her helmet visor as she crashed through the trees. Twigs slashed at her with ear-piercing raking noises, leaving behind bursts of pain where they penetrated her uniform. Would she ever reach the ground? she wondered, her mind filling with nightmarish visions of human shish kebob. Her risers jerked, giving her whiplash. Crunching sounds added to the brutal beating as she flipped upside down. And stopped.

The hush was deep and immediate. Bree dangled like a discarded marionette while her brain tried to catch up to what had happened. Powdery snow floated in the air, forming tiny rainbows where the sunshine pierced through. Then a whiff of pine-tree sap hit her like a bracing slap in the face. It spurred her into action.

One of her knives was a hooked blade created precisely for the purpose of slicing through tangled risers that bound her to the tree. Hoisting herself up, bent double, she went to work cutting cords. It was an awkward position. Her stomach muscles burned and trembled, but she couldn't rush her selective hacking unless she wanted to do a Humpty Dumpty on the frozen ground, a good fifteen feet below where she hung.

One last cut, and she flipped over. Hitting the ground boots first, she absorbed the shock of landing as she'd been taught by falling onto her side. Using that momentum, she rolled into a clump of underbrush—dead twigs and old leaves clogged with snow. She discarded her mask but kept on her helmet. On her belly, she drew her 9mm and waited, straining to hear who or what was around. Her descent had been so noisy that anyone within miles would have heard it.

Her breaths sounded like thunder; her heartbeat was even louder. But other than that, all she heard was the hiss of wind passing through the branches high above her. No shouts. No shooting. Not yet.

Bree tore open a Ziploc-type bag containing her radio. With her thumb pressed over the transmit button, she whispered loudly, "Scarlett, this is Banzai." She released the button and listened. Nothing. She tried again. "Scarlet, Banzai. Do you read?"

This time when she released the transmit button, she heard two clicks. Her heart jumped, and she wanted to whoop for joy. Two clicks meant yes. Three clicks meant no. If Cam was clicking, it meant she didn't feel safe enough to talk. Bree chanced one more whispered transmission. "You okay?"

Three clicks came in reply.

Aw, hell. Was Cam badly injured, or were North Korean soldiers surrounding her? Or both?

"I'm coming for you. I know where you are." Well, she had a reasonably good idea. Okay, maybe a fuzzy idea, but she had to stay positive, to keep the faith. She waited a while for Cam to respond, in hopes she could get to a safer place and pass along her coordinates. But nothing. Not a sound. Not even the clicks.

It was time to raise the rest of the team. "*Iris,*" she

transmitted. "This is Razor-one." Static. "*Iris*, Razor-one." More static. "*Anyone* . . . this is Razor-one." Nada. She tried five more times with the same result.

With a sinking feeling she eyed the trees surrounding her. Beyond them were tall hills. It didn't make for ideal conditions for communicating with anyone. With a flick of her thumb, she turned on the beacon that anyone listening to Guard frequency would hear. Even the enemy. She had to risk it, though. Search-and-rescue teams wouldn't launch a retrieval effort unless they knew you were alive.

Bree let the beacon warble for as long as she could stand before cutting it off. The other prerequisite for the launch of a rescue operation was a location. As soon as she made radio contact, she'd pass hers along. The hand-held GPS in her pack could triangulate three satellites to calculate position within fifty feet. Pretty darn *Star Trek*, she thought. Too bad she couldn't program the unit to "beam her" back to Kunsan Air Base.

Pain soared out from her cuts and bruises, taking root in a sharp hammering in her temples as she stowed the radio. Her flight jacket and g-suit were tattered. Snow had found bare skin at her wrists and neck, stinging pinpricks of cold. She hurt, too. Everywhere. Some of those aches and pains were gashes from the trees. Others were bruises from bailing out. But before she could tend to her wounds, she had to erase all evidence of her landing here. With both friendly forces and the North Koreans on their way to find her and Cam, she wasn't about to give the bad guys a head start.

Her breaths rang harshly in the wintry silence as she yanked the mangled parachute out of the trees. After hacking the silk loose away from the remaining cords, she rolled it into a tight, wadded-up ball. Now she had a blanket or shelter if she ended up having to spend tonight in the open. In the patchy shade of the woods, she sorted through what she wanted to take with her: olive-green woolen mittens and a hat, a survival kit loaded with water, medical items, and maps. Then she discarded what she didn't think she'd need, like the life raft, the discarded parachute pack, and her helmet. Those items she shoved deep into the bramble bushes and snow so no one would find them easily. After checking for chambered rounds in her 9mm pistol, she replaced it in her holster. Then, using a compass, she jogged in the direction of the hills where she'd last seen Cam's parachute.

She ran all afternoon. Except for brief pauses, taking cover to analyze the next chunk of woods for threats and a place to hide before racing onward, she kept moving long after her energy ran dry, her survival kit smacking against her hip, her gear rattling. The terrain was hilly and wooded and fought against her every step of the way. But she couldn't stop, even when it was apparent that Cam wasn't answering her repeated attempts to reach her. A sense of urgency drove Bree, a feeling that she was running out of time. Plans and backup plans formed in her head. She'd find Cam, pull her into a hiding place if she wasn't there already. Then she'd patch up her wingman, if she was hurt, and figure out how to keep them both alive until they could pass their location on to search and rescue.

As the day wore on, she began to worry that someone had spotted her and was on her tail. The hunch intensified hour by hour and made the back of her neck prickle. For the hundredth time, Bree stopped to scan the desolate landscape around her. A lone bird warbled; a crow screeched. No people; not a soul in sight, but that didn't mean they weren't around, looking for her. The memory of the news reports of dazed, brutalized soldiers released from the North Korean prison camp invaded her mind. She shrugged off the horrible images—they'd only shake her up when she needed her wits about her. Standing, she drank deeply from her water bag as she studied the hills ahead that were her goal. It wouldn't be far now, she thought, and took off again at a full run.

Only when it was dusk did she finally stop. The air had chilled. The scent of pine filled her nostrils. No scents of human habitation came on the slight breeze. Listening and seeing as best the fading light would allow, she searched the area around her. It was empty, utterly remote, but the gnawing dread that she wasn't alone lingered.

She took out the radio. "Scarlet, it's Banzai." *Cameron Adele Tucker, answer me, y'hear?* Never in her life did she want so badly to hear someone on the other end of the line. The wind swished high above in the pines, where stars glinted icily, the way they did only in a winter sky.

With the volume control rolled way down, Bree listened for chatter, a signal. "Scarlet, you up?" she asked in a low voice. And waited, her heart slamming. "This is Banzai. Do you read?" Faint static only. Maybe Cam had left her radio off for the night so the batteries wouldn't run out.

Then . . . three clicks answered.

Three? Bree's heart lurched. Something was wrong. She wanted to get back on frequency and ask Cam a million questions, but if her friend could talk, she would have. "Hang in there, girlfriend. I'm on my way."

Radios worked better at night. Maybe this time she'd have luck if she broadened her plea. "Anyone, do you read? This is Razor-one" She tried a few more times in hopes that someone could hear her and she couldn't hear them—like when the mountains back home interfered with making cell phone calls.

Behind her, a twig snapped. Bree's head jerked up. Fumbling for her gun with thick mittens, she spun around, pulling the 9mm from her holster. Past her misty breaths, she saw three pairs of eyes glinting in the shadows behind the trees.

Yellowish eyes. Unblinking. The kind that belonged to animals, not people. They stared, unblinking, their bodies barely visible in the shadows. Were they wolves? No, too small. Probably foxes or coyotes. Or wild dogs. Yeah, the size and shape fit the dog category. Not that it mattered—she didn't plan on being dinner for these oversized pups.

One of them whined slightly and licked its chops. She could relate to the hunger. It'd been a long time since that candy bar. "Shoo. Go on. Get!"

When they made no move to leave, she took the initiative.

She kept her aim on the dogs as she backed up, carefully. A bark would carry for miles. But the dogs followed, their eyes intently focused on her. One of them growled. Bree released the safety on her pistol. It made a crisp click, loud in the quiet woods. That's all it took to spook the animals. They darted away like wraiths in the twilight.

When she was sure they were gone, Bree lowered her weapon and saw how tightly her finger pressed the trigger. That's how close she'd come to shooting at them. Stupid, stupid. She was too jumpy. Not only would noise have drawn attention, pumping valuable ammo into a pack of starving wild dogs would have been a total waste.

Bree holstered her weapon, checked the heading on her compass. She'd better get moving, even though she lacked a moon to give some light. The next creatures she encountered might not be so easily dismissed.

Riddled with bruises and sore muscles, hungry and cold, she pushed her pace. Exhaustion numbed her after a while, but she maintained a near run. A horizontal smear of shadows stained the ground ahead. Bree stepped into it and her foot kept going, followed by the rest of her.

The plunge took her down a steep bank. She landed in a heap just short of the edge of a fast-running creek.

Close call. Loose dirt and rocks continued to tumble past, plunging into what she'd bet was extremely icy water. Bree wanted no part of that swim. Cold, she could live with. Shivering, she could handle. But hypothermia would kill her.

She grabbed hold of a sapling and dug in her heels. It was all that kept her from slipping into the stream as she climbed back uphill, tripping and cursing as she went. She held a first-degree black belt in tae kwon do, a Korean form of martial arts, but there were times, like now, when she was convinced that she didn't have an ounce of grace in her entire body.

Her teeth started to chatter. She'd been resting for only a few minutes and already she was shivering. Her toes were going numb, but to make a fire was unthinkable. She had to stay low, real low.

The parachute, she thought, yanking it out of her pack. The silk would camouflage and warm her, something she'd learned in Survival Evasion Resistance Escape training, SERE, where she'd been beaten and interrogated in a simulated prison camp and then half starved while trekking for four days with two classmates through the Rocky Mountain National Park. It was one of those brutal courses from which you were proud to have graduated and glad you'd never have to repeat. But now she was damn grateful for every day she'd suffered that summer. The training would save her life.

She found some scrub for shelter. The branches were prickly and dry and smelled sharply of resin. Her body rested, but her mind couldn't. Images kept surfacing of her parents' faces when they would find out that she was missing in action. Bree was sure they knew by now. The story would be on every news channel, everywhere on the Internet: two women, in enemy hands. Bree squeezed her eyes shut and sent a mental message to her parents. *I'm alive. Alive!*

An owl hooted in the distance, and then again, farther off. Other than the lonely sounds, the night was one of black, crystalline silence. It was so dark that it made the air feel thick.

Bree hunched her shoulders and shuddered. Wasn't she a bit old to want to hold someone's hand in the dark? Who'd guess that an F-16 fighter pilot, a USAF Academy graduate, needed to sleep with a night-light?

That's when Bree noticed she'd tucked her gun to her chest. A steel teddy bear? Without a night-light, she had to make do.

She lowered her head to her knees, resting her head on her folded arms. Reality, hunger, and exhaustion melted away, and she began to dream. Then the sensation of slipping on ice made her entire body jerk, waking her. The crackling of twigs in her hideaway touched off a distant chorus of quickly silenced barking and yips. The wild dogs! They'd followed her. Naptime was over.

She pushed to her feet, checked the glowing needle on her compass, and set off, making a mental note to keep watch for a small log she might be able to use as a club if the dogs attacked. It would make less noise and accomplish the same objective as her pistol.

Dawn arrived without fanfare. Weak gray light trickled over the horizon until it had stained the entire eastern sky.

Her stomach rumbled. She was hungrier than she'd ever been. Ravenous, she cast her gaze about, looking for something that looked alive and edible. There wasn't much around that she recognized, and she wasn't that hungry to risk poisoning herself. So, she tried to pretend that she didn't want to eat the nearest tree, raw and whole, and distracted herself by imagining . . . pizza, long strings of oily, melted mozzarella falling as she bit into the slice. After the pizza fantasy, she started on fudge brownies . . . iced fudge brownies . . . with chocolate chips!

The daydreams of food were so clear and real that when a savory scent came to her, borne on the breeze, Bree sniffed the air like a starving stray. The scent of garlic wafted past, pungent and strong. Spicy kimchi made from aged, pickled cabbage. Bree had tried it, didn't quite care for it, but she'd do just about anything to have a bowl of it now. Saliva filled her mouth instantly. For a second or two, gluttony, longing, alarm, and confusion battled for supremacy in her mind. Alarm won out. The food might smell good but the entire situation stank.

A nearby rock outcropping formed a small shelter. Bree wedged herself between the stones, drawing out her pistol at the same time. Her breaths echoed sharply off the rocks. She waited. Listened. The smells meant she'd come near a village, or maybe a camp of some kind. Her heart thumped against her ribs, and her mouth was dry. From within her makeshift fort, she took a long drink from her canteen, blotted her mouth with her sleeve, and took one more 360-degree look outside. Then she got out the radio. "Scarlet, Banzai," she whispered. Counting to five, she tried again. "Scarlet, this is Banzai."

Two clicks interrupted the soft static. Two beautiful clicks. *Thank you.* Bree closed her eyes and let out a breath. Cam had heard her. She'd made it through the night. "Hey, I'm on my way," Bree said under her breath. "I'll be there soon. Stay low. People nearby. A village, I think."

Three clicks answered her. Three? Bree stared at the radio in her hand. What did that mean?

Maybe Cam was already in the hands of the villagers, and she was injured, too hurt to speak. Or maybe they were helping her. Bree's hopes lifted. Maybe they'd help her, too. Why not? Their countries weren't at war.

Or . . . were they?

She heard a soft bark, almost a snort, like air expelled from a muzzle. The dogs again.

Her heart turned over. Those damned dogs. They'd stayed on her tail the entire night! Maybe they weren't wild dogs or Korean coyotes. Maybe they were tracking animals. It meant her instincts were right: Someone knew where she was, every step of the way.

If it had been only humans after her, she'd have stayed put, hoping they'd pass her by. But you couldn't fool dogs' noses. If they passed her, they'd find her.

She decided to go for it and try to lose the dogs.

Every muscle in her body protested her sprint through the trees. Sweat formed under her flight suit, but cold air stung her eyes and nose. Dogs barked and yelped in the distance. She leaped into a narrow stream and ran up the middle of it, splashing through icy water. She'd get the dogs off her scent and worry about her frozen feet later. But there they were, skinny dogs bounding along beside her, their tongues lolling, their yellow eyes sparkling, as if this was a fun game. "Chase the Yankee," maybe? Well, it beat "Eat the Yankee," or whatever other games the dogs' owners might want to play with her.

Bree veered toward the opposite bank and dry ground. The dogs followed, barking loudly. It would seem she should be feeling hopeless right about now, but the worse her odds became, the more resolve she felt. *I serve in the forces which guard my country and our way of life. I am prepared to give my life in their defense*. Article One, U.S. Fighting Man's Code of Conduct. She'd first memorized the code as a freshman cadet at the Air Force Academy, but the words hadn't taken on their true meaning until now.

Her grandfather had told her stories of POWs who met the horrors of captivity with guts and attitude. If USAF representatives had to come to Chester, New York, to deliver the bad news to her parents, then by God, Bree wanted them to be able to say the same about her.

The sound of a truck engine broke the rhythm of her boots. A road! Where? Bree stopped so fast that she skidded over the slippery creek bank. She landed hard on her butt, stayed down, and rolled, scrabbling in on her elbows and knees into the brush. She couldn't run blindly onto a road and risk countless people spotting her. Pistol drawn, she peered out of the bushes, hoping to pinpoint the location of the truck. She was shivering. Wet and cold, her feet throbbed, rubbed raw in her squishy boots. Snow had worked its way between her flight suit and jacket. She gritted her teeth and waited for the ice to turn to water, which she knew wouldn't feel much better. But at least her exhaustion had vanished with a renewed rush of adrenaline. Terror could be so . . . energizing. Still, she wouldn't recommend it to anyone. For health reasons.

The dogs found her hiding place. Their paws scrabbled on the hard ground as they circled her. Bree held her breath. True, the dogs knew where she was, but she hoped, prayed that the people who owned them would somehow miss her. *Even when you think it's all over, when you don't have a chance, never reveal your hiding place.* She'd learned that in survival school. There had been stories of enemy soldiers tripping over the boots of Special Forces personnel in the jungles at night, never knowing they'd stumbled over anything more than a tree root. She was going to stay in place until circumstances forced her to move out.

The truck stopped. A door slammed. And another. Bree heard male voices next. She knew a little Korean, enough to get by in the local market and restaurants, but not enough to follow a conversation. She relied on body language, and in this case, the tone of voice to understand.

A wet-nosed dog muzzle thrust through the shrubs. Bree smacked it with the heel of her palm. The beast expelled its breath in a half sneeze and jumped backward, yipping. But the skinny legs and muddy little feet continued to encircle her. She heard the whistle of air going in and out of their noses.

Beep, beep, beep. Bree strained to figure out the sound. When one of the men began talking in rapid Korean, she knew what it was: a cell phone. Then she heard it—the word "Yankee."

No more doubts. They knew she was here.

Their heavy footsteps crunched closer. Bree flattened her body on the ground. The bridge of her nose itched. She fought an overwhelming urge to scratch it. The wait to see what the men would do now that the dogs had given away her location was interminable. She'd never understood the true meaning of the word until that moment.

Twigs snapped. One man coughed. And then Bree smelled a cigarette. She remained frozen in position, praying they would pass her by, praying they didn't notice the dog's interest. If luck stayed on her side, her pursuers wouldn't hear her heartbeat. She sure as hell didn't know how they couldn't, though, with it thudding so loudly against her ribs.

Then she heard the hiss of the lit cigarette hitting the snowy ground. At the same time, the branches sheltering her gave way and a hand shot through the bushes.

Fingers closed over the back of her collar. Bree reached back, slammed her hand around the thick glove. Hunch-ing down, she heaved on the arm and threw the man over her head.

The momentum helped her to her feet. And then she exploded from the bushes like a flushed quail and ran like hell.

Chapter Three

Bree dashed toward the trees. The men had a truck. The only way to up her advantage was to choose the type of terrain their vehicle wouldn't be able to handle.

She threw a wild glance over her shoulder. The man who'd tried to grab her was sprawled on his back, gasping like a line-caught tuna, while his partner stared after Bree with such obvious shock that it was almost funny. Obviously, he hadn't expected a woman.

Bree yanked her wool cap lower over her matted hair. With her gun tucked to her chest, she ran uphill. Her pursuers wore civilian parkas, not military uniforms. They weren't soldiers, or at least not openly so. Not that it mattered. They could still haul her off to prison, making sure to manhandle her just short of actual bloodletting before dressing her up for the customary televised propaganda interview. But she'd give them nothing to use.

They might force her to say she was sorry for flying over their country, but everyone would see in her eyes that she wasn't. She'd never apologize to a regime that had for the better part of a century kept their own people on the brink of starvation, while a privileged few lived a life of luxury enviable in any economy, in any country, all while they threatened the rest of the world with incineration by nuclear weapons.

Barking interrupted her thoughts. The dogs were back, running with her, their breath puffs of mist, their eyes shining with delight. One of them snatched at her sleeve, trying to slow her down. "Get lost, Fido!" Bree yanked her arm free. The dog ducked before she could whack it with the butt of her pistol.

The men behind her were on the move, too. She could hear the truck's engine, and it was coming closer. *No!* If these people captured her before she could rescue her wingman, what would happen to Cam?

Another one of the dogs leaped at her. It grabbed her sleeve, and hung its full body weight from her arm. She tried to shake it free as the second dog latched on to the back of her jacket. Her strength flagged as the extra weight dragged at her. Gasping, she stumbled forward. Her lungs burned; her chest ached. Water streamed out of her eyes and down her cheeks, stinging her windburned skin. But she would not give up!

Bree struck back at the dogs with her pistol. A muffled thump told her she'd smacked the dog's shoulder and not its skull. It yelped and fell away. Without missing a step, she started beating at the dog clamped onto her jacket.

The truck gained on her. It was white with extra-fat tires meant for rugged terrain and barreled over ruts and bumps and through the smaller trees as if they were nothing.

Bree bolted into the trees where the trunks grew closest together. *Drive through this, bucko.*

And he did, knocking down the pines as if they were saplings. The landscape opened up—a clearing where it appeared a long-ago forest fire had created a meadow. Bree slowed, searched left and right for cover. And found none.

Bree gritted her teeth and decided to make the dash across the open field, whacking at the persistent dogs as she went. She'd throw one off only to have another attach itself to her and slow her down. Finally, she hit one hard enough to send it to the ground. It didn't get back up.

A startling twanging sound ripped through the air. Something rustled above her, and then dropped around her. At first, she thought tree branches had fallen. But it was a net! It had come from the truck, from a catapult attachment on the roof.

Bree felt like a fly caught in a spiderweb. The snare was made of heavy, rough twine. She struggled to break free as the dogs raced around her, triumphant and barking, a frenzied game of ring around the rosy. She flipped them off. "Say it to the finger!"

Four men got out of the truck. Two of them she recognized from earlier. The guy she'd thrown on his ass wouldn't meet her gaze, she noticed with muted satisfaction, and flicked her wary attention from their faces to those of the newcomers. They appeared to be civilians, too.

Bree hunted for the edge of the net, but the hem had pulled tight, closing off the bottom. The only option was to cut her way out. She drew out her pocketknife and began hacking away. The net's webbing was thick, heavyweight. She worked feverishly. The two new men walked toward her with alarming purpose. There was no question in her mind that they planned to take her into custody. Her heart turned over. She'd already sliced open a small hole, but she needed more.

Come on, come on. She tried to cheat and stretch the hole before it was wide enough. Pulling on the outer edges of the tear didn't expand it an inch. The rope was too strong. She slashed at the webbing, her forehead soaked with sweat. The woolen cap itched at her skin. A few more cuts and she'd be free.

"Drop your knife," the taller of the two men ordered. It took her a heartbeat to realize that he'd used perfect English. A North Korean educated in England, she guessed.

Bree dropped the knife, but only to draw her pistol. Stealthily, she slipped the 9mm out of her pocket. Article Two, Code of Conduct: *I will never surrender of my own free will.*

Bree released the safety and waited for the two men to reach her. One was a heavyset goon of a man with a vacant face. The perfect Igor, she thought. He was big, and he had an even bigger gun, a kind of Chinese-made automatic rifle she recognized. He held it limp-armed, pointed down, but Bree knew that could change in a heartbeat.

The taller man appeared to be the boss. His parka was a few steps up in quality from Igor's, and his features were fine, almost patrician. The dictator's nobility, she guessed, the look of a greedy pig who satisfied his needs before those of infants and children. She knew all about his type. May they rot in hell, or whatever form hell took in their religion—if they even had a faith. And if they were atheists, may they rot anyway, and their brethren, here and around the world. They were why she'd joined the military, to keep people from having to live under their oppression, with no hope of ever breaking free. If these men thought she'd be their biddable little puppet, they were way off base. *I will never surrender of my own free will. If in command, I will never surrender my men while they still have the means to resist.*

The men stopped about twenty feet away. "You are not what I expected," the taller man remarked.

Well, neither are you, she thought. She watched warily as he beckoned to the two other men who'd hung back near the truck before turning back to her, examining her from head to toe. "A female, but you'll do," he said.

She'd do? Bree puzzled over that while the pair approached eagerly and accepted a small sack from him. Good Lord. What had he just done? *Paid* them for her?

Gah. It sure looked that way. It was like watching a transaction take place in the market. The men smiled, their heads bobbing in appreciation and respect. Cigarettes dangled from their mouths. Their hands were rough and dirty, used to labor. Locals. Farmers, maybe. Backing away, they whistled for the dogs—another question answered—the mongrel ownership issue. Then the group disappeared into the woods. So, Mr. Suave, Pay-peasants-for-pilots was a bounty hunter. He examined the hole she'd made in the net and then her, shaking his head as if she were a disobedient child. Bree frowned. Really? Is that what he thought? *We'll see how disobedient this bullet feels going down your throat, creep.*

"If you return me to my people, they'll reward you," she tried, thinking of the blood chit in her right pants pocket. And of the radio that couldn't seem to transmit past the hills. "Let me use your phone, and I'll call them."

"No."

"The Geneva Convention states, regarding the treatment of prisoners of war—"

He interrupted her. "You are not a prisoner of war."

You could have fooled me.

"I will now free you from the net. Drop your weapon."

Not that easy. Bree tightened her hand around her pistol.

The boss nodded at his monster accomplice, who lifted his machine gun. Bree heard the click of a safety, saw the red line of an infrared sight track upward. But she couldn't see where the beam ended, because Igor aimed between her eyes.

She swallowed. "Okay. Okay." But she took her time. Every little step counted when it came to resistance; she'd learned that in POW training. Ever so slowly, she opened her hand. Finally, the pistol hit the ground by her boots with a solid thump.

Igor stepped forward, grabbed the hem of the net—but not her pistol, she noted. With a mighty grunt, he lifted the heavy webbing over his head, holding it high, obviously expecting her to walk out from beneath it. While his hands were occupied, Bree scooped up a handful of mud and threw the dirt in the men's faces. As they struggled to wipe their eyes, she scooped up her pistol and took off running.

Bree ran harder than she ever had. Although the snow in this area barely covered the ground, it slowed her down. Pressing her elbow to her ribs to assuage a stitch in her side, Bree tried to increase her pace but couldn't go any faster. Her lungs hurt and her body burned with fatigue. Her energy had finally bottomed out. Shock, untreated cuts and bruises, hunger—everything had conspired to suck her dry. Igor was hot on her trail. She didn't dare chance a glance behind her; she knew who it was by the sound of his big boots.

The truck followed, too. She turned, fired at the tires. Dust kept her from telling if she'd scored a hit. She swerved her aim to Igor, but he was closer than she'd thought.

Igor swiped at her, missed her collar, but pulled off her woolen cap. Blinded momentarily, she felt her finger press the trigger as he slammed it from her hand. The gunshot rang in her ears. She ran, mourning the loss of her weapon. But Igor had the advantage of height and food in his belly. His next strike caught her by the jacket. He reeled her in.

She tried to unzip the jacket to win her freedom at the expense of what she had stored in the pockets, like a wolf that gnawed off its leg to escape a trap. But she stumbled and Igor tackled her.

They tumbled over the hard ground. Bree knew she was gaining bruises and lacerations, but pain didn't register as her fear factor soared. She was about to be captured, or killed. The reality of it sank in hard. Article Three: *If I am captured, I will continue to resist by all means available. I will make every effort to escape and will aid others to escape.*

She fought back, kicking and punching, moves she'd used only on the practice mats in martial arts workouts. She struggled free, but Igor threw her to the ground. She landed on her stomach, and it knocked the air out of her. He flipped her on her back. The toe of her boot caught him on the chin. In the corner of her eye, she saw him go down. And she was off again, running hard.

The ground around her popped and fizzed. Confused, she watched dirt spray up in clods. A second later, the retort of a gun explained it all. They were shooting at her.

Something slammed into her calf, felt like a fist. It knocked her leg out from under her. She rolled on the ground, clutching her calf. Her hand came away bloody.

The cloth was torn. Then the pain kicked in, a delayed reaction to the gunshot wound. *Ah, God. Please. Don't let me die yet. . . .*

She crawled, collapsed, and pushed to her knees again, inching forward as the men gained on her. A deep sense of regret swamped her. She thought of all the things in life she'd never experience: falling in love, marriage, having kids. She thought of the friends she'd never see again, the places she'd never visit, her parents' grief when they learned of her death. USAF representatives would make another visit to Chestnut: an officer or two, and this time a chaplain, dressed in crisp blue uniforms. Her mother would be the one to open the front door to the sight of those grim-faced men with their sympathetic eyes, because Bree's father would be in the shop in the barn working on someone's car. "Mrs. Maguire, we're sorry . . . so sorry . . ."

Bree crawled, gasping. The men's boots appeared in her blurred vision. Igor grabbed her by the collar and hoisted her to her feet. She mashed her heel onto the top of his foot, bringing her elbow backward, his privates the desired target. But he jerked her backward, into his body. Something cold and round pressed into her temple.

A gun.

Bree went still as the bounty hunter walked toward her. Breathing hard, the gun pressed to her head, she weighed her options. Hell, she weighed Igor. She'd learned how to handle imprisonment and interrogation. She knew how to resist. Most of all, she'd learned how to *survive*. She was a fighter pilot, a valuable resource; her country wanted her home, alive. It was looking more and more likely that this pair wanted to keep her that way, or they'd have killed her already. Her only hope was that Cam would somehow escape this pair's notice, and live until she could be rescued. *Because I won't be able to help you, Scarlet.* Bree swallowed. *I'm sorry.*

She glared at her pistol, dangling from the bounty hunter's hand, before slowing raising her gaze to his dark eyes. He walked toward her, pulling something from his pocket. A hypodermic needle.

"There's money for you if you give me back, unharmed. A lot of money," she bargained desperately, breathlessly, recalling again the blood chit. "You'll need the paper in my right thigh pocket. Go on, take it. Have a look."

The bounty hunter came for her, his arm raised. "You are what I want. Not the money."

Bree started to struggle. Igor jerked her against him, reminding her of the gun pressed to her head. She hated the gasp that escaped her dry lips as the needle sank into her upper arm. It burned. Immediately, she felt woozy, and fought futilely against the effects of the drug.

Her limbs went weak. The ground felt spongy, and she was floating . . . floating . . .

The bounty hunter sheathed the needle and spoke to Igor in rapid-fire Korean. He sounded impatient, angry. He probably hadn't liked chasing her all over the countryside.

Igor wrenched her upright and threw her into the back

of the truck. She landed on her stomach, and tried to push to her knees, but her arms and legs didn't seem to be working right. She could lift her head and little else. A layer of hay and assorted bundles covered the flatbed. On the sidewalls were round iron handles, like what you'd use for harnessing livestock. Well, she thought drunkenly, she'd be riding to their destination in utter, bovine comfort.

"I draw the line at a nose ring," she slurred huskily against the pain in her leg and the effects of the drug. Igor gave no indication that he understood English or had heard her at all. A pair of wide hands smoothed down her hips.

She went rigid at Igor's touch. Teeth clenched, she submitted to what appeared to be a thorough but thankfully asexual pat-down, hoping she'd hurry up and pass out before he changed his mind and committed an act far worse. Igor found her second pocketknife, the blood chit, map, and compass. He found her tube of lip gloss, too, treating it equally with the rest of her gear—as if it were all worthless. Wiping his hands as if she were dirty, Igor stomped out of the truck and swept the rear door closed. Bree heard it lock.

Hay made a flimsy shield against the chill of stainless steel. Where the bullet had grazed her calf, it stung like killer bees. Hay poked between her boots and damp woolen socks. It's nothing, she told herself. She didn't feel it, any of it.

She wouldn't feel what they'd do to her later, either.

Bree fell forward as the truck lurched into gear and bumped violently up the wooded slope. Rolling onto the road didn't much improve the ride. Apparently, the North Korean dictator had fed his dollars into nukes and not the roads.

Bree did a push-up and got her knees under her. It wasn't only the truck that left her swaying. She was losing her coordination; she had to think about moving each body part. Staring at her hands half buried in the hay, she saw that they were blurred, both of them—no, all four of them. She blinked and then there were eight hands. Somehow, she made her way to the back wall, nearest the cab. Her arms buckled, but a lump cushioned her fall. It was more solid than a bag of hay, not as lumpy as a sack of potatoes. And it was warm.

Bree lifted her head. The lump was an unconscious American soldier slumped against the wall. A pilot, like her.

Bree squinted, dragged fingers down a cool cheek. A smooth cheek. The face spun in a drugged kaleidoscope, but she could make out the features. "Cam," she whispered, grabbing her collar before she slumped sideways and passed out.

Chapter Four

Bree exploded out of a dream into blinding white light and utter silence. She sucked in a breath. The sound of the abrupt inhalation rang in her ears. Her heart pounded even louder.

Instinctively, she flung out her hands, but something held her arms in place. It was light . . . not dark, she thought, anchoring her mind to reality. Not the river from her childhood, the canoe, but she was just as trapped.

Bree swerved her attention upward from the sides of the luminescent white box that contained her. Pipes and intricately twined wires lined the ceiling, high above. The irregularity of the stone surface suggested that it was a cave or an area dug under the ground. A vague sense of pressure in her ears suggested it was located at some depth.

A high-tech dungeon?

Good guess, she thought. She was eight-way, hand-tied to a gurney. Her flight suit was gone. The closest thing she could come up with to describe what she was wearing was a white rubber suit, riddled with wires and who knew what else. What was it designed to deliver? Electric shocks? Direct nerve stimulation? Her imagination did a good job of filling in the blanks. A fog clung to her brain, dulling her thoughts, but nothing hurt—and she knew plenty of spots that should have been hurting: lacerations left from the forest landing, the bullet wound on her calf. As far as she could tell, she hadn't added any new injuries to the list.

She swallowed, her mouth dry, and tried to come up with a plan. She'd been in sticky situations before, but it was going to take a boatload of creativity to get out of this one, though it didn't hurt to give the basics a shot, first. "Help!" she shouted. "*Help!* Can anyone hear me?"

"Too well." The bounty hunter peeked over the edge of the box-bed. It must be on a raised platform because she couldn't see him from the shoulders down.

"Let me go!" she yelled.

The man exhaled and adjusted his clear protective goggles. "I don't know which I care for less, your pleading or your wingman's cursing."

"Where is she? Is she here? Let me see her!"

"I put her to sleep."

"To *sleep?*" Bree choked out. Cats and dogs were put to sleep, not people.

"*Sleep* sleep," he clarified. "Well, perhaps a little deeper than that."

The bounty hunter lifted a needle to the light. A trembling droplet sparkled on its tip.

"Wait!" No more drugs. She wanted something she could fight, where the odds were more in her favor; she couldn't defend against the meds. "I'll cooperate," she lied.

When the man's needle paused in midair, she stalled for time. "We were part of a peacekeeping patrol. We have nothing against your people. Our countries are not at war."

"This is true." He tapped the needle thoughtfully. And then he lifted his eyes. "Let me be frank, Captain. We share something in common: distaste for the ruling government here—although the term 'government' hardly applies to this particular regime. The Democratic People's Republic of Korea," he said in a mocking tone, and lifted the needle.

"Wait." She cleared the hoarseness from her throat. "You're a rebel?" If he was a radical, a dissident, then she was a hostage and not a prisoner of war. The distinction meant that all the rules had changed. In other words, there were none.

"I'm a scientist. The type of work that I do requires aggressive subject acquisition, but there are few places to find young, healthy, robust people for my needs, people who won't be missed. Your peace patrols presented the perfect opportunity. I could acquire the subjects I needed while placing the president in a delicious pickle."

A pickle? He had to be joking. "That pickle could lead to nuclear war!"

"So, what if it does?" He shrugged. "My laboratory is deep underground, hardened for a direct hit. I have power and supplies to last through an Armageddon of a thousand years."

She shook her head, trying to absorb it all. "Did you do it?" She had to know. "Did you shoot me down?"

"Ah. And how did I accomplish the deed? Your wingman had the same questions. The answer is yes, and with shoulder-launched missiles, available easily and everywhere, even here in this ignorant, arrogant little principality. Try not to look so surprised. I can read everything in your face, you know. Every emotion. It is a good thing I do not have the need to interrogate you, Captain. You would have made my job an easy one."

No, you bastard, I wouldn't have. She had a wingman to protect. A friend. She'd never have let Cam down. Or betrayed her country. All her life all she'd ever wanted to be was a soldier to serve her country and its ideals. Bree knew she looked inconsequential to some, but appearances were deceiving. That her captor didn't recognize that made him far more vulnerable than she was with her supposed transparent expressions.

"Now, to sleep," he said. The needle he held disappeared from sight. To where? Something powerful entered her bloodstream and gave her the answer. "More correctly, I will place you in suspended animation. Biostasis is the common term, and one you may have heard, although technically your biological functions are not completely suspended." He ran his gloved hand over the smooth white edge of her coffinlike box as if he thought it was a thing of beauty. "The cryopod," he said with reverence. "It will maintain your body temperature at the defined level, while these tubes, here, will fill your body cavities—stomach, intestines, lungs, and the like—with supercooled fluid. In that manner, you will continue to exist, indefinitely, unaware of the passage of time, while aging proceeds at such a slowed rate that you could live nearly forever in the state." His eyes shone with promise, excitement. "Or at least that is my goal once I perfect my life's work."

Once he did? It wasn't perfected yet? Bree was spinning now, falling into a black hole, but she had enough adrenaline left to push her pulse faster. She tried to free her legs. The restraints tightened around her jerking limbs until she imagined her bones snapping under the pressure.

"Keep still!"

"Why are you doing this?" she gasped.

"To be able to say that I can." The fanatical determination in the man's eyes chilled her to the bone. "Don't worry. It will be for only a day or two. A week at most, depending on how well you are doing. And what then? I'll thank you and your cohort for your time and set you free where your people will be sure to find you. Enough talk. I am behind schedule."

A clear lid descended over the pod. Her eardrums wrenched with a pressure change. She was closed off to everything outside, as if she were in the cockpit of the

F-16. In a way, it was reassuring. It meant that her captor did indeed have decent technology at his disposal. Maybe, just maybe, she would wake up at the other end of this.

But as soon as the door sealed, the interior of the pod whirred to life. Tubes and needles with fiber-optic-illuminated ends moved into position. One straw lowered to her mouth. She pressed her lips together, turned her head as far as the neck brace would let her.

The scientist rapped on the glass and shook his head. "Keep still!"

A gas of some kind entered the pod. It smelled sweet. *Another drug.* A silent scream of outrage ripped through her. She wasn't ready to die, not this way, captured and caged.

If I am captured I will continue to resist by all means available. I will make every effort to escape and will aid others to escape.

Bree held her breath, her heart slamming against her ribs. Tears stung her eyes, and her lungs felt ready to explode. She knotted her hands into fists, but the instinct to survive was too strong and she couldn't keep from sucking in a breath.

The sedative took effect immediately. To pass out was to give in, and she wasn't ready for that. With all that she had, she struggled to stay awake, to stay *alive,* fighting with the zest for life and the strength of will that had been hers since birth. Sass, her grandfather had called it.

The straw scraped along the seam of her compressed lips, found the corner of her mouth, and invaded. A cold salty-sweet liquid squirted inside. Bree spat it out, until it began to gush and she couldn't keep up. She coughed, inhaled a lungful of the vile stuff. It went up her nose. She was suffocating. Arching her back, she thrashed about in her restraints.

Somewhere above her, her captor watched the drugs take her down. Somewhere above him, she could only hope, God watched them both. It was her last thought before the growing darkness choked out the light.

2176

Chapter Five

By all accounts, it was a peaceful night. A full moon illuminated the water of the East Asian Sea, where swells undulated in a timeless rhythm, curved, luminous, and dark like the backs of tarnished silver spoons. But far below the surface, a sleek black shadow raced over the sea floor. The *Sea Snake*.

Onboard the UV800, the coastline of the Asian Kingdom showed up clear and three-dimensional on the forward navigation display. United Colonies of Earth Commander Tyler Armstrong maintained his vigilance at the controls. It had been fourteen hours since he'd left the UCE-SS *Invincible*. Fourteen *long* hours, Ty admitted, rubbing one hand over his scratchy jaw. But the *Sea Snake* was designed for stealth and not for comfort.

Terrain-following guidance allowed the underwater vehicle to stay close to the sea floor, necessary for avoiding the notice of the infamous, enviable, and efficiently brutal Han forces, protectors of a secretive and isolationist kingdom that wanted little to do with the world outside its borders. His goal was to slip through the border without anyone knowing, and then go back out the same way. If all went as planned, Prince Kyber, the acting Han ruler, wouldn't know that tonight ever happened.

Luckily, the UV's depth and its almost-nil silhouette made detection almost impossible. Almost, Ty thought.

During the crackdown on sea terrorists, known in the aftermath as the Pirate Wars, the UCE Navy had seen the loss of two military UV-800s, six men between them. Luckily, the pirates lacked both the brainpower to operate the commandeered UVs and the infrastructure to maintain them, averting what could have been a catastrophic loss of technological knowledge. On the downside, what the sea dwellers lacked in wits and tech they made up for in barbarism. They'd caught the UV crew, tortured, and killed them.

Ty had been the first to find the bodies.

He shut down the gory images that flooded him. Mental self-censorship. As a SEAL commando, he'd had a lot of practice at that game, even for the missions that went as planned. But tonight's venture was a different kind of hunt, he reminded himself. He was after treasure. Off the record and off the clock.

Treasure Legend said that two pilots missing since the end of the Korean Peninsular War were in fact still alive, their bodies preserved and hidden in a bombed-out cave now submerged by the East Asian Sea, which, like other oceans, had risen slowly and steadily over the past couple of centuries. That those POWs, dead or alive, had never been returned home and repatriated had always bothered him. It was inexcusable that no one had searched harder for them. "Never leave a man behind." That was his unit's motto. If no one else would do the job, he would.

Hell, Armstrong, admit it. You're a tomb raider. You want to feel the rush of snatching artifacts right from under ol' Prince Kyber's nose.

Yes, there was that, too, he thought, his mouth tipping in a self-satisfied smile. Men like him had raised ships from the bottom of the sea, uncovered lost millions from secret vaults, raided tombs, discovered secrets beneath the pyramids. But no one had ever salvaged a live person along with the mysteries of the past. Ty wanted to be the first.

Last year he'd found his name in the top ten of two lists: world-class adventurers and the UCE's most-eligible bachelors. The latter, he knew, had far more to do with his father's permanent position as the UCE's supreme military commander than his own efforts—or more accurately, his lack thereof—to marry. Yet, there it was. Ty could only hope that *United Colonies Extreme Sports* was a better judge of his interests than *People*. He'd climbed Everest, twice, and had won a spot on the race-hike across Antarctica in the '68 Olympics; he'd ridden the currents boiling out of the cone of an active volcano in the Pacific Rift, free-fallen from near space, but when it came time for socialites and social events, duty had a way of intervening. Or he made sure it did. He was a dedicated UCE fighting man, after all.

His dangerous job served him well as a good excuse, but in truth he avoided romantic entanglements because he'd never been able to shake the gut feeling that something different and far better lay in store for him. Was whimsy to blame, or his ego? He didn't know, but none of the women he'd met so far had "permanent" stamped on their foreheads. If loneliness was the trade-off for living with a sense of destiny, so be it. He had a knack for finding activities to fill the void.

Like this expedition, he thought. He'd wanted to uncover the truth behind the legend of Banzai Maguire for years. Now, finally, everything had come together, thanks to a grateful pirate lord whose life he'd spared. Compensation was the last thing on Ty's mind at the time, but when offered a highly accurate, underwater map of the region as thanks for saving the man's life, he didn't hesitate to take it. Only fools turned their backs on providence. Without the chart, he knew he stood only a slim chance of finding the submerged cave, the most likely location of the two missing pilots. As if that weren't enough, the appreciative pirate insisted he hadn't come close to paying off his blood debt. While Ty didn't take him up on the offer of his daughter and a rather large collection of jewels, it was nice to know someone in the Raft Cities thought he owed him a favor. Only he hoped he never found himself in a position to need it.

Ty opened the map. One sweep of his hand made the pirate's chart glow in three-dimensional detail. What was it really like, inside the Asian Kingdom? Some said the citizens were prisoners. Others believed that no one wanted to leave a land that was Shangri-la. Ty could only guess. Few had seen inside the borders since the Bai-Yee colonial wars over a century ago ended with the Asian Economic Consortium breaking from the UCE. One of Kyber's Han ancestors had led the revolt. They'd declared independence and kept their borders sealed ever since—with the exception of an occasional foreign bride imported by the Han family. But the blue-blooded queens never reported back with details. Maybe part of the prenuptial agreement was a vow of silence. On the other hand, if it really was paradise that they'd married into, maybe they didn't mind.

Outside the tiny vehicle, submerged rocks towered. Ty marveled at the immensity of the boulders, and at occasional carcasses of buildings destroyed in the war. He was surprised no one had carted off the pieces, for salvage if nothing else. Everyone else in the world had dismantled their sunken coastal cities. If Kyber hadn't kept up with housekeeping, it meant anything could be here, lost and forgotten. Including a couple of pilots.

The UV mirrored the seabed's gradual rise toward shore. Ty slid two fingertips over his map to a shadow he hoped was the opening to the underwater cave he sought. One look ahead confirmed it. Sediment kicked up by the UV's maneuvering reduced forward visibility to almost zero. An error now would mean disaster: capture and a DNA-check, which would connect him to his father, one of the most powerful—and hated—men on Earth. The political fallout of his stealthy mission would be ugly, something Ty didn't want to imagine, let alone experience. He'd rather free-fall with a frozen parachute.

Ty secured the UV800 in an underwater niche hidden from the entrance to the cave. Silent jets would keep her in place until he was ready to return.

Ty pushed away from the console and gathered his equipment. He tightened swim fins over his boots, locked night-vision goggles on the frame of his facemask. His SEAL commando training made him equally adept in operations at sea, air, and land—thus the name SEAL, an acronym in use nonstop since the unit's creation in the early 1960s, long before the United States became the United Colonies of Earth, long before the SEALs were tasked to pursue and destroy terrorists in every sea, in every world port; and long before he broke out from under his famous father's shadow, making a name for himself as an officer who'd earned every medal and every promotion on his skill and not his name.

Suited up, Ty shimmied into a cramped pipe and sealed it behind him. Bracing himself, he opened a hatch. The sea roared in, pummeling his body. Where the temperature regulators in his wet suit were perhaps a little slower to react than they should be, he felt the press of cold salt water. Adjusting his mask and goggles one more time, he kicked his legs and finned toward his goal.

Normally, he'd have two men keeping watch for him from inside the UV, but tonight he was on his own. Rebreather gear captured his exhalations, preventing bubbles from rising to the surface and alerting anyone who might be watching. Ty doubted anyone was, but he was taking no chances. Using the pale green luminescence of his night-vision goggles, he scanned for threats.

Rocky pillars defined the entrance of the cave, but he wouldn't have seen them unless he'd known exactly what he was looking for. The landmarks he saw next matched the information on the map. Ty gave a kick of his fins, flattened both hands on a ledge. Rocks scraped against his wet suit and mask as he squeezed through a narrow opening that opened into a larger area. The water was shallower here. The surface flickered above him. With his marine pistol loaded and ready, he finned toward it.

He broke the surface, his pistol held at the ready. Water trickled off his goggles and mask as he peered into the darkness of a cave. The area was in worse shape than he'd thought. He assumed he'd find one large room. But the ceiling had collapsed, forming stone dividers with fissures wide enough to insert a remote camera but not for him to enter. Or maybe the builders had structured the lab this way. He'd never know. The people who'd worked here in secret were dead.

Ty hoisted himself up to dry land. After pulling the breather from his mouth, he left the apparatus hanging from his weapons vest. His fins fit in a holder at his hip. He smeared the entire length of the waterline with a paste containing EWTs—early warning transmitters in the form of microsized computers designed to "talk" with the communicator and computers he wore on his wrists and belt. If someone breached the line, Ty would get an instant warning.

The air was still, silent, and ripe with salty dampness. In the distance, he heard faint trickling. How long had it been since anyone had stepped here? How long had this air existed, undisturbed? As he searched the chamber, he felt the weight of history pressing down on him. They were here, those two pilots. Dead or alive, they'd be a great find.

Ty scaled the first fallen wall and dropped into a dark chamber. He entered a room so large that his goggles couldn't illuminate the far reaches. Exploring the area section by section, he walked for quite a while on a platform before he realized it had once been a wall. Where it had buckled and lifted, it almost hid a cylindrical white container, large enough to hold a human being.

His pulse picked up speed. The container was similar to the kind used in early experiments in bio and cryo suspended animation. From within the pod, faint lights glowed. Power? Possibly it had sustained what lay in the pod all these years—if the juice had continued uninterrupted. Would he find a live body inside or a mummy? His money was on the mummy. His hopes were on the living body.

Ty approached the pod in measured, reverential steps, as if making his way to an altar. A layer of sand hid the glass. With a gloved hand, he moved aside the silt, revealing the snug interior. The oyster, he mused. Did it contain a pearl?

He wiped away the silt and looked inside. His oyster did indeed contain a pearl, perfect and whole. It was Banzai . . . Banzai Maguire. She existed. She was alive!

Fingers splayed on the clear cover, he savored the sight of his treasure. Her eyes were long-lashed and closed, her hair, glossy and dark, swept back from a pale face. No, that old photo hadn't done her justice.

"Sleeping Beauty," he murmured.

The pilot from the past might be a legend to most, but she was a woman to him. He'd never admit it, though. Navy psychiatrists didn't take kindly to combat soldiers who pined after dead women they'd never met. But he'd met her—had loved her and *made love* to her—in his imagination. And she'd remained there, in his mind, from the first time he read her tragically shortened biography, relegated to a footnote in a comprehensive data-volume on twenty-first-century warfare he'd received as a gift from his father.

He'd grown up, of course, left home, gotten an education, gone on to fight in a war, but the impression Banzai made on him had never waned. A beauty who could kick some ass? Now *that* was a woman. Over the years, it had become somewhat of an obsession to find out what had happened to her. And now, it appeared, he had.

If only waking Sleeping Beauty required a procedure as straightforward as a kiss. But it did not. Working quickly and using the pod as a table, he opened the medical kit he'd brought with him. Wishful thinking, he'd thought at the time, but now he was glad he'd listened to his optimism.

His equipment and weapons clattered in the silence. The entire pod was too large for the UV; he'd have to remove its occupant, but he'd prepared for that eventuality. He'd revive her enough to get unassisted respiration. He'd brought extra rebreathers for the return swim. It would have to be strapped to her face, but the water would help keep her body temperature down in the critical hours after waking. If you made a sleeper too hot too fast, he or she died on you. Full speed in the UV, the *Invincible* was six hours of driving time away. There, Ty would have access to a ship's typical complement of medical personnel. It meant he had to keep Banzai alive for those hours. And, perhaps, her wingman as well. Those core-curriculum courses in cryobiology he'd taken at the university before abandoning his premed studies to join the UCE Navy at the beginning of the Pirate Wars would finally prove their use.

Yet book knowledge didn't equate to hands-on experience. Of that, he had none. He risked killing the pilots if he broke them out of stasis in less than ideal conditions.

Was it moral to risk it? Should he leave them be?

Ty's gaze traveled back to Banzai's face. He'd seen sleepers before; her expression should have been serene. It wasn't. He was no expert in female-emotion interpretation, but in Banzai's face he saw anger, and sadness, too. If he were to hazard a guess, he'd bet she'd choose the risk of him waking her over spending the rest of her days asleep in this underwater cave.

Slipping his night-vision goggles over his eyes, Ty stood. "I'm going to find your wingman. Then I'll bring you both home."

Home. It had a nice ring to it. But "home" would be a far different place than what she'd left.

Ty went in search of the second cryopod. He crawled, climbed, or walked into every area large enough to hold him. When that yielded nothing, he inserted a viewer on a long flexible cord through cracks in the fallen walls. It allowed him to see where he couldn't reach. The other sections of the cave had not fared as well as this one. It looked like seawater had filled the areas at one time before receding. Bomb damage was heavy, with fallen equipment sharing space with rocks, broken pipes, and twisted steel girders. The other pilot was here; Ty knew it. But he'd need heavier equipment to investigate and more men to assist him.

Ty sat back on his haunches and exhaled. He couldn't find Cameron Tucker. The disappointment wasn't nearly as sharp as when he'd found the mutilated UV drivers in the raft city, but his guilt emanated from the same source. And, as it was on the raft mission, time was his enemy. He'd better get out—and get Banzai out—before someone figured out they were here.

He returned to her pod. Revival from biostasis followed a rigid series of steps, but the most important one to remember was letting the pod control the recovery, intervening only in a case of complete mechanical breakdown. Impatience on the waker's part had left more than a few sleepers at the mercy of what was at best a dicey resuscitation. Even in modern times, biostasis was an imperfect art. But they were getting better by injecting microscopic computers into the body before and after stasis. In Banzai's day, true nanotech had still been a vision of the future.

Ty reinstated power to the outside of the pod, sat back, and waited. Although he couldn't see it, he'd started the slow process of waking her. Changes had begun on the molecular level. Inside her body, fluid chilling the internal organs warmed.

Time passed. Ty watched Banzai's skin turn from chalky to pink. As her face lost its waxy stiffness, her mouth relaxed. He looked at her lips, soft and full, and his chest clenched with an odd feeling. It finally hit him that she was real. Banzai Maguire. A woman from another time, a time long past. Someone who should have been dead all these years but had slept through them instead.

The last time she was awake, the United Colonies of Earth were still the United States, a nation that resembled and even remembered its revolutionary roots. Fifty white stars flew on the flag; people watched Fourth of July fireworks and knew the words to "Yankee Doodle" and "The Star-spangled Banner,"—or most of them, at least. But in modern UCE culture, Americana was notably absent, the fact reflected in the flag itself, a simple block design: a white globe on a blue square in the upper left corner of a solid red banner. Totally revised, the national anthem further celebrated world unity and peace. No one sang the old songs anymore.

Ty, on the other hand, knew them all. Whether or not his fascination with Banzai Maguire was the cause or a consequence of his interest, he felt a certain kinship with those who'd lived in the precolonial era of the late twentieth and early twenty-first centuries. While his boyhood friends had gazed at holo-wall images of the nuclear-fueled Century-Saber craft that regularly flew round-trips to Mars, in Ty's bedroom models of F-15 Eagles and F-22 Raptors dangled from tacks stuck in the ceiling. (His mother hadn't been pleased with the damage done to the holoscreen, but since he'd rarely used it, the issue faded.) The country had no colonies in those days. It hadn't spanned half the world; it still retained its roots as a struggling young nation with principles, which had freed itself from a bloated, imperial power.

A bloated, imperial power like the UCE itself was now?

Ty frowned. That charge was unfair. The UCE had brought stability to the world. There hadn't been a major war fought since the late twenty-first century. But had the UCE created peace at the expense of something more precious?

Late at night when he'd been out on patrol, the officers' talk often turned to that subject, a trend far more dangerous than the grumbling of the enlisted men. They were leaders, the officers, loyal men tasked with incredible responsibilities. To be effective in their role, they had to believe in the power from whence their orders came. Ty saw their private doubts as the first symptoms of eroding faith.

Certainly, they weren't the only ones who were disgruntled. As always, the UCE had raised taxes on the colonies to finance the costly upkeep of its far-flung empire, and the military needed to keep the peace. But for the first time, the colonies balked against the taxes levied on them, and several threatened to protest by refusing to buy UCE goods. Boycotts would weaken an economy overly dependent on exports. Panic gripped the white marble halls of New Washington, spurring tough curfews and restrictions on organized public gatherings. And it only made things worse.

But the UCE wasn't the only source of discontent. Similar troubles plagued the Euro-African Consortium as well. If the same was happening in the Kingdom of Asia, no one had heard about it, but it didn't mean it didn't exist. To Ty, one thing was certain: Change was afoot in the world; he smelled it as accurately as he could scent coming rain. After so many years of calm, was the UCE prepared to weather the coming storm?

Ty had asked that very question of his father, Supreme UCE Commander Aaron Armstrong, late one night when Ty was visiting on leave and they'd both had a few too many drinks, spurring them into sharing private thoughts that discretion normally kept masked.

"It's surprising to see how rapidly a panic will sometimes run through a country," his father had murmured in reply. "All nations in all ages have been subject to them. Yet panics, in some cases, have their uses. They produce as much good as hurt. Their duration is always short; the mind soon grows through them, and acquires a firmer habit than before."

The general noted Ty's perplexed expression. "Thomas Paine," he explained. "A patriot of the American Revolution."

Ty wondered what was in his father's liquor. "You think unrest may be good for the country?"

A veil fell over his father's eyes. Ty could no longer tell what was in them. "Those are his words, son. Not mine."

It was obvious that his father wanted to distance himself from the statement now that he'd uttered it. And Ty let him. A man in his father's position had few people to trust. Ty would hope that he'd trust his son, but it appeared that he didn't.

Trust Ty with what, exactly? A few wandering scotch-laced thoughts? That's all the words were.

Ty glanced up to find his father watching him with an expression he wasn't sure he liked. "I love this country, Ty."

"I don't doubt that, sir," he'd put in quickly.

"I will never allow anyone to weaken it." The general's blue eyes turned as cold as the chips of ice in their drinks. "Never."

Ty lifted his glass in a toast, in part to lighten the atmosphere that had become strangely intense. "To Paine and his words. May we find good lessons in the past—if we need them." Then he'd drunk a mouthful of expensive scotch and exhaled. "Reminds me of that expression: Hindsight is twenty-twenty."

His father had lifted a brow. "If hindsight is twenty-twenty, then foresight is a brand-new pair of Buschnell-Irwin binoculars." He finished his drink. "Best on the planet. Unfortunately, too few people own a pair." The older man rose, more slowly than usual, as if bearing the weight of years and responsibility on his shoulders. "Good night, Ty."

That conversation had happened many months ago, but Ty still thought of it. "Ax" Armstrong, many called the general—for his decisive, incisive, but sometimes bloody strategies of fighting terrorism and controlling the UCE's colonies. Others said he was a dove clothed in hawk armor, using the largest military in the world to further his personal vision of peace. Still others claimed he'd like to oust the president and turn the UCE into a military dictatorship. Sometimes Ty thought the less he knew about his sire the better.

Would the UCE weather the coming storm?

It was Ty's duty as a military officer and his father's son to make sure it did. Crouched by the cryopod, he studied his gloved hands, clenched into fists, until Banzai's vital signs strengthened. When her pulse was steady and she breathed on her own, he opened the lid and prepared to slip a breather over her face. It was time to move out. They had no seconds to waste.

Gently, he undid her restraints. Her eyes flickered open—two slits appearing where her lids had been swollen shut. Her irises were brilliant green, though he knew the drugs in her body were responsible for the hue. As the meds wore off, the irises of her eyes would fade to a less intense color. How much less, he'd have to wait and see. What would those eyes think of the twenty-second century?

What would they think of him?

Maybe he should have shaved.

"Up we go," he told her. "Departure time is now." He slipped a hand behind her head and lifted her upper body off the pod bed. Her eyes widened, dazedly searching his face. He cradled her head as he wondered if she could process what she saw. "Welcome back, Sleeping Beauty," he murmured, and fastened the breather over her lips.

Then his gauntlet comm bleeped in warning. Something had set off the Early Warning Transmitters.

Ty heard water splashing at the entrance of the cave. Adrenaline shot through his body. Angry shouts erupted, coming closer. Kyber's men, Ty thought. Who else would they be?

He had a split second to decide whether to drag Banzai with him or leave her in the cryopod. He decided that she'd be better off with him.

A dozen hulking soldiers stormed in dressed in black body armor and toting the best weapons money could buy.

"You there—halt!" they shouted in Hannish, the Kingdom of Asia's adopted and meticulously honed dialect of English. Their accent sounded too polite for the circumstances, but they were anything but cordial when they saw him pull Banzai into his arms and swing away from the cryopod. He dove with her behind a pile of rocks and rubble.

There, he ducked down and cocked his pistol. "I'm armed!"

Instantly, violent concussions ricocheted off the stones. Lasers and bullets were everywhere. So much for his warning, he thought, and threw himself sideways and into an adjacent blockade of rubble, leaving Banzai lying hidden on the stone floor. *He* wanted to be the target, not her.

On his belly between piles of rubble, he returned fire until he'd emptied a clip. Discarding it, he replaced it with another.

The firefight was intense. With every passing second, the soldiers gained ground. Ty hadn't brought enough ammo to outlast this kind of battle. Salty sweat ran in rivers down his temples. He swiped it out of his eyes, fired, and took down a couple of his attackers. Wounded, they writhed on the ground. He aimed again . . . and heard empty clicks. He was out of ammo.

It didn't take long for the soldiers to figure it out.

They pulled him out from behind the rocks, greeted him with a hailstorm of kicks. Then he was down, rolled into a tight ball, a last-ditch protective position to keep steel-toed boots from crushing his skull. Unfortunately, that left his kidneys wide open.

Bright lights flashed behind his eyes as their assault caught him in the back, ribs, and gut. Pain lanced deep. The agony was especially vivid when they found the same place twice, which seemed to be on purpose.

He'd heard that when you were beaten like this, shock deadened the pain. Bullshit. The next guy who told him that was dead meat.

His next thought was of Banzai, lying groggy and vulnerable behind the rubble. What would happen to her? Was she all right?

He held a picture in his mind, of her green eyes, full of wonder yet barely open. She could be dead already. He hoped she was, if Kyber's monsters meant to turn on her next. Soldiers could be brutes. A woman was always at the mercy of . . .

As Ty slipped out of consciousness, his mind centered on the irony of it all. He'd found the ultimate treasure, only to give her up to barbarian soldiers of the world's most powerful dictator: the very people who'd appreciate her least.

Chapter Six

". . . blood pressure falling . . ."

"Temperature low . . ."

"I need vasoconstrictors . . . now."

"Introducing nanovasoconstrictors, Dr. Park."

"Watch the pressure."

"Watching . . ."

Bree listened to the voices, not sure how long she'd been aware of them. She'd been drifting, for what amount of time she didn't know. Forever. A billowing marshmallow dream . . .

Strong hands gripped her upper arms, lifting her and pulling her up. She would have fallen backward, but he didn't let her.

"Sleeping Beauty . . ."

The familiar voice resonated inside her mind, luring her out of the fog. The soft white clouds floating all around her disintegrated. She glimpsed startling blue eyes, white teeth. "Welcome back. . . ."

From where? Had she been gone long? He seemed happy to have her back, though. A sweetly poignant and inexplicable certainty told her that she already knew this man, though she seemed to be having some trouble remembering who he was. It didn't seem to stop her from wanting to kiss him. His mouth moved closer; warm breath whispered against her cheek. As longing flared inside her, she hungered to complete the contact. But white clouds enveloped her before she could.

A cold hand swatted her on the cheek. "No sleep," a person ordered as if training a dog. "Eyes open."

". . . consequences of stasis . . . too long asleep . . ."

"Some of them never wake up . . ."

"Keep her alive." A new voice, also male. But this one came from the room, not her mind. "Banzai Maguire must not die."

Must not die . . . ? Was she dying? Was this what it felt like?

Something draped over her mouth, wet and cold. It felt like she was underwater. Bree arched her back and tried to breathe . . . to reach the surface. She couldn't find it! No air! A coil of panic wrapped around her and yanked tight. She fought the feeling of suffocation, struggled. *No!*

She sucked in a breath and jerked awake. Gasping, she lay there, eyes fluttering, like a grounded fish.

"She is awake!"

"Pulse eighty-five. Respiration rising rapidly!"

"Keep it down!"

"Sedative?"

A woman answered in a British accent. Her voice was the most familiar. "No. Too soon. I want her to stabilize. Her body must remember how."

Time passed, but not in linear fashion. Reality skipped forward from one scene to the next like a movie on a scratched DVD.

A while later—how long, Bree didn't know—a gentle hand brushed her cheek. "How do you feel?"

Been better. Her lungs hurt. Her arms and legs tingled with a million stabbing needles, which grew worse if she tried to move. She quickly figured out that wasn't something she wanted to do.

She'd rather sleep. Turning away from the prodding and poking, she tried to press her head into her pillow. Her throat was sore, and her mouth was cotton-dry. Her joints ached. Holy Christmas, it was whiplash, a nightmare hangover, and the flu all rolled into one!

Knuckles brushed her cheek. A woman's hand. "Do you hear me? Do you understand? You *must not* sleep."

Why? Outside, there were poking hands and frantic orders. Inside her head, there was undemanding tranquility. Peace. It wasn't hard to choose between the two worlds. . . .

"If you dip back into slumber I may not be able to bring you back." The woman's tone turned officious. "The prince will be very unhappy if you allow that to happen."

"Very," a deeper male voice said. Him, again. "*Keep her alive. Banzai Maguire must not die.*"

Good man, she thought drowsily. She liked his philosophy.

The male voice triggered another memory, until only a fragment of a dream. "*Welcome back. . . .*" He was her rescuer. She must have opened her eyes for a moment, and seen him, a muscled hunk with a marine haircut, high cheekbones, and those bracing blue eyes. He'd had a little scar on his upper lip; she remembered that now, too. But that was all. He must be with the Special Forces. When she was better, she'd find out who he was, and thank him. . . .

Someone was tapping on the cheek again. "Please. There is only so much we can do, Captain Maguire. The rest must come from you."

Captain . . . Captain Maguire.

Bree Maguire.

Banzai.

Bree's eyes shot open. She'd been captured, tortured. Now, apparently, she was in the hands of rescuers. She remembered little of it, and none of how she got here.

Where was "here"? Bree had trouble focusing at first. It was as if she had a piece of gauze laminated to each eye. When her vision finally cleared, she lifted her head. Mistake. Trying to move reminded her of being back in the cockpit of the F-16, battling nine g's worth of force.

Lying flat on her back, she looked around. Her hospital room was enormous, furnished sparely but luxuriously with ultramodern furniture that looked like it belonged on a cover of *Architectural Digest*. Integrated into and almost blending with the wall closest to her bed were computers, or medical monitors. This place had cost some money. It definitely wasn't a military hospital.

As her vision improved, Bree turned her gaze toward the source of the voice she'd heard most often, the one she sensed had been talking to her in her dreams for the past few . . . was it hours? Days? She'd lost track of time.

The woman smiled at her, radiating warmth and genuine concern. She was Asian and fashion-model gorgeous, maybe in her late thirties or early forties. Her folded arms and white outfit shouted "physician." But her sultry, British-accented English, the huge black pearls in her ears, her flawless skin hinted at luxurious living. "I am Dr. Park," she said, sensing Bree's question. "Dae Park."

A Korean name, Bree noted. They must have brought her back to Seoul.

A woman walked up to Dr. Park and handed her what looked like a pocket-sized computer. She was younger, younger than Bree, but she, too, wore the white clothes of a physician, and was tall, beautiful, and sophisticated like Dr. Park. If it weren't for her earrings, huge opals that seemed to glow from within, Bree would have thought the new woman *was* Dr. Park.

Other women moved around the room, too, farther away and busy with various tasks. All four were dressed in simple dove-gray scrubs.

And all four were younger replicas of Dr. Park.

Bree squeezed her eyes shut. Opened them. Seeing double was one thing, but this was ridiculous. Yet the other women were poorer "copies" of the original: They were shorter, their clothes further down on the scale of quality, their skin and eyes duller; some, their mouths slack. They appeared suited to their menial tasks, in contrast to the two—no, three—women dressed in white. Yet another "sister" glided past Bree's bedside to confer with Dr. Park. She, too, was dressed in white and wore expensive jewelry. In all, there were seven women. Seven sisters. Impossible.

Bree closed her eyes to erase the hallucination, and marshmallow softness enveloped her.

"I gave you a little more for the pain, Captain."

Bree jolted back to awareness. Dr. Park's voice came from a different direction. She must have blacked out again. "It will help," the doctor said. "Tell me if it does not."

Bree didn't care. All she wanted to do was return to the big powdery-soft marshmallows. She didn't even like raw marshmallows. Burned to a crisp over a campfire was the only way to go. But these were big mothers, spongy and inviting. All she had to do was fall . . . deep . . . deep . . . deep . . .

The voices started to shout again. "Keep her up. Up!"

Reality fast-forwarded again, and she woke to more chaos. This was a hospital. What was so wrong about a patient wanting to take a nap? She heard the loud thumps of boots crossing the room. Strong hands lifted Bree, forcing her to her feet.

"Your Highness!" one of the women gasped in astonishment.

Your Highness? Even if this was a civilian hospital in Seoul—where the air force might have sent her for specialized care that the military hospitals couldn't provide, care that Bree for some reason needed before they could airlift her home—South Korea didn't have a monarchy, or even the ceremonial trappings of one like England. Or did they?

"You say she will not stay awake? I will keep her awake." He pulled Bree to his side. "It is something I am good at." He swept her close.

Bree stretched out her hand and flattened it atop an abdomen as hard as his thick belt, which pressed into her ribs. She twisted her head to see the man behind the voice, but she was too close and he was too tall, giving her only the quickest glimpse of a hard jaw and broad shoulders. He wore black, all black. She, on the other hand, wore beige pajamas, a thin, formfitting outfit that somehow kept her warm.

"You are a stubborn creature," he said in her ear.

It took Bree a moment to realize that the man was talking to *her*. No guy had ever called her a "creature" and made it sound like an endearment.

"Come, you can do better."

"Trying . . ." Her voice was raspy, almost a whisper. Maybe she'd screamed during the torture that she didn't remember and shredded her vocal cords.

He supported her while forcing her to walk, his big hand cupping her elbow, her other arm sandwiched by their bodies, as if she were a drunk who needed sobering up. Maybe he'd feed her coffee. That would help. How long had it been since she'd had caffeine? *Too long* was the only answer. She was twenty-eight. She felt eighty-eight.

But the longer Bree held her eyes open, the better she felt. Taking a deep breath—it felt somehow good to stretch her lungs to capacity—she noted that smells were starting to come back to her. They'd been absent before. The air was clean and dry, filtered, like airplane air. Dr. Park smelled like flowers. The man smelled like leather and warm skin, a masculine scent that she liked, layered with a faint sweet soapy aroma.

"So, she wants to sleep?" the man prompted Dr. Park.

The physician replied with a wry smile. "I'd rather she didn't, Prince Kyber, and told her so."

The man gave Bree's shoulder a squeeze. "You will soon learn to listen to Dae. There are many physicians, but there are none better than she."

Dr. Park was so fair that it was easy to see the man's praise coloring her cheeks.

"I have not heard from you for hours. Give me an update," he demanded.

"There has been atrophy, of course. But we've already begun treating it. In addition to pulse stimulation, she'll need strength training."

"Good. We will start it now. Step, step, step," he urged.

Bree stumbled, then caught the rhythm by watching their feet. His: polished black boots. Hers: white slippers. Again, she craned her head to glimpse his face, but poor balance said no to sightseeing and walking at the same time. Her coordination was nonexistent, and she couldn't get her legs to hold any appreciable weight. What had the North Koreans done to her? "I have to think about every move I make." Her voice was scratchy, but understandable. "It's like I'm learning to use my body all over again."

"You have survived an incredible ordeal, Captain Maguire. But you will get well. I hope you will have as much patience in your recovery as we have confidence in it," Dr. Park added in a tone that made it easy for Bree to believe her. "Our medical science is the most advanced in the world. Every day will see you stronger. We've regenerated some of your lost muscle mass already, and what physical damage remains will heal."

Bree's neck ached. Her head, too, now that she thought about it. But the pain had a dull edge, as if some medication worked equally hard to keep her from feeling its full force. *Please, not a head injury*. A bad CAT scan was the kiss of death for a pilot. She would rather have flown anonymously for an entire career than lose her wings for war-hero status.

Bree cleared her throat. "What about my head? My brain? Will the damage be permanent?"

Will I fly again? That's what she wanted to ask, but she wasn't ready to hear the word "no." For someone who had never expected to wake up again, she sounded a wee bit ungrateful about surviving. But all she'd ever wanted to be was an air force pilot. If she couldn't do that anymore . . . what would she do with the rest of her life?

"We won't know what effects are permanent, if any, for some time," replied Dr. Park. "Your greatest challenges lie ahead, as we continue with your physical and emotional therapy." The physician and her white-coated twins watched Bree with pride. "But look at you already. You are walking."

Hardly. Bree's legs trembled under her weight, her heart straining. "It's like I haven't worked out for a hundred years."

There was a bit of awkward silence, which her escort quickly filled. "One hundred and seventy."

Bree groaned. "It sure feels like it."

"Prince Kyber!" Dr. Park scolded him in a shocked tone and brought her finger to her lips.

Bree on the other hand appreciated a man with a warped sense of humor. And she was glad to see he was unrepentant in the face of the dismayed medical people.

"Why wait?" he asked the women. "She is strong."

"Your Highness, Captain Maguire has suffered tremendous trauma. At this point, I'm hesitant to add more." The second sister had spoken. Bree locked eyes with her knowing, empathetic gaze. She was a shrink. Bree would bet her bottom dollar.

As if on cue, the original Dr. Park said, "This is Dr. Park—Min Park. She is also assigned to your well-being."

Another Park. It was a popular Korean surname. But

the women were identical. They were sisters. If not for the age difference, they'd be twins.

The second Park wore her hair long and loose. She looped it over one shoulder as she bent her head in greeting. "As your psychiatrist, I look forward to assisting you, Captain Maguire."

Ha. Bree knew it. She *was* a shrink. Bree was two for two. But despite her awkwardness with the idea of a psychiatrist assigned to her, Bree found the woman's kind expression comforting.

"With all due respect, Your Highness," Min said, "I think our patient is ready to return to her bed."

Kyber ducked down and reached for Bree's legs. His forearm hit the back of her knees. In one graceful motion, he swept her off her feet and put her back in bed.

"Do as the doctors ask," he said. "Or I will walk you the length and breadth of this building if that's what is required to keep you awake." Then he flashed a smile, the kind of self-confident, devilishly charming grin that told her he recognized his effect on women. His black clothing looked more like functional body armor than surgical wear. She'd been following a series on TV called *Outrunners* about futuristic cops, and this man could pass for a cast member. Only he was better looking than the actors on the show. Much better looking. He worked out, and it showed in his muscled biceps and broad shoulders. Asian ancestry gave him smooth, burnished skin and slightly almond-shaped eyes. He wasn't 100 percent Korean, or even 75 percent. He probably had a parent of each race, and maybe more than that, a Caucasian grandparent or two, she guessed, recalling her own Eurasian blood. His hair was long, glossy black, and clasped at the nape of his neck. His eyes were stone gray, and utterly taken with her.

"It is a miracle she is alive," he murmured to no one in particular, transfixed.

Bree went very still. It was eerie, having someone look at her that way . . . as if she were an acquisition. A prize. Kyber saw in her something he wanted. Badly. So had her rescuer, she realized. The blue-eyed soldier's gaze had been little different.

Bree shrank from the attention. "I'm not the first pilot to be shot down. I did my duty, that's all. I'm nothing special."

Kyber crouched by her bedside. "You are the stuff of legends, Banzai. One of a kind."

"Actually, there are two of us. Cam Tucker is my wingman. How is she? Is she at this hospital, too?"

No one answered.

Bree smiled, shook her head. "Knowing Cam, she managed to get through this without a scratch, the little stinker."

Uncomfortable silence met her words, and everyone looked at everyone else but her. Bree stopped breathing, and her face felt hot. "She's not okay, is she?" Were they going to tell her that Cam hadn't made it? That the drugs that had so sickened Bree had killed her friend? "Is she alive? Just answer me that."

Min Park, the mind doctor, opened her mouth to speak, but Kyber's hand went up, stopping her. "We found you in an underwater cave one week ago. Until that day, I didn't know the cave existed. Records show that the site was once a North Korean laboratory. Heavy bombing reduced it to rubble. It complicated the rescue."

"They bombed the lab," Bree whispered. She remembered none of it.

"Anyone else who may have been with you in the cave either escaped at that time or was killed."

"Cam wouldn't leave without me."

Kyber's voice took a sudden tender turn. To Bree, the gentleness was out of place on a man of his size and stature. "They searched, Banzai, searched until a typhoon warning forced me to order an evacuation of the cave. I didn't want them stranded underwater with rough conditions at the surface."

Hope flared. "They'll go back to finish."

Kyber shook his head. "Those are some of my finest men. I trust them when they say they performed a thorough search. They found no bodies. Although the sea may have long since washed away any human remains."

Something in her chest knotted into a ball. *Ah, Cam . . .* It seemed as if an air force chaplain should be telling her this, not him. "What about the Americans? Aren't we searching the ocean? The divers will look. There has to be a body somewhere. I know Cam was with me. I rode in the truck with her." Bree had passed out on her! "Cam was there. She was there."

Min Park shook her head. "I'm sorry—"

Pressure built up behind Bree's eyes. "The bastards," she whispered bitterly. "They killed her."

Kyber's expression darkened. "Or took her, as they would have stolen you, had I not intervened in time."

Bree jerked her head up. The idea of Cam as a hostage carried a hell of a lot more hope than one of her dead.

"We have one man in custody. He claims to know nothing of another pilot." Kyber made a fist. "If he has lied, he will die. No one steals from the Hans."

He fumed, but as soon as he returned his attention to Bree, his expression transformed back to a disturbing mix of possession and awe. When he spoke, his voice had turned husky with reverence. "But, perhaps, I will keep the bastard alive—if only because he brought me to you."

Kyber brought his hand close to her cheek. Bree held her breath as it hovered there. But he didn't touch her. Making a fist, he pushed to his feet and strode from the room.

The doctors resumed their fussing over her, and Bree stared straight ahead. She worked hard at remembering the man who'd woken her the first time, the blue-eyed soldier. She'd assumed he was Special Forces, although now that she thought of it, she hadn't seen a uniform. He'd worn a black wet suit with no insignia.

This man was Kyber's "bastard." Bree scowled. If Blue Eyes had anything to do with Cam's disappearance, she wouldn't wait for Kyber to hurt him. She'd do it herself.

* * *

Ty woke with his cheek pressed to a cold stone floor. Something tickled and bumped his nose. He opened his eyes and focused on a pink muzzle with twitching whiskers. The furry head turned, and a black, beady eye stared back at him.

Groaning, Ty pushed off the floor. The rats scurried off into the depths of the surrounding underground dungeon. A summer palace equipped with a dungeon. How convenient. Ty supposed that the Hans didn't believe in taking vacations from pillage and torture.

He shoved a hand through his hair. The short strands were greasy and matted with dried blood. The floor was wet where he sat. A drop of water landed with a plunk. It came from above his head, foul-smelling. Ty hoped it wasn't seepage from the palace's sewer system. The dungeon stank so badly, he wouldn't have been able to tell if it was. Another drip landed. Tiny creatures wriggled through the puddles on the floor. Larvae? Ty quickly checked for open cuts and bruises, wiping the scrapes on his arm with the filthy tattered hem of his prison shirt, hoping he'd acted before any exotic diseases kicked in.

He exhaled and rubbed his forehead. He would have been home by now—with *her*. Instead, he sat in a cage, wasting time while someone else had what he'd wanted. That haunted him.

He should be less affected. He'd raided tombs before, hunted for treasure. There was always someone else who thought they owned what you were after. Robbery was always a risk. He'd gone into this knowing that. But this was different. It was Banzai he'd found. Banzai Maguire. She'd been right in his hands. He'd touched her, seen her face. Damn it, she belonged to him!

And now someone else had her.

Ty stood, staggering a bit before he found his balance. They'd beaten him again when they'd thrown him in the cell last night, but not too badly. The guards had known where to kick the toes of their boots so as not to damage a kidney or a rib.

He couldn't say the same about the soldiers who'd found him in the cave, but that had been over a week ago and something had changed since then. Kyber, his captor, wanted to keep him alive.

If not, Ty would have been dead already—or at least tortured to the point of permanent dysfunction. Instead, medics had arrived to patch him up. They'd given him nanomeds that started the process of healing his internal injuries and sealing his broken ribs. And then there was the matter of his new living quarters. This cell was luxurious compared to the places he'd stayed the past few days. Only one explanation existed: Kyber had learned the results of the DNA tagging, and thus Ty's pedigree.

Crouching, Ty used a pebble to scratch a tick mark onto the stone surface of the wall. One day down; how many more to go? It had been seven days—no, eight—since they brought him here from the cave; he'd forgotten to include the day of interrogation when he got here, during which he'd been crammed into a cell too small to stand or sit. Total: eight days missing.

Ty's next thought was of his father. The general knew he'd gone off treasure hunting, but not where he'd gone to find it. Of course, now the secret would be out. Kyber was now in a unique position to make his rival squirm. The prince would take great pleasure in tormenting the "Ax," dangling his son and only heir in front of his nose. Ty wondered how long the emperor-prince planned to hold him hostage. And what the UCE would have to give Kyber in exchange for his freedom.

The muscles in Ty's jaw tightened as he imagined Kyber savoring his rare appearance on the world stage, declaring the son of the UCE's number-one military man a trespasser and a thief. Even Ty couldn't deny it was the truth. Kyber had caught him red-handed. Although the UCE could—and probably would—argue the point that Ty was justified in stealing back what was rightfully theirs.

And, by God, he *was* justified. The claim to the missing pilots belonged to the UCE. Those pilots were a shining symbol of the past, the UCE's past. Banzai's reappearance would motivate and inspire all who came to see her. She was worth too much to the UCE to leave behind, especially in the hands of an intolerable tyrant who wouldn't understand what he possessed, who wouldn't know how—or even want—to use the pilot-hero to her full potential.

Ty explored further and found some old graffiti scratched into the wall, the legacy of those who'd previously suffered this cell. It looked like a few of them were here a while, based on the deepness of the etching, and the amount written. *D'ekkar Han Valoren*. Kyber had imprisoned another Han? The name was scratched out vigorously and replaced with *Deck*. Along with a few other illegible scribblings were several references to *Shadow Runners* and a very bold *Freedom!* Had "Deck" been part of a rebel group? And down near the corner, in large lettering in a different handwriting was *Kyber sucks!*

Ty's mouth curled. Another satisfied customer in the Kingdom of Asia, he thought.

Ty paced, analyzing his options. He was a combat veteran. He'd been in worse scrapes. He'd get out of here, and not in a body bag. He intended to walk out of Kyber's prison, and before the Kingdom of Asia could thoroughly humiliate the UCE.

Ty swore. The Kingdom of Asia? More like the Prison of Asia. No one got in, and no one got out. But Ty was determined to be an exception.

He limped back to the wall of the cell. It was made of moist, dirty stone. Yet, it was an illusion. Within its unsophisticated confines, no doubt, lurked some of the most advanced microscopic robotic technology found in the world.

He stopped, pressed his palms to the wall. Closing his eyes, Ty tried to gauge any temperature fluctuations, texture, vibration. He felt nothing out of the ordinary, but the cement more than likely contained "smart dust," programmed to track his every breath, his every move.

Everything but his thoughts.

Ty smiled. That was his one advantage over Kyber, those private thoughts. Little did Kyber know that every last one of them centered on the treasure Ty had lost and was dead-set on taking back.

Chapter Seven

It was almost dawn, an observation Bree made based on the glowing numbers of a clock built into the curved clear table near her bed; the room had no windows. It was her third night since coming awake again, becoming aware, but it was the first night she couldn't sleep. Tossing and turning, she tried to puzzle out the strange circumstances of her hospital stay.

Almost every one of her conscious moments over the past two days had involved some sort of physical therapy. In one respect, she'd welcomed the exertion. It distracted her. Left alone, she spent her time beating herself up over her role in Cam's fate. If she'd been more observant, reacted quicker, looked harder, who knew, maybe her friend would be alive. Of course, there was that reedy little voice of dissension that assured her she'd done all she could.

On the other hand, if she was feeling guilty, then she must be feeling better. She knew herself well enough to figure that out. And now that she was feeling better, she wanted out of the hospital.

It wasn't that she had complaints about the care. Meals came regularly and were nutritious and tasty—although the too-obviously genetically bioengineered pitless avocados and the cute apple-sized watermelons with edible peels were more than a little strange. And Kyber's all-female medical team of identical twins acted as if she were the center of their lives. What more could a patient want?

Access to the outside world.

Where were the intelligence people? They were usually the first on the scene, even before the shrinks and chaplains showed up, so they could begin the lengthy process of debriefing a freed POW. And why couldn't she use the phone?

Her "fragile physical condition" was always the excuse the doctors gave her. Granted, for a while, she *had* felt fragile, and didn't argue with the diagnosis, but she wasn't feeling that way anymore.

Maybe she could wander the halls a bit before the sisters came on duty, chat with the doctors and nurses working the graveyard shift, and see what she could find out about using the phone. *Good idea, Maguire.*

Sitting up, she swung her legs off the bed. There was no wooziness this time, another sign that she was on the mend. A faint humming noise caught her attention. It was barely audible, lower in pitch and volume than a mosquito.

Something glinted to her right, and a silver sphere floated into her field of vision. At first, in the dim light, she thought her bleary eyes were playing tricks on her. But, it was a sphere, and it was bobbing . . . all on its own.

In midair.

It rotated, laser-sharp lights glowing, and paused to hover in front of her face. "Pip!" it chirped.

Bree lifted her finger to touch it, and changed her mind. How *was* the thing floating? No hospital she knew had that kind of technology. It begged an answer to the question: Where was she?

"Lights on," Bree said, as she'd heard the sisters Park do. The walls and ceiling glowed brighter, providing the room's lighting from an opaque, almost luminescent material resembling white crystal. The furnishings and tech reeked of money. The setup bore less resemblance to a hospital room than it did a converted bedroom in an opulent home.

All the more reason to take a walk.

Wobbling a bit, she stood. Her muscles ached some, but all things considered she felt pretty darn good. Not great, but good enough to find a telephone. And, if she was lucky, a Coke and a Milky Way. Her caffeine level was dangerously low.

She crossed the room to the huge double doors that everyone used to come in and out. The sphere followed her. "Pip! Pip!"

She ignored it, as she'd ignore an annoying, yapping dog that she didn't know. It seemed harmless, but it might have sharp teeth.

The doors were heavy. Bree leaned her shoulder against one and pushed hard. Then she tried the other. No dice. Running her fingers along the frame revealed no knobs, handles, or dead bolts. She was locked in. Trapped.

She didn't like the feeling. At all.

She tried again, shoving her full weight against the door. It didn't budge. She slammed her hands against the surface. "Open!"

"Pip!"

Bree pushed away from the door and looked down her nose at the floating ball. "I don't suppose you have any ideas."

"Pip!" A thread of light shot out of it and into her right eye.

A violet splash of light blinded Bree. Her pores went electric as she staggered backward, covering her eyes. There was a commotion outside the doors. Her hospital staff pushed them open and swarmed into the room.

Dr. Park's gaze traveled from the lights turned on in the room to where Bree now stood, spitting mad. "Captain Maguire. What's wrong?"

"That *thing* flashed something in my eye."

"It was a routine scan, nothing more."

"I don't care what it was. Never mess with a pilot's eyes. If that little disco ball tries to shine any more lights without my express permission, I'm going to see how it likes playing Ping-Pong."

"Pip!" The sphere bounced close to Bree's face, and she blocked it with the heel of her palm. It thudded into her hand with a clanking noise, as if she'd knocked something loose inside. "Pip!" It came at her again. She drew her arm back.

"Pip, go!" Dr. Park shouted, and the sphere soared off. "Please don't be alarmed."

Bree rubbed her palm. "Keep it away from me."

"Pip is your triage nurse, my robotic assistant."

"A what? A robot?"

The ball was back, hovering near Dr. Park. It rotated, its tiny lights pulsating. Some sort of wireless communication was going on between the sphere and Dr. Park's handheld, which seemed to confirm the woman's explanation about the scan. "When you arose from bed on your own, Pip reacted to your unpredicted behavior. It's programmed to monitor your vital signs during the night."

"And ring the bell if I get loose, hmm?"

Bree's slang seemed to baffle the elegant physician, as it often did the man named Kyber. What was with these people? Did they live in isolation, too? "I tried to get out but couldn't open the doors. Why am I locked in, Dr. Park? Am I a prisoner or a patient?"

Kyber strode into the room. As always, he was dressed impeccably in black, but his hair was damp, as if he'd come straight from his room and a morning shower. The helper sisters clustered near the door, fell to their knees in a bow. He dismissed them without a second glance.

Bree turned on him before he could say anything. "I was given an invasive examination. Without my consent." She thrust an accusing finger at the sphere. "By that."

"It was merely a scan," Dr. Park protested. "Completely benign."

Kyber acted outraged on Bree's behalf. "You did not forewarn her, Dae?"

"My apologies, Your Highness. I'm so used to Pip and its kind that I didn't take into consideration that she wouldn't know."

"You delay me from telling her the truth, and yet you treat her with technology she can't comprehend. Days have passed. She is stronger now, both physically and emotionally. The time has come for her to learn the facts of her situation."

Bree's attention jumped from the man to the woman and back again. The "facts"? Her "situation"? Come to think of it, what *was* her situation? Why was she isolated, locked up overnight? How come she hadn't seen a single person in an American uniform during her entire stay?

You're still in North Korea.

Ice flooded Bree's veins. All at once, all the puzzle pieces fell into place: the strange hospital room, the weird accented English, the lack of contact with anyone she knew. She was imprisoned somewhere in North Korea. Why hadn't she seen it before? Kyber claimed the blue-eyed diver had tried to "steal" her. But maybe the North Koreans were the hostage takers, and had abducted her from the hands of the U.S. rescue team! And they hadn't caught Cam. No. Somehow, Cam had got free. That's why she wasn't here, not because she was dead.

How come it took her this long to figure it out? How could she be so stupid? So trusting?

They've been calling you by your name, fighter call sign, and rank. The enemy wouldn't know her name.

Unless she'd given it to them during interrogation.

His English is flawless.

Okay, so he had British schooling. His father, whoever he was, wouldn't be the first enemy of the United States to buy his son an Oxford education.

Kyber's expression showed that he'd noted the dawning horror in her face. "Banzai . . ."

Bree stepped backward. "You're North Korean."

"I am not. Let me assure you that you are in friendly hands. We are not the people who captured you. We are not North Koreans. Or South, as we allowed you to believe. Much has happened to you, some of which you will not be able to comprehend all at once. We were in danger of losing you; your condition was fragile. My best medical people advised that further trauma could jeopardize your recovery. I didn't want to do that." His voice gentled. "I want you to get well."

Something in Kyber's eyes gave her pause. Sincerity, graveness, those qualities would be hard to fake. But that's what she saw reflected in Kyber's gaze. Nothing in his expression indicated malice. "Who are you?"

He shared a brief, insider smile with the doctors, who appeared more concerned than amused. "It is not too often I am asked that question." The worker-bee sisters who had paused in their chores reacted to Bree's question with alarm. But, clearly relishing the moment, Kyber dipped his head in a gallant bow. "I am Prince Kyber of the Han Dynasty, ruler of all Asia."

Ruler of all Asia. Oh, please. She'd heard that North Koreans were egocentric, but this was for the birds.

He lifted his head. "You do not believe me."

Well, duh. "I need to contact my commanding officer to let him know I'm okay. Phone or e-mail is fine. I don't care."

"I am afraid I can't have you do that."

Bree folded her hands over her chest. "Can't? Or won't?"

"Can't."

She'd expected won't. "Why not?"

"Because he or she is dead, Banzai. Everyone you once knew is dead."

Her stomach took a sickening plunge. It was hard to catch her breath. "I . . . don't believe you."

He waved at the empty bed behind her. "Perhaps you would like to sit."

"That's okay. I can take this standing up."

But Kyber continued to act reluctant about spilling what he wanted to tell her, and since she had the feeling that he wasn't normally a man who wavered, it didn't bode well for what she was about to learn.

Squaring his shoulders, he clasped his hands behind his back, paced a few times in front of her, and stopped. "The underground laboratory in which you were put into stasis was bombed. Bombed heavily."

"That's what I understand," she said.

"Rubble buried you in the cave. The pod protected you and kept you alive. Somehow it maintained power. But your rescue . . . it was delayed." Kyber, his hands still clasped behind his back, studied her for long moments. "You were trapped in stasis for 170 years. I rescued you, and now you are safe."

Bree never stuttered, but she did now. "S-say again?"

"You were trapped in stasis for almost two centuries. It is 2176."

"Twenty-one seventy-six," she confirmed. "The year."

"Yes."

The other women looked on, grave and concerned. Either this was an elaborately concocted scheme to brainwash her à la *The Manchurian Candidate*, or Kyber was telling the truth and she'd done a Rip Van Winkle and slept through the last 170 years. She wasn't sure which scenario was more far-fetched.

Bree pushed her hair away from her face. It fell around her shoulders. She took a lock in her fingers and stared at the strands, her heart beating hard. Her hair had grown longer. She'd noticed yesterday, but had been too sick and too tired for it to sink in. For years, she'd worn her hair in a jaw-length bob, both for the ease of wearing that kind of style with a helmet and because it looked good on her. But her hair was longer than it ever was, reflecting months and months of growth. The hair on her legs had grown in, too. It was fine hair, but she always waxed. And she'd just done so a few days before the mission. It shouldn't have grown back for months. . . .

A thousand rapid-fire thoughts flickered through her mind. Didn't the scientist who captured her say she'd age while in stasis, but at a much slower rate? Did 170 years in the pod equate to approximately one year in normal time?

An awful feeling of dread grabbed at her chest. Mom, Dad, her older sister, Brittany . . . were they dead? Had they died believing that *she* was dead?

What about Cam? Her best friend. Bree hugged her arms to her chest and stared hard at the floor. Cam had probably died in her pod. How could Bree wallow in self-pity knowing that? She fought off a sharp wave of guilt. Survivor's guilt. She was all too familiar with it.

She felt stinging in her hands and realized that her long fingernails had cut into the flesh of her palms. Opening her hands, she stared at bright smudges of blood.

The third Dr. Park grabbed a vial of something and swabbed the wounds, her dismay visible.

Bree lifted her head. "Show me something with the date. Money, a calendar, anything."

Min took a note-sized piece of paper from her front pocket. "My schedule book."

While the other woman cleansed Bree's wounds, Bree looked at Min Park's book, which was about the same size and thickness as a printed photo but glowed like a computer screen, and was flexible, too. With a brush of Min's fingertip, a faint musical chime sounded and a forest in autumn appeared. Tiny trees in incredible, three-dimensional detail. Then the image broke into squares and reformed as a calendar floating a few hairbreadths above the base. A twelve-month calendar. The familiar layout was comforting, but the date was not. It said *August 27, 2176.*

"It's in English," Bree accused. "Or is that just for my benefit?"

"More precisely, it's Hannish."

"I've never heard of it."

"It didn't exist in your time. When Asia erased its borders in 2043, it required a unifying language free of the past. We speak a dialect that adheres strictly to the version of English spoken in London at the time of our revolution. The first Han king was married to a Scot. He'd lived in London for many years. He felt that declaring English as the national language would be easier than trying to combine myriad dialects—or having to choose one from among many. Yes, there was opposition, but it eventually died out after a generation or two. It was a brilliant choice, Hannish. It unified us. Language does not a civilization define, Banzai. Regional culture lives on in many ways. I support and encourage it."

Kyber had an answer for everything. She didn't want answers. She wanted to poke holes in his airtight claims, to catch him in his lie. A lie meant she had a chance to go home.

The truth meant she'd lost everything.

Except her country. "I can still go home. Does the United States know you found me? They'll want to repatriate me."

Kyber's gray eyes had that sympathetic look to them again, the look she was beginning to dread. It meant he had something to say that she wasn't going to like. "The United States is no more, Banzai. There is the UCE, the United Colonies of Earth. It grew out of the country you once knew."

The unease that had so far been lying like a cold rock in her stomach expanded. The room was cool, but she'd started to sweat. "It doesn't matter what they're called, that's where I belong."

"No." Kyber's expression hardened. "They'll want you back, but they don't deserve you."

"Isn't that my choice to make?"

"Not as long as you remain uninformed. The UCE is not the U.S.A. It would be incredibly naïve to confuse the two." Kyber lifted a hand. "Medcom. Show world map."

The entire rear wall of the room pixilated into a screen with resolution that made the picture she'd watched on her brand-new satellite-imagery, high-definition TV look like a 1950s black-and-white.

On display was a world map in intricate three-dimensional detail. Glowing sapphire borders marked the borders of various countries. The cities themselves were clearly visible. The first difference Bree noticed was the encroachment of the oceans on the coasts. The seas had risen, as everyone had predicted. Then she noticed that the myriad nations she was used to seeing were gone. With a few exceptions, the countries of the world had consolidated into several enormous entities.

Kyber flicked on a handheld beam of light. "A lesson in geography, Banzai." His light circled the continent of

Africa before making a ring around Europe. "The Euro-African Consortium, overseen from Paris by the United Nations. Or does the consortium oversee the perpetually inept U.N.? Nobody knows." He gave her a long-suffering sideways glance. "No one can tell." The beam of light bounced across the Atlantic Ocean. "Here lies the Dominion of Tri-Canada. Poor Canada, when will you come out of your quarantine?" Kyber sighed. "Maybe never. A full century after suffering a massive plague, they cower behind a veil of seclusion in self-imposed isolation. Perhaps they don't want to attract the lusty interest of their neighbor in the south."

The light tracked downward, swinging around the United States and nearly half the rest of the world: Mexico, South America, Antarctica, Iraq, Iran, Turkey, and the Middle East. "This is the UCE, Banzai. The United Colonies of Earth. But all that unites this distended, overextended malignancy are the taxes wrung from its more capable colonies."

The United States was an imperial power? It had colonies? It was inconceivable that the United States had turned into what it most hated when it broke from England in the 1700s. Incomprehensible, that America would turn its back on the principles that had set it apart as the cradle of independence and freedom for hundreds of years.

Grandpa Vitale would roll over in his grave.

Now Bree knew what Kyber had meant—this wasn't the U.S.A. she knew. She stared at her fisted hands. Tears didn't seem an appropriate response. She felt too empty. *The United States is no more.* Something else to mourn. Add her country to the long list.

But if there wasn't a U.S.A., where did she belong? Surely there were remnants left of her old home. But she didn't know enough about this new world to find them. If in fact it was a new world. The only proof she had of that was Kyber's word and a collection of cool high-tech gizmos.

But he sure sounded convincing.

Kyber's beam of light swung south and west. "Australia, Earth's waste dump. All trash graciously accepted, human and otherwise," he spat before slicing the beam of light northward toward Asia.

Bree stopped him. "What about India?"

"Gone."

"Gone? How can it be gone?"

"The land is there, but it is mostly uninhabitable. So are Pakistan, Nepal, Kashmir, Afghanistan, and the southern edge of the Himalayas. How did it happen? Terrorists set off a small nuclear device in Bombay. It destroyed the financial district. India blamed it on Pakistan and lobbed a bigger one back. By the time they were done, a billion people were dead. That was over a century ago."

Except for the old nightmares that visited her in the dark, nothing scared her. No Fear was her motto, and the fighter pilot's creed. But now her hands were shaking. "God help them," Bree whispered.

"On this planet we don't agree on much, but most say

that war saved us all. The damage done was so far beyond what anyone could comprehend, or stomach, that to this day no country has ever again threatened the use of nuclear weapons. Our conflicts can be bitter, and bloody, but they are conventional."

Bree felt the beginnings of a headache. Dull pain pulsed behind her eyes. It reminded her of her physical debilitation, that she was not yet well. But she had to keep her focus squarely on Kyber and the information he passed on. Her gut told her it would mean the difference between living through this, or not. Bree walked over to the bed and sat on the edge. Leaning an elbow on her thigh, she dropped her chin onto her palm.

"She needs a drink," the self-proclaimed prince declared.

"Yes, of course." Dr. Park gestured to one of the helper-sisters. "Joo-Eun. Bring water."

"Not water." Kyber lifted a hand. "A *drink!*"

"No, no, Your Highness. She cannot drink. Not alcohol."

His mouth twisted in a mulish frown. "I would say she could use one."

"I would say you're right," Bree agreed. Who cared if it wasn't good judgment? Who cared if it was 6:00 in the morning? Shock had made her downright giddy. "Make it something strong."

Everyone stared at her—the medical people with dismay, Kyber with a twinkle of amusement and approval in his eyes. He snapped his fingers. "Bring my best vodka!"

The doctors rubbed their foreheads as Joo-Eun ran off to comply with the prince's orders. It added to the surrealism of the situation.

"Proof, Kyber," she said, lifting her head. "I need it."

"And proof you will have. One hundred proof!"

Had he just made a joke? Holy Christmas, he had.

Despite her grief and anxiety, Bree felt her mouth twitch. That humor again. He had the same bad sense of timing as she did. Got her into trouble all the time.

If only he were joking about the rest. The seriousness in his eyes told her that he wasn't.

"Not that kind of proof, Kyber. Come on, Buck Rogers got a ride in a flying car, and all I get is a slide show and a history lesson? It's going to take more than this to convince me that I slept for almost two centuries."

Kyber lifted his hands helplessly. "Your English . . . if only I could decipher it."

"I want proof that what you're telling me is true. Proof that I can see with my own eyes. You have some cool gadgets, but for all I know I'm still in North Korea."

"You are *here*." The wall distorted and reformed into a panorama of forest and sky. "My summer palace," he said.

As in, not his winter one? But Bree didn't make the comment. She guessed there were still people in the world who owned more than one palace. Only she'd never run into any.

A huge mountain dominated the scene, dusted with white at the peak. "This is a sacred place, Banzai. In Korean mythology, the son of the Lord of Heaven descended to earth, right here, and the first Korean empire began. Now *I* am here." He gave her his most charming smile. "In the summer months, at least. Here on the slopes of Paekdusan, the weather stays cool."

Paekdusan! "That's in North Korea. Up by the Chinese border."

"Three hundred and fifty kilometers northeast of what used to be called Pyongyang," he confirmed.

You lying bastard. "You said you weren't North Koreans."

"I told you the truth. The former capital of the People's Democratic Republic of Korea is now called North Han City, and has been for over a century."

Bree pressed her fists together and pushed them against her mouth. The map disappeared, and the wall screen panned out over a vast wilderness. It was full summer outside, blue sky, puffy clouds, green trees, and it made Bree's heart ache for her home in Chestnut. Then the camera sped up and ascended the side of the volcano. At the very top of the volcano was a huge, deep blue lake that filled the crater, ringed by stony crags. A cluster of cabins stood near the shore. The word *cabin* didn't do the exquisite buildings justice, but they appeared to be made of wood. Soft smoke curled out of the chimney of one.

"Chonji," Kyber said. "Lake of Heaven. It sits there, at the summit. It is one of the deepest and coldest alpine lakes in the world. We'll go often. You'll enjoy our swims there as long as you stay close to the hot springs." His even, white teeth gleamed. "I will make sure that you do."

"You make it sound as if I'm staying."

He spread his hands. "Where else will you go?"

Her chin jutted up. "Home."

"Where is that? Somewhere in the UCE?" He said the name with disdain.

The United States is no more. Bree tried to keep her face blank of the emotions swirling inside her.

The wall once more formed into a view of the world. Kyber reaimed his beam of light at the map. "My kingdom is a land of peace and prosperity." His eyes turned smoky; his voice deepened and warmed. Bree couldn't help thinking he'd use that tone of voice in bed with a lover. His light caressed all of Asia, circled a shrunken Indonesia and Philippines, slid up to Siberia, Mongolia, and around the eastern half of Russia. "We have the highest literacy rate, the lowest infant mortality rate, and the longest life span in the world. There is no better place to live than here."

"You make your kingdom sound perfect," she said.

"It is."

"Don't you wish?" she said under her breath, giving in to a fit of petulance. Finding out that you'd lost just about everything you had, and then learning the little you thought was left didn't exist either—well, it made a girl grumpy.

"Actually, I do wish, Banzai. Let me say rather that my kingdom is perfect most of the time—but that is another matter, one that has to do with politics, of which I had my fill last night." He glanced at both Drs. Park, who had been following the conversation and Bree's distress with physician-ish disapproval. "Parliament troubles in Australia. Macao again. Greedy energy brokers. It's been this way since my grandfather's reign in the thirties," he told Bree. "I have yet to decide on a solution."

"The thirties?" She tried to trap him. Math could catch the best of liars. "That was almost eighty years ago. Your grandfather would have been a little kid, if he was born at all yet."

"It has been only forty years, Banzai."

"How's that?"

"The 2130s. Not your 1930s."

He'd done it again. The perfect answer.

"If you're the prince," she asked him, "who's the king?"

"My father is the king." A few seconds of silence ticked by. "He lives here in the palace with my mother, the queen. But his condition leaves him unable to rule."

"His . . . condition," Bree hinted, looking for more.

Kyber was fond of long-winded answers, but on this topic his reticence was obvious. Family issues. Bree let it go at that. "You're a hereditary leader, though. You hold no elections. Your people have no choice in leaders but you. You're a dictator."

She knew she was being reckless with her words. Kyber held all the cards; she had none. With a wave of his royal hand, he could have her head lopped off right where she stood. And yet, it didn't scare her. Nothing did anymore.

She felt empty. No fear, no grief. Thrust into a strange new world, she had nothing to lose but her principles. She wouldn't sacrifice those; they defined her. She was an American soldier, even if there was no more America. She'd hang on to what she believed until the end.

She waved her hand at the luxury surrounding them. "I joined the air force to rid the world of so-called leaders who live in luxury while their population suffers."

"Suffers!" He reared back. "My people are happy. Blissfully so. If I opened the borders, none would leave. I'd have to fight back a tide of refugees from everywhere else."

Bree snorted. "I'm sure Genghis Khan said the same thing. And Stalin."

Too bad Joo-Eun hadn't returned with the vodka. Bree needed that shot. Maybe the whole bottle. Or, maybe her grief was coming out as anger, and she was taking it out on Kyber.

The emperor-prince puffed out his chest. "I am not your average despot. I'm . . . an autocrat with a heart, a tyrant with a conscience. Come, Banzai, surely this is as obvious to you as it is to my own people." To his full-of-himself stance, he added a killer smile.

The man was hot, Bree decided. The trouble was, he knew it. If only she were as convinced of the facts of her situation as Kyber was about his looks.

Kyber turned to the doctors for support. He spread his hands wide. "She does not believe me." Sighing, he strode over to where Bree sat on the bed and hoisted her into his arms.

"Oh . . ." She grabbed his shoulders for balance.

"My people are happy, Banzai. They do not suffer. I will prove it to you now!" The room spun as he swung around and carried her out the door.

Chapter Eight

Dr. Park protested. "Your Highness! She must rest. She's been up too long as it is."

Kyber shifted Bree's weight in his arms, but he didn't put her down. "Dae, you act as if we haven't spent the past week trying to keep her awake!"

Bree settled the argument. "I feel fine. I'm going." It was a chance to get past the locked doors. She didn't care about the specifics.

Granted, it felt a little weird: Kyber holding her. As a rule, men didn't carry her places. But she sensed nothing untoward on Kyber's part. He acted like a perfect gentleman.

Also, working with men all her life, she'd mastered the tricky art of compromise—when to give in, and when not to, to preserve the egos of Mars *and* Venus.

She slipped her arms around Kyber's broad, leather-clad shoulders. "As soon as we're out of sight of Dr. Park, you can put me down. I can walk, but if they think I'm having trouble, they'll try to make me rest." Whether it had been one year or 170, she'd been in bed too long.

"Dae is not happy with me," Kyber admitted. "I have no doubt I will hear about it later."

Bree craned her head to peek over Kyber's shoulder. The women watched him carry her swiftly away, their faces pinched in varying degrees of concern. "Are they sisters? The younger ones look like a set of sextuplets."

"No. They're clones, not sisters."

"Clones." Good Lord.

"But not Dae. She was my father's muse."

The slight change in Kyber's tone hinted that the physician might have been more than a muse to the king.

"My father considered her so brilliant, so beautiful, he had to have more of her. So he had more made. Nine altogether. But as in any reproduction, I've learned, the copies are never as good as the original. Dae's first clone was also brilliant, but not right to be a surgeon. Hand-eye coordination concerns. But her talents suited the field of psychiatry, where she has done quite well. The second genetic copy made an excellent medical technician. The other fourth, fifth, and sixth, in decreasing levels of abilities, were fit to be servants only, as you saw."

"You said nine? Where are the others?"

"They were put to rest in childhood. Inadequate brain function."

"Put to rest? You mean euthanized? *Killed?*"

"That is correct."

Bree stared straight ahead. "They were people. . . ."

"No, Banzai, they were clones. But the topic spurs debates all over the kingdom—and the world, as I understand it. In your time, people debated whether or not those still in the womb were people. This is no different. As our machines become self-aware we will undoubtedly debate their humanity, as well." His voice turned thoughtful. "They are important, those debates. What decisions we make will ultimately define us as a civilization."

Her impression of Kyber so far had been of a big, good-natured, good-looking—and maybe a bit simple—man who loved his power and status. Two new qualities made her rethink her original opinion: ruthlessness and razor-sharp intelligence.

The clone issue, however, nagged at her. "What did Dr. Park think of your father making copies of her?"

"I don't know. I never asked." He pondered that for a moment. "I would think she'd take it as the compliment that it was."

Bree wondered what Dr. Park thought about Kyber's father killing off versions of herself. Weren't doctors supposed to respect life, *any* life? Maybe Kyber's father kept presenting copies *of* Dae *to* Dae as gifts, and she liked having the extra help around. Bree could think of a few times when a clone of herself would have freed up some time and gotten her out of a few annoying obligations. And maybe the king kept secret the ones he had to return to the store.

Kyber set a fast pace. Two men dressed in black body armor followed him and Bree. Bodyguards, she guessed. But they seemed invisible to Kyber, as did Joo-Eun and the other three subservient sisters in the hospital room.

"We are leaving the medical wing now," Kyber told her. The hall they entered was enormous, its floors and walls made of creamy marble shot through with honey-colored veins. "The area is sealed off from the rest of the palace. It exists as a hospital to serve my family, and for the isolation of infections, if required."

"No cures for disease?"

"We have cures for most of them. But new diseases appear every year, designed by the terrorists in their labs. Those cause us trouble, from time to time."

"The terrorists or the diseases?"

"Both." Kyber carried her to a pair of massive double doors. There, the guards who had escorted them from the hospital wing stopped to confer with guards behind the doors. The woodwork around the frame looked like teak, carved intricately with scenes from Korean folklore. It fit the theme of the palace: an odd mix of ultramodern West and ancient Oriental.

The guards pulled the doors open, revealing another vast hall. The same marble that covered the floor in the hospital wing formed benches and sculptures that seemed to rise up out of the floor, fully formed. Doors off to each side looked like they led to bedrooms. Bedrooms upon bedrooms. She thought of the tiny little house in Chestnut, New York, where she'd grown up. The wood floor under the carpet squeaked. The radiators clanged early on winter mornings when her mother turned up the heat, waking Bree to the smell of breakfast cooking. That was a home. How could this palace ever be a home . . . to anyone?

Kyber's palace was a castle in the truest, fairy-tale sense of the word. Outside the grand windows, she saw towers and turrets. Beyond were mountains and forest. But it was very clearly summer. The sky was robin's-egg blue; birds flitted back and forth. Freedom, she thought, her chest constricting. Would she ever taste it again?

Art prints lined the walls of the grand hallway of the residential area. *The Persistence of Memory*, *The Hallucinogenic Toreador*, and more—all prints by Salvador Dali. So, Kyber was a fan of the artist. In a way, it figured: She felt the same way around the paintings as she did with the emperor-prince. Dali art always made her a little uncomfortable, as if she were peeking at the artist's private fantasies, and seeing in them a few of her own to which she'd rather not admit. And there was that one of the melting clock. *The Persistence of Memory*. How apropos, considering what he'd told her about her situation.

"You like Dali," Kyber noted in his deep voice.

"I find him . . . interesting. Disturbing, sometimes." She let it go at that. "Your reproductions are fantastic."

Kyber chuckled. "They are not reproductions."

He owned the world's supply of Dali paintings? As she worked at absorbing what he'd just said, he carried her through another set of open double doors and into a vast chamber where a foyer of black granite danced with reflections of lavish tapestries, pieces of oriental furniture, and towering celadon vases—all ancient and priceless, she'd bet. In the center was an indoor fountain that was large enough to be a swimming pool. The grandeur was breathtaking.

"My private quarters," he announced, carrying her finally into a somewhat smaller living area that still had to be at least two thousand square feet. Pale orange covered the walls. Bree's sister, a decorator, would have wrinkled her nose at Bree's choice of words and called it "pumpkin."

There was no marble in sight. A floor of rough-hewn wooden planks bore the muted sheen of hand waxing. Plush rugs lay scattered here and there, with an enormous white flokati rug holding the place of honor before a massive, rugged fireplace made of river rock. Stale wood smoke and a faint incensey smell scented the air. It was as if she'd entered the lair of a barbarian forest king. Maybe, Bree thought, that's exactly what she'd done.

He carried her to a pair of French doors that opened to a balcony, and swept her outside with him. There he set her on her feet and strode across the balcony to the railing. The wind was strong, and it brought a sound like the roar of the sea. Only it wasn't the sea of water, but a sea of humanity.

For as far as she could see, people filled the square below and the streets leading to the palace. There were thousands of them gathered. Bree had no words to describe the spectacle. She'd never seen anything like it in her life.

When the crowds saw Kyber appear and raise both hands over his head, they broke into a cheer. It was deafening. The cheering took on a rhythm that pulsated in her ears. Then it became clear what they were chanting.

"Kyber, Kyber, Kyber . . ."

He savored their adulation for a few moments. Then he brought his arms down. The cheering silenced, and he filled his lungs with air. "Are you happy?" he bellowed.

The roar that followed was louder than before. Bree grabbed hold of the railing behind her, worried that the vibration shaking the balcony would cause it to fall.

Kyber glanced at her over his shoulder. "See? They're happy."

Bree swallowed. "Yeah. I see that."

She also saw the boxy aircraft that took off vertically from a pad down below. It lifted into the sky, slow and controlled, and flew past the balcony. Bree knew on sight every airplane in the world. She'd never seen one like that. In the distance, near forested hills, cars and assorted other vehicles skimmed over a gleaming road, fully levitating.

It wasn't 2006—she knew that much.

No, Dorothy wasn't in Kansas anymore.

Kyber offered his hand to her. "Join me. They want to see you."

"They know I'm here?"

"Yes." He lowered his chin. "Come. Let them see that you are safe."

She looked at the crowd, then back at their ruler. If she joined him, would it signify a betrayal of everything she stood for?

Kyber waited for her, his arm extended, palm up.

Bree hesitated. She'd had a life. Before. A good one. But there came a time when you had to put the past behind and keep going. A new beginning didn't mean giving up who you were.

But who are you? What are you?

Bree could honestly say that she wasn't sure anymore; and she took that first step toward Kyber. A second step brought their hands together. He stared at her so intently, for a heartbeat she thought he'd kiss her. But he pulled her to the edge of the balcony and raised their clasped hands toward the sky.

The thundering cheers surged in volume. At first it was wild cheering, and then it turned rhythmic, growing louder and louder. "Banzai . . . Banzai . . . Banzai. . . ."

Chapter Nine

The applauding and whistling continued without signs of letting up. After a while, Bree ached to escape the noise—and the unabashed hero worship—but the cheering didn't bother Kyber. In fact, he seemed to thrive on it.

Well, let him, she thought. He'd obviously earned their adoration. This was Shangri-la, the Garden of Eden, everything he'd said it was, obviously. She should be grateful she was here, and not with the rebel who'd tried to steal her.

She wished she were happier about it.

Her hand throbbed in Kyber's powerful grip. He pumped his other fist in the air to thunderous applause. It was obvious they'd keep on cheering for as long as their king remained on the balcony.

Behind them, an assortment of Kyber's staff waited at the entrance to the balcony. The men and women were of various races and nationalities, and a mix of those, as well: Asian, Caucasian, Indian. Their expressions reflected both patience and alertness. They were used to this.

Bree thought of tactfully extricating her fingers from Kyber's hand when a flash caught her eye. Low. Off to the right. In the crowd. Fireworks, was her first thought. But two white streaks of phosphorescence flew toward the balcony, and the beginnings of a collective gasp from the crown muted the cheers. Bree's fighter-pilot instincts kicked into full throttle. Not fireworks—it was an attack.

Bree jerked her hand from Kyber's grip. She used her full weight to shove him away. But it took a foot hooked behind his legs to take him down.

Kyber's body took the brunt of their fall. With his arms around her, he rolled her away from the railing.

There was a flash of light and then a one-two boom. His hands shielded her head. The lack of heat and shrapnel told her that the missiles, or whatever they were, had missed. The midair explosion turned the crowd's chants to screams.

Kyber's staff was on the move. Feet thundered on the balcony. Guards shouted, positioning themselves while the staff hurried to assist. Kyber lifted Bree to her feet and pulled her into his bedroom.

"Someone attacked you," she gasped as he made her sit in a soft chair.

"Tried to attack," Kyber corrected. "The balcony has a molecular barrier. Nothing can penetrate. Well, I suppose it could if a bomb were powerful enough—"

"I thought they liked you!"

"They do!"

"They sure have a funny way of showing it." She sank deeper into the cushions. Her protective instincts were in high gear. Adrenaline continued to pump through her and made her shake.

"Those were small-time terrorists, Banzai. Hoodlums. Escapees from Newgate, Australia, or maybe malcontents from Macao. Or possibly supporters of my half brother—which doesn't rule out the first two possibilities, and in fact strengthens the odds of a connection. D'ekkar and his supposedly shadowy friends . . ." He shook his head.

Kyber obviously didn't think very highly of his half brother if his expression was any indication. "But likely it was your appearance that encouraged them, whoever they are, to set off their daytime fireworks."

"Oh. Blame it on me."

Kyber's mouth twisted into a near smile. "You drew attention. They wanted a share of it. The missiles they used were more for show than damage."

She sank deeper into the chair. The adrenaline was fading now, and in its place came bone-deep exhaustion. Or was her wiped-out condition more a factor of information overload? "They would have done some damage if they'd landed in our laps."

"But they didn't."

A member of the staff appeared behind Kyber and cleared his throat. Dressed in black except for a small, oval gray hat, he was tall and lean and all business. "Your Highness."

"Yes, Kabul."

"Security is tracking the mischief makers."

"Ah. Very good. Message me when they are in custody."

The staffer bowed and then departed. "That was my chief of palace security," Kyber told Bree. "He will take care of everything. Now, do you feel strong enough for a tour of the palace underground? You expressed worry about my safety. I want you to see some of the measures I have in place in the event of a security breach, should they ever need to be used, which I doubt highly. But a tyrant must never underestimate the cleverness of his detractors, yes?"

"I guess so. You're the first tyrant I've met."

"Ah, a virgin. I promise to handle you gently." He took her by the arm and tugged her across the room.

Bree wasn't used to feeling speechless around men. But Kyber's audacity and arrogance were so unapologetic and so part of his personality that she couldn't get angry with him. She couldn't even work up a decent blush in response. Unless she was still in shock from the episode on the balcony. Not that it was a bad thing, she thought dazedly. She was beginning to think there was a definite advantage to her state of shock. It took her mind off the grief. And if she ever were to admit she was scared, the shock would numb the fear, too.

She stumbled. Kyber swept her off her feet and into his

arms. She protested. "My coordination needs a little work, but I can walk."

"In a moment. First you must fall." He spoke to the air. "Open access!" A trapdoor opened in the wood floor, and Kyber dropped her into it.

Bree landed on a thick mat. A heavy thud told her that Kyber had fallen behind her.

"If I ever had to evacuate my quarters, I would come here," he said. He helped her to her feet, then added, "And then I would run." Then they were off and jogging through the cool and dim bowels of the palace. "How are you doing?" he asked.

She spoke between gasps. "Good." Excellent, for a 198-year-old.

"Here, I would stop and board my magcycle."

Kyber's "magcycle" looked like a cross between a jet ski and a Harley. It sat on a road, or track, gouged into the stone floor. Gleaming coils lined both sides of the track.

"Halbach arrays," he explained as he pulled two helmets off the wall, one for him, one for her. "Permanent magnets. They create inductive current in the coils."

She shook her head. "Refresh me on the physics."

"It means all we need to do is move to achieve levitation. It's the same method used by magcars all over my kingdom. And in my space program, we use a similar track to accelerate the space planes to takeoff velocity." Kyber jumped onto the magcycle. Twisting in his seat, one arm outstretched to help her board. "Sit behind me, and strap in. Yes, the thigh straps—there. And one more around your waist."

She did as she was told. It would be the height of irony to survive what she had, only to die her first week here because she didn't buckle her seat belt. She didn't see any handles to hold on to and rested her hands on Kyber's hips, motorcycle style.

Kyber squeezed something on the handlebars. Blue-white streams of energy slithered around the coils below. *Whoa*. Bree tucked her feet up on the footrests.

The vehicle rolled forward over the coils on small wheels until it reached about the speed of a fast walk. "Hold on," Kyber warned and the magcycle surged forward.

Bree heard the wheels retract. Kyber must have felt her arms tighten around him. "Levitation transition velocity," he yelled over his shoulder to be heard with the wind noise.

It was true. They weren't riding on the track, but were flying inches above it. The wind rushed at her face. Her hair whipped around her jaw and shoulders, where the helmet didn't cover.

They reached what felt like their peak speed, and held it for some time, before the vehicle started to slow. Up an incline, around a curve to the left, and the darkness gave way to light, as if they'd come to a station. The magcycle continued to slow. The wheels came down and it dropped down and hit the track.

Kyber drove the vehicle to the end of the track, where

he and Bree dismounted. Bree's legs were shaking with fatigue and excitement. "That was a great ride." She took off her helmet and shook out her hair. "Thank you."

"I would not want you to think that all I could give you was a slide show and a history lesson."

Bree tucked her tangled hair behind her ears. "Well, you came through. It felt . . . good to fly again." But that thought brought an uncomfortable sadness. She shoved it aside and poked her thumb at a staircase leading to the ceiling. "Where are we?"

"Below the medical wing. Your room. But the magtrack leads to many other stops under the palace, including my safe room, where I would join with my security team, if necessary, and maintain communication with every area of the palace and my kingdom in emergency conditions." He reached for a control panel inset in the wall and pressed an icon that looked like a corkscrew. The magcycle rotated on its wheels until it had turned 180 degrees. On its own, it rolled down the track. It hit levitation velocity and shot off into the darkness.

"It returns to the starting point on command. The magcycles—there are three—can also be summoned from any station in the palace." His gauntlet device chimed. "Yes, Kabul?"

"The troublemakers are in custody. Shall I have them brought to the dungeon after questioning, or question and release them?"

Kyber thought on that for all of two seconds. "See what information they're hiding, then, yes—a stay in the dungeon will prove rehabilitating. The message must be clear that I won't tolerate any mischief with the potential to harm Banzai Maguire."

"Yes, Your Highness. Kabul out."

"You have a *dungeon?*"

Kyber spread his hands. "What despot worth his weight in suffering would dare be caught without one?"

Then he chuckled at her surprise and shook his head. "Banzai, Banzai. I am teasing. My dungeon is rarely used, and when it is, it is to teach a lesson. In fact," he said, his self-satisfaction obvious, "the thief who tried to kidnap you is learning his lesson as we speak."

Since there were no windows, Ty judged the passage of time by the rise and fall of the temperature. The heat and humidity in the cell increased as the day wore on, and with it the stink. Since he was sweating like a pig and the place stank to holy hell, he assumed it was afternoon.

Ty dozed with his back propped against one of the walls, and as far from the hole in the floor that served as his toilet as he could. Shouting jolted him awake. He sat up, wiping one hand over his whiskered face. Guards pushed two dirty, frightened men past his cell. One man's eye was swollen shut. The other prisoner was bleeding from his mouth. Well, well. He had company. And fresh from interrogation, it looked like.

Ty pushed off the floor and went to the bars. "So, what did you two do?"

One of the guards smashed a baton against the bars, missing Ty's fingers. "Back off!"

The man with the swollen eye shrugged. "Lobbed a rocket at the Banzai Maguire celebration."

"The Banzai Maguire celebration?"

"Haven't you heard, man? Banzai Maguire." The guard shoved him along. "She slept for two centuries and the prince revived her," the man shouted over his shoulder. "A miracle."

Blood rushed to Ty's head, and his heat-induced languor evaporated. *Banzai.* He gripped the bars. "She's here? She's safe?" He swallowed, squeezed his eyes shut in thanks. Then it hit him what the man had said. "You shot a *rocket?* Was she nearby?"

"Shut up, UCE scum!" The guard whacked the bars with the baton, knocking Ty back. Then, as if looking for an easy end to the conversation, he brought his baton down on his prisoner's head. Without a sound, the man pitched forward. It wasn't a fatal blow—the guards knew how to stop short of killing you, Ty had found out the hard way—but the rebel was going to feel it in the morning.

Ty's blood boiled as he watched the guard drag the unconscious rioter to a cell. He shouted at the one who remained on his feet. "The rocket! Where did it hit?" His voice echoed through the dungeon. "If you hurt her, I'll rip out your throat!" He shook his cell door, wishing he could tear it apart.

At last, he swore and pushed away from the bars. Kyber had put Banzai Maguire on display. Wasn't he taking any precautions to keep her safe?

Jamming his hands through his hair, Ty paced. Losing your treasure was one thing, but seeing it neglected by the thief was another entirely. *She,* he corrected himself. His treasure was a woman, a living, breathing woman, and a beautiful one at that.

She's here.

That realization brought Ty to a halt. Suddenly, the local terrorists didn't seem as big of a threat to Banzai Maguire as the reputedly lusty ruler who had brought her to his lair.

Kyber invited Bree to dinner. He greeted her dressed in a softer, more casual version of his usual all-black leather outfit. Someone had lowered the lights and put on soft music.

"Dr. Park tells me you napped this afternoon," he said as he escorted her into the living-room area of his private apartment. "For seven hours. I feared I would have to come wake you and take you on another forced march."

Bree laughed. "I thought I was just closing my eyes for a few minutes. It didn't feel like I slept that long." But, then, neither had the 170 years she'd spent comatose. "I guess adulation and fireworks wear me out."

Kyber made a sound that sounded like a snort.

"You wouldn't by chance have coffee, would you? And don't tell me no one drinks it anymore. I'll die." She thought of bringing up the subject of Milky Way bars, but chose to take it one step at a time.

Kyber looked delighted and proud, as if she'd asked for

the moon and stars and he could provide them. "Yes, of course. I grow the best coffee on Earth in my plantations."

"Everything you offer is 'the best.' As if you have anything that isn't."

"I will take that as a compliment." A hint of pleasure added an extra sparkle to Kyber's magnetic smile. "And, Banzai, it seems I anticipated your request."

He gestured to a plush, multicolored rug spread with pillows by a floor-to-ceiling window with a view of the forest that surrounded the palace. On a tray sat a squat engraved silver pot with a spout that held the promise—and the scent—of rich coffee.

"Coffee," Bree said, bringing her hands together.

"Join me." Kyber settled his muscular body next to one of the pillows. His black boots scraped over the rug as he crisscrossed his long legs in front of him. Then he offered her a hand as she dropped down to sit next to one of the large, soft cushions.

Bree thanked her lucky stars that she'd somehow fallen into the hands of a rich and powerful man whose favorite pastime seemed to be making her happy. In fact, it was the only thing that had gone right in the past 170 years. She hoped her family watched over her from beyond the great divide, and saw the generosity and kindness of her rescuer.

If only her luck had extended to her research into Cam's whereabouts. "I didn't only sleep today," she admitted.

"Ah. What else did you do?" He made his inquiry in an

indulgent way that told her he knew the answer but would rather hear it from her.

"Dr. Park taught me how to use the computer." Which took some doing; the keyboard as Bree knew it was absent. "You gave me free access. I could go anywhere, see anything."

"Why not? I do not censor what my people read and learn, and I especially don't limit their access to the Web. What better way to prove that the best life is here?"

Maybe it was, she thought. "I watched a lot of news." In her first hour, she'd seen civilians clashing with UCE military—big goonlike dudes with black-and-silver-encrusted uniforms and automatic weapons. It seemed the UCE wanted to tax the use of the Interweb. One "colony"—strangely enough, the one that overlay the area of the old contiguous fifty states—had threatened a boycott of UCE goods if the tax went into effect. It was almost an exact repeat of what the British tried to do in pre-Revolutionary America. The Stamp Act was going to tax *anything* printed: newspapers, even decks of cards. It had led to violent protests, and eventually to the revolution itself.

She asked, "Have you ever heard the expression 'history repeats itself'?"

Kyber poured coffee. His expression didn't change. "Do you think it might?"

The people she'd seen on-screen might as well have been redcoats and colonists. "I think it already is. But I'm not a fortune-teller. I can't predict what will happen."

"But you have a unique perspective on our times, Banzai. Because you are from another."

Was part of her value to Kyber as political adviser? She hoped not. Her view of the world consisted only of what she'd seen, read, or downloaded. It wasn't enough. She wanted to know what else was out there. What it was really like.

Muted light, filtered by the woods outside the window, accentuated Kyber's exotic appearance as he prepared the coffee. To their cups he added honey, cream, and a cinnamon stick, without asking what she preferred. She didn't comment. She had the feeling this prince wasn't used to serving others. That he was preparing her coffee at all, with such devotion to detail, was enough to keep her in appreciative silence.

"Thank you," she said and took the offered cup. In silence, they sipped and gazed outside at the woods. A river ran through the trees. Half hidden in the pines was an ancient pagodalike tower.

"What do you think?" he asked.

"It's beautiful."

"I think you will like the mountain, as well." The scene changed instantly to the white-topped volcano she'd seen earlier.

She almost choked on the coffee she sipped. "I thought the view was real. . . ."

"Horace, remove holo," he said.

The volcano vanished, and a courtyard took its place. "This is the 'real' view." An enormous triangular black-bottom pool sparkled in a sunset. Nearby were tables and chairs set in a garden. Rainbows flickered in the mist of a marble fountain. "Would you like the barrier removed?"

"The barrier?"

"Horace, fresh air."

At Kyber's command, outdoor smells of flowers and grass flooded the room. A warm, moist breeze rustled Bree's hair.

"The window is a membrane made of microscopic computers," Kyber said, as if he were describing something as everyday as a glass of water. "The computers respond to commands to let in the outside air, or not. Or they can function as a display screen to show anything I like. Horace," he said, "Show the Great Wall."

The image transformed into a view of the Great Wall of China, making it appear as if they sat in the center of it. In the distance, the path snaked away into the mountains until it was lost on the hazy horizon.

"I like the garden," she said hoarsely. At least she knew it was real. "Who's Horace, by the way?"

"My computer. He maintains my private quarters to my liking, and interacts with the palace computer to provide service and security, as necessary."

Bree looked around the bedroom. "The walls were a different color this morning. Orange. But now they're white. Nanocomputers, too?"

He nodded. "Would you prefer the pumpkin?"

"*Pumpkin?* You know pumpkin?"

He lifted an elegant black brow. "The hue," he explained.

"Yes. I know." She sighed. "My sister would have loved you."

His other brow lifted.

"She was a designer." He had no idea what she meant—she could tell. "Never mind. White's fine." Now she'd thoroughly confused him. She gulped down more coffee, half praying it wouldn't suddenly transform into apple juice. All her life, she'd worshipped technology. Now she felt as if she were overdosing on it. It was everywhere; you couldn't escape computers, because most of them were microscopic and integrated into almost every part of the palace. She'd read that in the future, nanotechnology would change the world. Computers would no longer sit on a desk, or slip into a briefcase. They would *be* the desk or the briefcase, integrated into every area of life, even inside the body, repairing cells, administering medicine. She knew that there were microscopic medical computers coursing through her veins at that very moment. It was why, after so long asleep, she could function almost normally.

Kyber called out, "Horace, open the door," and a small army of servers entered the room on silent, slippered feet.

Transfixed, Bree watched the preparations take place. Plate by plate, the servers arranged a feast of food before them, presenting the food in what resembled the traditional Korean way. Bowls of every size held delicacies, more than a few containing the bioengineered substances she'd eaten in the hospital. Covers protected some bowls, steam wafting from beneath the lids; others were open and contained morsels that either were chilled, salted, and dried, or preserved with some sort of liqueur, judging by the scents.

A woman wearing a snug, curve-conscious gown that was Thai in appearance lit candles. Incense gently sweetened the air. Tiny silver-tasseled rings dangled from her long, pierced fingernails. Her nail polish changed from one color to the next as she worked. Then, she remained crouched on one knee until Kyber met her gaze. He shook his head at her, an almost undetectable movement, and the woman rose.

"Thank you," Bree told her. The woman's curious gaze hesitated on her before she hurried off, as if she didn't know how to react to such open acknowledgment.

As quickly as they came, the servers vanished.

Kyber chuckled.

"What?" Bree asked.

"You thanked her."

"For the food. Was that wrong?"

"Under the circumstances, not at all." Kyber smiled at her, his gaze warm. "You see, she asked if I desired company tonight. Female company."

Ah, so that's what that little round of nonverbal communication was all about. "So, you turned her down and I thanked her." Bree's face warmed, and then she laughed. "Oh, well. I didn't know you had a harem."

"Not a harem, no. Nothing that formal."

"But you have women . . . at your disposal."

"Why, yes."

Bree's head filled with images of Kyber in bed, making love with several women. She couldn't tell if she was embarrassed, offended, or a little bit jealous. "Did she mean now or later, by the way? The female company."

Kyber acted affronted. "Later, or course. I would not have considered that she . . ." Curious, he searched Bree's face. "But, if that is what you desire—"

She held up her hands. "No, thanks. I'll stick to the food. Anyway, I prefer men. And one at a time. But don't let me stop you. Do whatever you want."

"I already did," he said, quieter. "I declined."

She shook her head at him. He knew too well how to walk the fine line between sexual flirtation and coming on too strong. And yet, she sensed he was trying hard to be on his best behavior, wanting more to impress her than to bed her.

Kyber filled two tiny glasses with a clear liquid and gave one to Bree. "Vodka. I offered you proof earlier but did not deliver it. One hundred proof."

She touched her glass to his. "To proof, then."

"To proof," he returned. His gaze held that odd hunger again, the awe and fascination, and all because she was from the past. It made her a relic, something valuable. Coveted.

She had nothing in this world. No family, no career, nothing. And, apparently, nowhere to go. Not only had the UCE turned away from its American roots, she was a throwback to a time they seemed to want to forget. But if she stayed here, she'd be more than a mere addition to

Kyber's eclectic collection of servants, mistresses, bodyguards, physicians, politicians, and advisers. He'd treat her with the utmost care, as befitting a valuable and hard-won addition to the palace, like a fragile antique vase or a priceless ancient brooch. Maybe others saw her that way, too. It hit her that her "value" might serve as a bargaining chip, one she might have to use if she ever needed to barter for anything, including her life.

"Another?" Kyber asked tentatively.

"Why the heck not?"

Kyber refilled her glass, and his own. When he touched his glass to hers, he asked, "What were you pondering so hard?"

She laughed softly. "My new life as a kept woman."

" 'Kept' woman? Is that what you think you are?" His gaze hovered somewhere between wicked and hopeful.

"Being coddled, pampered—I'm not used to it." She downed her drink. Her eyes watered less this time. She shook her head. "What would Cam say to that? Banzai Maguire, kept woman. I can almost hear her laughing." She pictured Cam's bright smile, and her throat constricted.

"Cam Tucker. Your wingman."

"And my best friend," Bree whispered. She poured vodka into her glass and drank it down before she realized what she'd done. "Wow." She shook her head. "Strong." She offered Kyber the bottle. "Give me your glass."

The prince shook his head, his gray eyes unusually soft. "No, but you go ahead, Banzai."

And she did. A little sloppily. Beads of vodka shimmered on the carpet. She ran her finger through them. They reminded her too much of tears.

Kyber speared a piece of meat with his fork and offered it to her. He was sober, she thought; she was getting drunk. "Being pampered, coddled—this doesn't appeal to you?"

"I don't know. I don't know what it's like."

"Try it," he murmured, touching the morsel to her lips.

She took the meat off the fork with her teeth. Kyber's eyes darkened, his gaze fixed on her mouth. His sexual attraction to her was obvious. The temperature inside the room went up a few degrees, and Bree suspected it wasn't due to a computer problem with the air-conditioning. She washed down the meat with some more vodka.

Kyber offered her a second bite. "I could get used to this," Bree confessed, her speech slightly slurred.

"And you will. I will see to it."

Her words flowed almost as freely as the vodka. "All my wishes granted. Anything I desire. As long as I live here on display, like something in a freak show." She beckoned to an imaginary audience. She could hear the jeers and applause. "Come, see the woman from the past. Come one, come all. I don't know, Kyber. I don't know if this is for me."

She refilled her little glass. She was beginning to feel a little light-headed, but her mood had turned so dark that she didn't care.

Kyber appeared to tamp down his temper. "I will always protect you," he said in a controlled voice. Or maybe it was his gritted teeth that made him sound in control. "I rescued you. Now, I offer you sanctuary."

"From what? From the world? From everything that's out there?"

"All that's worth having, Banzai, is *here*."

He made the statement with such conviction that even if she hadn't spent hours on the Interweb she'd have found it hard to argue. "Including me?" she asked, frowning at her glass.

"Ask the trespassing UCE pig who tried to steal you."

"The man who almost kidnapped me is from the UCE?" Suddenly, she was fascinated. However tenuous, there was a connection between the United States and what the country had become. "Why did he want me?"

Frowning this time, Kyber filled both of their glasses with vodka. He swallowed the contents of his glass before he answered her question. "He claims you belong to the UCE. And now, so it seems, the UCE does as well. They have already filed a formal request to have you brought back."

"That was fast."

"Word travels."

Bree felt like the rope in a tug-of-war game. "Did he come here specifically to find me? Was he part of a search team?" All she could think of was Cam, and the chance that this man from the UCE might know her whereabouts. Hope, absent since Kyber told her that his men had searched the cave from top to bottom, flooded back, filling the void inside her. "Did you ask him if he knew of anyone else in the cave? Maybe he saw my wingman's pod."

Or, Bree thought, he'd found Cam's pod empty. It had been almost two centuries. What if, during that time, years ago, someone had found her and freed her? Maybe Cam had searched high and low for Bree, but couldn't find her. Finally, she'd had to give up, and went on to have a full and happy life. Bree liked that scenario better than the one of Cam's body decomposing under leagues of cold seawater. "He might know, Kyber. He might be able to help us." *Us*. Just like that, she'd aligned herself with the leader of the Asian Empire.

"Banzai," he tried, gently. "He's a tomb robber. A treasure hunter. He's rich and bored, the playboy son of the highest-ranking military officer in the UCE."

"So, what was he going to do with me if he found me first? Sell me?"

"It does not matter! You are here. You are safe."

Bree remembered that streak of ruthlessness she'd seen in Kyber earlier when they'd discussed the clones, and contrasted that with the statement he'd made in the hospital room: *"Perhaps, I will keep the bastard alive—if only because he brought me to you."*

"And you've got him locked up."

"Yes."

"The son of the UCE's top military man . . ."

"Yes."

She leaned forward. "Isn't that causing a wee little bit of international tension?"

Kyber downed his drink. "Gloriously so," he said on a gust of air. "And I'm enjoying every minute of it."

"Are you going to give him back?"

"Eventually, yes."

And when he left, Bree would lose the only other person she knew who might have information about Cam.

She pushed aside her glass. She could hold her own in any bar, but she had no intention of falling more under the influence than she already was, not now, not with Cam's life possibly at stake. "I want to see him, to talk to him. About Cam."

"Beware of putting all your hopes into finding your friend. You set yourself up for more disappointment."

She squared her shoulders. *If in command, I will never surrender my men while they still have the means to resist*. "I'll take that chance."

Kyber stared at his empty glass and brooded. He seemed to be vacillating between wanting to temper her rising hopes without crushing them, and wanting to appease and please her without sacrificing his principles. After a long while, he spoke. "I am an open-minded man. I will prove it to you, Banzai. I will invite the trespasser to dinner. Give me a few days, and I will arrange it."

"Thank you," she said.

Kyber narrowed his eyes at her. "Five minutes in the man's company and you will understand everything I have told you about the UCE."

Chapter Ten

Bree spent the hours not engaged in physical therapy in front of a computer embedded in a desk made from a foot-thick slab of glass. In her quest to find information leading to Cam Tucker, she'd learned more about her new world. The people of 2176 had settled Antarctica, and lived on the bottom of the sea. They'd built space stations as big as cities, traveled to Mars and Saturn, and put a few colonies on the moon, too. But nowhere did Bree find anything about an audacious blond bombshell of a southern belle who'd walked out of a cave dressed in a flight suit.

Elbows propped on the desktop, Bree dropped her chin into her hands and watched a digest of the day's news stories. " 'We have no new information,' state those close to Supreme UCE Commander Aaron Armstrong, whose efforts to free his son of all charges stemming from illegal entry into the Kingdom of Asia have so far met with failure. Negotiations will continue, sources say, though at the time of this report, they have broken down."

The image cut to a severe-looking man dressed in a crisp black trench coat and a high-crowned, General Patton–type hat trimmed in patent leather. He had sharp cheekbones and a hard mouth. The general strode to a sleek waiting car with a woman clinging to his arm. She wore a black scarf wrapped around her neck and pulled over her mouth and nose. Dark sunglasses kept the rest of her face hidden as security people ushered the couple into their vehicle.

The general looked as impossible and arrogant as Kyber said he was. Kyber said he had designs on the UCE presidency, now a government-elected, not a people-elected position, and that he wanted to see a military dictatorship in its place—with him in charge, of course. Now his son was biding time in Kyber's comfortable dungeon, waiting for the posturing to cease so he could go home. But maybe, before he went home, Armstrong's son would be able to tell her about Cam. All her other efforts thus far had failed. She was beginning to see Tyler Armstrong as her only hope, her only link to Cam, and the cave in which they were hidden all these years. But would the younger Armstrong help her? With a father at the military helm of the greatest imperial power the earth had ever known, why would he bother?

Somehow, she had to make him *want* to bother.

But how?

Joo-Eun, one of the subservient Park "sisters," entered Bree's hospital room, her arms laden with flowers and a beribboned box. Bree turned in her chair. "Wow. What's all this?"

"Gifts. From Prince Kyber." Joo-Eun's smile was sweet and shy.

Clone. No matter how hard Bree tried to block it, the word intruded when she saw Joo-Eun. The girl didn't have a father or mother; someone had created her in a lab. But, though the girl was a little slow on the uptake, and Bree took special pains not to speak to her as if she were a child when in reality she was seventeen, Bree had made a vow not to treat her differently than anyone who'd started life in the traditional egg-and-sperm way.

She sensed that Joo-Eun had noticed, and that in return, the girl had given Bree her loyalty. Bree hoped so. Friends were valuable when you didn't know who your enemies were.

The bouquet was a fragrant cluster of three dozen long-stemmed aquamarine roses. Another marvelous, bioengineered feat, she thought. Tucked within the flowers was a note in Kyber's handwriting. *Tyler Armstrong will join us for dinner at 8:00 p.m.*, it said simply.

Bree's heart skipped a beat. Tyler Armstrong. To her, he was no longer the blue-eyed diver-thief; he was the man who would tell her how to find Cam.

Joo-Eun gave Bree the package next. "It would please the prince if you wore the dress to dinner."

Bree tore off the ribbon and lifted a bundle of rustling

fabric from the box. Shaking out the dress, she held it at arm's length. "Whoa. It'll please me, too."

The gown was a floor-length gorgeous lavender confection made of diaphanous silk and pale amethyst gemstones. Despite the knots in her stomach and her lingering numbness, something melted inside her as she contemplated wearing the gown. Kyber had made no secret of his romantic interest in her, but so far, she'd pretended not to notice and he hadn't pushed it further. Did the gifts foretell a turning point? Choosing Kyber would be as good as consigning herself to staying here, and that's what she couldn't do. As long as hope existed for finding Cam, she wanted no promises holding her back.

But letting go for one night didn't mean surrendering all her nights to come, did it? Bree clutched the dress in her hands and touched the shimmering fabric to her face. What plans Kyber had made after dinner, she didn't know, but he sure was doing everything right.

Guards appeared outside Ty's cell just after the heat peaked for the day. He'd been dozing with his back propped against the wall—more specifically on the scrawled letters that spelled out *Freedom!* He didn't consider himself a superstitious man, but he figured it couldn't hurt, sleeping next to the upbeat graffiti.

Stiff and sore, Ty got up warily and waited for them to unlock the gate. The guard who opened the cell was a moose of a man whose ancestry appeared to be the same as some of the pirates Ty had fought in the Raft Cities.

Many of them were of Indonesian, Malaysian, or Maldivian ancestry who hadn't thought to—or wanted to—resettle on the mainland after the ocean took their island homes. Ty empathized with their plight, if not the piracy.

"UCE. You, shower," the big man grunted, as if speaking to Ty was too far beneath his level of contempt to bother using full sentences.

Ty lifted his brows. "A shower? No kidding." He rubbed his T-shirt. It clung damply to his skin. Sweat had long since erased the bloodstains. "What's the occasion?" If he was getting out, good. But if he had to leave Banzai here, not so good.

The guard didn't answer, instead stood back to let him pass by, wrinkling his nose at Ty's stink. Ty scratched his beard. "Will your disinfectant kill lice?" He pinched something in his fingers and studied it. "These look like lice. Or fleas." He thrust his fingers at the guard. "What do you think?"

The guard arched out of his way. "Go," he growled, pointing farther down the dank passageway between the cells. Ty suppressed a smile, squared his shoulders, and strode on ahead.

Two other mooselike men waited for him with ion-rifles in their hands. They fell in step with him, and did not meet his eyes. Ty studied their faces, however, analyzing their level of tension, their size and strength. He shifted to study the doors and exits, and the location of additional men. No, not yet, advised his SEAL's intuition. This was not the right time to make a run for freedom. And he might not have to take that chance; if they were giving him a shower, things were looking up.

Or, down. Kyber might like to clean up his prisoners before he put them out for public execution.

Ty walked with the guards to a shower room that looked as if no one had used it in a century. A guard commanded the water on. As it swirled down a drain in the middle of the stone floor, it took with it decades' worth of grit and God knew what else.

Barefoot, Ty stepped under the spray. Lifting his face to the stream, he closed his eyes. Little else had ever felt this good, he decided.

"Clothes off!"

Ty opened one eye at the guard. "If only the women I meet would say that."

"Off!" The guard jerked his rifle butt menacingly.

No humor, Ty thought. He stripped off his T-shirt and baggy, tattered prison pants. Taking his time—he'd waited long enough for this—he soaped his body, scrubbing the sterilizer into his skin, stopping shy of abrasion. Then he did the same to his hair and scalp. By the time he stepped out of the shower, he felt ready to face whatever they had planned for him.

The guard threw him a towel, which he tied around his hips. They climbed a staircase made of stone that ended near a magtrack with pristine silver coils that indicated infrequent use. Here, the air wasn't thick with rot. Ty thought he smelled pine trees. Somewhere, a window or door was open to the outside.

Another hundred paces brought them to a room similar to the ones Ty had sat in during interrogations. Yet here, a young woman waited for him with a pair of sharp scissors in one hand and a razor in the other. She pointed to a stool. "Sit there, UCE."

He gave her a salute and took a seat. Silently and efficiently, she cut his hair and shaved his beard. Brown clumps of matted hair spilled onto the floor and his bare feet. Within minutes, his hair was trimmed, not quite to military specs, but shorter than it was.

"Nice job," he remarked, rubbing his smooth chin and cheeks. "What's next? An oil massage? A sports rubdown?"

"Come, UCE." She turned on her heel and left the room.

Ty rolled his eyes at the guards and followed. "Yes, ma'am."

He followed her up yet another flight of stairs. Judging by the freshness of the air, he'd say they were now out of the dungeon proper. Life was improving by the minute.

In a locker room the size of a small closet, he found a brown shirt and pants made of thin, soft fabric. They were ugly and functional, and a little too small, even accounting for his weight loss, but a giant step up from prison wear.

When he'd dressed, the woman handed him a mouth-cleaning kit and a bag of toiletry items. She abandoned him in another room with a real sink, a toilet that wasn't a hole in the floor, and a wall of mirrors. "You have fifteen minutes, UCE."

"I'm a man. I only need two."

She ignored his smile and slammed the door.

Exhaling, Ty faced the mirror and began running a comb through his wet, freshly trimmed hair. He didn't know what Kyber had in store for him, but he had decided he was going to show up looking good.

Chapter Eleven

Prince Kyber of the Hans and his magnificent palace were a balanced mix of East and West. For tonight's dinner with the UCE hatchet man's only son, it was clear he wanted to emphasize the Asian part of his heritage.

Fruits and flowers decorated a long, polished dining table made of teak inlaid with jade and mother-of-pearl. Volleyball-sized clear spheres held live butterflies and exotic moths. While Bree's previous meals with Kyber were eaten using conventional Western silverware, tonight's utensils consisted of solid gold chopsticks and spoons. Tiny gold dishes to hold sauces and red silk napkins highlighted the goldware.

Kyber had changed the walls to a dark yellow to complement the gold. The window screens tonight were open to the real view, the outside courtyard bathed in the colors of the sunset. It was a mild evening with the barest touch of autumn in the air.

Kyber pulled out her chair. As she sat, Bree's gown swirled around her legs, the amethysts making little bell-like sounds. The dress's sleeves were designed to fall off the shoulder, but a "smart bra" held the bodice in place. Joo-Eun had pulled Bree's hair into a twist, securing it with two jewel-tipped sticks. Wisps fell around her jaw and neck. Bree felt good. Pretty. It was the first night since waking in this world that she felt remotely lighthearted. Nothing like good food, gorgeous clothes, and handsome men to erase your self-pity. Well, one handsome man. The other was still missing. "Where is Tyler Armstrong?"

"He will arrive soon." Kyber settled himself in his chair in front of a place setting of gold and sapphires. "He is dressing for dinner."

"Dressing for dinner?" Bree sipped from a goblet of icy water. "You treat your prisoners well."

Kyber smiled and said nothing. The benevolent dictator, Bree thought. The kindhearted tyrant.

She hoped the decent treatment had put Armstrong in a good mood; she desperately wanted to talk to him about Cam. And more. He'd be another view of a world she knew little about. The UCE . . . the U.S.A. . . . she wondered if she'd find similarities between them that the Interweb and Kyber's prejudice were unable to reveal. A part of her wanted to find a connection; she missed her home. And yet, she felt obligated to Kyber for all that he'd done for her. That familiar tug-of-war. She struggled, wondered how she'd settle it. But soon, Tyler Armstrong would arrive, and she'd learn the answers to all those questions and more. Nervously, she rubbed her hands together.

A light on the gauntlet computer Kyber wore on his left forearm flashed and beeped. "Yes, Kabul."

"He is here."

"Allow him in."

A couple of Kyber's leather-clad bodyguards entered the room. Between them was General Armstrong's son.

The guards left her would-be kidnapper alone in the foyer and retreated to the double entry doors, where they took up a position to either side.

Armstrong glanced back at the guards, as if not believing they'd left him. He walked to the dining table with slow and deliberate steps as if trying to conceal a limp. Bree narrowed her eyes. Something was off. His clothes didn't fit. His pants were too short. He was leanly muscled and athletic, but gaunt, thinner than the pictures she'd seen of him on the news. His hair was a little longer, too.

Her heart gave a jump when she met his ice-blue eyes. She wasn't sure what she was expecting to see in them, but the emotional intensity she found there startled her. If was almost as if he had feelings for her.

Bree's heart gave her ribs another swift kick. Ridiculous, she thought. Tyler Armstrong couldn't have feelings for her; he didn't even know her! He was the pirate, and she was the gold. That hadn't changed from the very first time she'd seen him. If anything, his fascination with her and his hunger to have her were sharper than before.

Wasn't it?

She realized then that she was staring at him. *Say something, Maguire.* "Thanks for coming to dinner, Mr. Armstrong."

That appeared to amuse him. The little scar on his upper lip stretched with his half smile. His gaze lingered on her face. "You look lovely. I trust your care is adequate?"

She swallowed against a dry throat. Why did she feel so shy? Men normally didn't fluster her. This man somehow did. "Thanks, yes. More than adequate. Prince Kyber has generously opened his home to me."

"Yes, I have," Kyber cut in. "Sit, Commander Armstrong. Please." The prince waved at the only other empty chair, on the opposite side of the table from where he sat next to Bree.

Armstrong slid into the chair. He remained stiff and serious, and on guard, as if he expected something to happen at any moment. But his military rigidness faltered some as servant after servant brought in platters and bowls of food and set them out on the table. Savory smells thickened the air. Bree watched Armstrong's expression. The man's jaw moved, and he pressed his lips together. His gaze sharpened, his eyes never leaving the food. He was hungry.

Her heart gave a little twist. When was the last time he'd eaten?

A servant murmured to her, wanting her to indicate her

choices from the feast. "I don't care. Pick a selection for me, please." As soon as the servant went to work filling her plate, Bree pushed a tray toward Armstrong. "Try the meat buns," she told him. "They're delicious."

Almost a little too eagerly, he grabbed one of the steaming buns and tore off a large bite. Chewing, he ate more before swallowing the first. He wasn't hungry, Bree thought. He was starving.

"Would you care for wine?" a server asked Armstrong.

"Please," he mumbled between bites.

The woman filled his goblet. Armstrong gulped it down. The polite way he dabbed at his mouth with a napkin was at odds with the ferocity with which he attacked his dinner.

Bree tried to make conversation and break the ice so she could get to the more serious questions about Cam. "Prince Kyber called you Commander. That would make you the naval equivalent of an air force lieutenant colonel, wouldn't it? That's the way it was in my time."

Armstrong glanced up sharply. He stopped chewing. His attention went to Kyber before coming back to her. Then he mumbled something and went back to eating.

She tried again, reaching for common interests. "I am—I *was* in the United States Air Force."

"I know," he said.

"A pilot."

"Yes."

Bree gave a silent sigh. He didn't want to talk, and that didn't bode well for getting any information out of him.

If she'd been thinking ahead, she could have gotten this information from the Interweb, and used it to make him more comfortable. "So, do you fly, too? Are you a naval aviator? Or just a boat type?"

He spoke as he shoveled food into his mouth with the chopsticks. "Tyler Armstrong, Commander, eighty-twelve, one-one-seven-sixty-two-twenty-two. April third, twenty-one-forty-six."

When questioned, should I become a prisoner of war, I am bound to give only name, rank, service number, and the date of birth. Article Five: The American Fighting Man's Code of Conduct. The articles existed to give guidance to captured soldiers, and while he wasn't an "American," Armstrong had followed the code to a tee. Kyber told her he'd thrown the commander in jail for trespassing and attempted theft. But Armstrong acted as if he were a prisoner of war.

Was he?

Bree took a closer look at him: the ill-fitting clothes, the thin brown fabric that stretched too tightly across his shoulders. Her gaze traveled to his face. He was tired and drawn. Under his left eye and on his right jaw were yellow and green smudges. Old bruises. They'd beaten him.

Shame and shock squeezed her chest. *I'm so sorry. I had no idea.* Now she understood why he wouldn't answer her questions. He thought she was trying to interrogate him. *I will evade answering further questions to the utmost of my ability. I will make no oral or written statements disloyal to my country and its allies or harmful to their cause.*

Bree put down her chopsticks and stared at her plate. She'd lost her appetite. She'd expected dinner with a rich and spoiled treasure hunter, whom she could sweet-talk into giving her information about Cam. But that's not what she got. It felt wrong to be dressed in an expensive gown, eating gourmet delicacies, while dining with a beaten-up captive in scruffy clothes, dragged up here only because she'd desired it.

Bree sat still as she listened to the two men eat. The tinkling of chopsticks brushing against china. The softer music in the background. No one spoke.

Kyber? He seemed pleased with himself. *See?* he seemed to say. *I am an open-minded man.*

And Tyler Armstrong? His sole focus was wolfing down as much food as he could, as if he thought he might never eat again. Suddenly, she wanted very much for the dinner to be over.

It took all her strength of will to forget her discomfort long enough to ask her questions. "Commander Armstrong." Her voice seemed to startle both men. "This has nothing to do with your specific duties. I hope you will be able to help me. I wanted to meet with you tonight, because you were the first one to find me in the pod. I wasn't alone in that long-ago mission. My wingman Cameron Tucker was with me." Her voice dropped. "Did you see her? Do you know where she is?"

Armstrong stopped chewing. She saw him swallow. Then, with slow and careful movements, he rested his chopsticks on the edge of his almost-empty plate. By sheer force of will, it seemed, he erased all emotion from his face, a skill she lacked. His eyes told her nothing, either; they were chips of ice. "Tyler Armstrong, Commander, eighty-twelve, one-one-seven-sixty-two-twenty-two. April third, twenty-one-forty-six."

"This is not an interrogation. It's a plea for help." She made fists on the tablecloth. "Cam Tucker was my wingman. She could be out there. Alive!"

"Banzai," Kyber said in a gentle tone.

She ignored his attempt to soothe her. "Do you know anything, Commander?" She hated the desperation she heard in her voice. "I don't need details. Just tell me if you know where she is."

Armstrong's eyes thawed. He looked as if he wanted to say something and then decided against it.

"What?" she demanded. "What do you know?"

He shook his head. "Nothing," he said quietly.

Bree's nostrils flared. She fought the almost overwhelming urge to grab his collar and shake him. "You mean you can't tell me. You can't talk. What if it were you, looking for someone in your unit? Someone under your command? You wouldn't give up."

A muscle jumped in Armstrong's jaw. He inhaled, held his breath, released it. And said nothing.

Ack! Bree pressed a fist to her stomach, as if that could somehow keep her from letting go of the last shreds of her composure.

Kyber brought his mouth to her ear. "I knew he'd disappoint you." He was slow to move away, as if flaunting his familiarity with her, eager to have Armstrong believe it was more. Then, smug, Kyber leaned back in his dining chair, leaving her to sort out the sorrow and resentment in Armstrong's eyes.

Just barely, she squelched the urge to explain that she wasn't sleeping with Kyber. She wasn't supposed to care what this stranger thought of her personal life. Why she did was anyone's guess.

Armstrong folded his napkin and placed it on the table next to his plate. With one last soulful look at his unfinished meal, he said, "I don't think I'll stay for dessert."

She caught his eyes and mouthed, *Eat*.

His gaze hesitated on hers. Then, with an oddly self-satisfied glance in Kyber's direction, he lowered his head to devour down the rest of his food.

Kyber sipped his wine and regarded his prisoner with what could only be hatred. But his animosity didn't appear to bother Armstrong in the least. It amazed her that he seemed to consider his loss of her more important than saving his own hide, which he wasn't doing a very good job of preserving, provoking the man who held the keys to the dungeon.

"Don't let it fool you," Armstrong murmured.

She frowned, shaking her head.

He waved a hand at the sumptuous feast. "The finery. Don't let it fool you. You're a prisoner here, Banzai, just as I am."

"I'm not a prisoner. I'm free to go."

Armstrong lifted a brow. "Really?"

"Yes, really," Kyber answered for her. "Banzai Maguire

is my guest, and is here by choice. She understands the dangers that exist outside these walls—and that with me, she is safe."

"You couldn't even keep your own father safe."

Kyber's face closed immediately, as it had when she'd asked about the assassination attempt that had left the king in an irreversible vegetative state. "You are out of line!"

"Well, could you?"

"Silence!" Armstrong had twisted the knife in what appeared to be a still-raw wound.

Kyber's chair scraped backward, and he stood. Dressed all in black, he was downright menacing. "You know nothing of the truth, you son of an imperialist pig."

"If you couldn't keep your own father safe, how will you keep Banzai out of harm's way?"

"You question my security?"

"Damn right, I do."

Bree groaned. *Boys, boys.*

"Must I remind you, Commander, that the very safety measures you question *stopped you* before you could steal Banzai away? Without proper medical attention, she would have died. Thanks to my security team, you didn't kill her."

"*Kill* her?" Armstrong shouted back, incredulous. He turned to her. "The UCE wants to repatriate you, Banzai. We want to bring you home. . . ."

Home. Her chest ached with the word. How she wished home still existed. But the country she saw daily on the news didn't resemble in any way the nation to which she'd once pledged allegiance. Where was her home now?

"Why do your countries hate each other so much?" she asked, finally expressing out loud the question dogging her since she'd arrived at the palace.

That elicited a moment or two of surprised silence.

"What I mean is—you two are enemies because your countries are at war. Right?"

"We are not at war," Kyber bellowed. "But if they send more delinquents to steal what's mine—"

"She is not yours," the commander yelled back.

"She certainly does not belong to you."

"I disagree."

Bree dropped her head in her hands. She could hear it now: *Is not . . . is too . . . is not . . .* "

"She was born in the northeast sector of the Central Colony," Armstrong pointed out.

"And she remained here, protected within my lands for almost two centuries. If the UCE wanted her, perhaps they should have shown a little more interest."

"The UCE didn't know!"

"But why so much hatred?" she interrupted. "Why can't your governments come up with a treaty?"

"There is a treaty," Kyber said. "The UCE refused to sign it."

"What treaty is that?" Armstrong demanded.

Kyber lifted an elegant brow. "The one drawn up after the UCE conceded defeat at the end of the Bai-Yee Wars. It sits in its airless case in the Royal Museum. The signature line that reads *The United Colonies of Earth*? Notoriously blank." He turned to Bree and explained. "My kingdom began as a league of Asian nations linked by an economic trade agreement. The Asian Economic Consortium. Fifty years of the West outsourcing high-tech jobs had brought us wealth and power that no one anticipated. The UCE wanted it. Wanted us. When they sought to tax what we gave to the world, we declared independence." He narrowed his eyes at the UCE commander. "And we bled mightily to achieve it. The Bai-Yee Wars. The fighting ended many generations ago. Now, we, the Kingdom of Asia, don't share with anyone. We don't need to. We have it all and in higher quality and quantity than anyone else on this planet."

Armstrong's mouth twisted. "Is that why you keep your citizenry in bondage?"

Kyber groaned. "The usual UCE refrain. It's all they can come up with in criticism. In truth, your people are the ones in bondage—shackled to out-of-control taxation and overgovernment."

"At least we can leave the country."

"Ah. That is the fundamental difference between our lands. My people do not want to leave."

"What would make this better?" Bree asked. A fighter pilot attempting diplomatic mediation. If ever a situation paralleled the bull-in-the-china-shop metaphor, this was it. "If the UCE signed the Bai-Yee treaty?"

"It will never happen," Kyber said.

Armstrong shook his head, apparently in agreement for

the first time with his enemy. "It won't," he agreed.

"That's too bad," she said quietly. It wasn't just bad blood that kept the two huge powers at odds; it was *ancient* bad blood, the worst kind.

"Meanwhile," Kyber said with a deep sigh, "I'm left to hold my own against the battering waves of aggressive territorialism."

"Bullshit! The UCE has no interest in your kingdom."

"The only thing that keeps my kingdom safe from colonial expansion is our sheer power."

"Our colonies provide the framework for a stable world."

Kyber rolled his eyes. "Is that the excuse your father uses when he has to use force police in your colonies? Your military has become a guard dog trained to turn on its own master. And I wouldn't be surprised if it does, *Commander,*" he added with disdain.

Armstrong appeared less sure now. Or maybe the hint of doubt seemed magnified in the face of Kyber's absolute belief and unshakable confidence. "The UCE and no other brought the world lasting peace." He gave the impression of being certain on that point at least. "And we owe it to the world to continue bearing the burden of keeping that peace."

Kyber turned away, waving his hand in disgust. His jewel-clasped ponytail whipped over a broad shoulder. "This table is no place for your propaganda. Take him away," he ordered his guards.

The sentries left their posts by the heavy double doors and came for the commander.

Unrepentant, Armstrong stood. The guards took hold of his arms and led him from the room. The polite nod of farewell he gave Bree held a hint of disdain.

Sleeping with the enemy. That's what he thought, she'd bet. But she tried hard not to care. She owed him no allegiance—or Kyber. Gratitude, yes, but not loyalty. She didn't belong in their world. The only thing that mattered was staying true to herself, and to Cam.

Bree turned her back to the open doors and walked to the window. She didn't see the beauty of the simulated scene, only her monumental dilemma. Tyler Armstrong was the only other person besides Kyber who could help her. He knew how to find the cave—and, she suspected, much more than that. She needed him to find Cam, but how would she get him to help? The dinner had been a disaster. She'd have to come up with a different plan.

Kyber joined her. "Do not listen to anything he says. You are safe here. Safe with me. I will not let any harm come to you."

"I trust you," she said.

Somber and silent, he rubbed his knuckle down her sleeve. "Something more troubles you."

"I'll live."

He took her by the shoulders and turned her to face him, regarding her in a distressed and proprietary way, as if she were a treasured pet who'd suddenly stopped eating. "I'll send another expedition to the cave. Will that make you feel better?"

"Yes!" Tears of gratitude should have filled her eyes

then, but perpetual numbness precluded a display of emotion. Dr. Min Park would tell her that crying was therapeutic, but Bree hadn't been able to work up a single tear since going down in her jet over North Korea. "Thank you. I owe you a lot, Kyber."

"Bah! Anything for your happiness, my pet."

His pet? Hmm. Her instincts had been right on; that was how he viewed her. But was it so horrible? He'd given her the best medical care, treated her with kindness and respect. And he'd offered her a life here, if she wanted it—a good life. A fabulous life, actually. No, it didn't come with the heady rush of protecting the skies in an F-16; there was no country to offer allegiance to, no sense that she was contributing anything vital. No challenges.

But she'd have safety here. Protection. Few people received a future so nicely prepared and gift wrapped. She should be happy. But restlessness and a sense of unfinished business, an uncompleted mission, wouldn't allow it. She had to consider her time here as temporary—for now.

This time, she changed the subject. "I learned more about my ancestors today," she said in a lighter tone. "I found names and locations for the ones that live in the UCE." Brittany's great-many-times-over grandkids, which made Bree their great-many-times-over aunt. "There's a branch of the family living in Canada."

"Tri-Canada's borders are sealed. There is nothing any of us can do about locating someone who lives within them. Not even me. As for your relations in the UCE, I will arrange for you to meet them when you are feeling stronger. But on neutral ground."

"Like where?"

"Not there."

"Why not, Kyber? I was born there." She stopped before more of her frustration over the failed dinner with Armstrong leaked through.

"It is the safest course of action, Banzai. Go to the UCE and you may never leave."

"Are you so sure of that?"

He was growing angry again. "They want you, Banzai Maguire, and not for good reasons. I cannot allow you to go. You're too valuable. I won't give you permission."

"So, you're not saying I *can't* go, only that I if I do, I don't have your consent."

He took her chin between his thumb and index finger and tipped her chin up as he bent his head toward her. His mouth hovered a fraction of an inch from her lips. She felt his warm breath, smelled the wine he'd drunk. Attraction kindled curiosity, and she let him kiss her—a soft, lingering taste of her lips.

He pulled back and murmured, "I require consent in all things, Banzai."

She flattened her hands against his chest. Kyber held her close, waiting to see what she would do. Or say.

Regrettably, it wasn't a "yes" to a night of great sex with one of the most powerful men in the world. Maybe, if she were lucky, it would have erased the distracting effect Tyler The-Unhelpful-One Armstrong had on her, but one night with Kyber might lead to more, and she'd become even more entrenched in a life she wasn't sure she wanted yet. She wouldn't lead him on; she owed him that much.

She dropped her hands and stepped out of his embrace. "I have some thinking to do."

Kyber let out a slow breath. "Damn the human animal's propensity to think."

She rubbed her hands together nervously. Her palms were damp. "I want to see Commander Armstrong again."

Kyber's mouth thinned. "So, that's what this is about."

She reared back. "What *what* is about?

"Why you wouldn't kiss me."

"I did kiss you!"

He circled his hand. "You know what I mean."

She rubbed a hand over her face. "Will you please stop thinking of everything in terms of sex? It's hard—you're a man—but try."

Kyber gave her his gloomy acquiescence.

She folded her arms over her chest. One sleeve dropped lower. She hitched it back up to her shoulder and folded her arms again. " 'When questioned, should I become a prisoner of war, I am bound to give only name, rank, service number, and the date of birth. I will evade answering further questions to the utmost of my ability.' That's Article Five of the American Fighting Man's Code of Conduct. Armstrong's not an American, but that's what he was following. It means he sees me as the enemy.

Or, more accurately, he sees you as the enemy, Kyber. I think I stand a real chance at getting something useful out of him, and right now I'll take anything, but I don't think he'll talk if you're around."

"You want to see him alone?" Kyber appeared horrified at the idea. "I said I will send another expedition to the cave. Isn't that enough?"

"If he knows where Cam's pod is, it'll help the searchers find her, right? Otherwise, they're digging blind. Let me see what I can learn from him."

"But alone? I will not allow it."

In desperation, she tried to come up with a solution that would ease Kyber's worries and allow her to speak to Armstrong without his presence. "I'll bring guards with me."

"The dungeon is no place for you."

"Then let me meet him somewhere else. Please."

Kyber turned away to gaze out at the torchlit courtyard, his brow furrowed in concentration. Just as the silence began to feel uncomfortable, he said, "I'll arrange the meeting elsewhere. But Kabul will accompany you."

Kabul, the chief of palace security? To Armstrong, the man's high rank might prove as intimidating as Kyber's. But what choice did she have? Running out of options and time, she had to find out what he knew about Cam. "Tomorrow?" she asked, her chin coming up.

Kyber sighed deeply. "I will see what I can do."

That meant he'd think about it. He was the boss here. He didn't have to ask for anyone's approval on any matter.

His wrist gauntlet bleeped. "Yes, Kabul?"

"Your Highness. We appear to have a terrorist interruption of the Interweb."

"Another worm?"

"It doesn't appear to be, no. There's been no breach of palace security. But I want to research it further before I say for certain."

Kyber walked away from Bree. "You said interruption. Of what nature?"

There was silence for a few seconds. Then Kabul said, "I don't quite know. Is your display on?"

"No, but I will put it on." Kyber spoke to the room. "Horace, show display!"

The courtyard faded as the molecular barrier closed. The huge windows turned white, bright white. It was strange to see the screens without an image. There was sound, though: a booming voice that was weirdly without gender. It was either a woman with a deep voice, or a man with a high one, and it seemed to have been caught in midspeech.

". . . we have spoken of good and evil today, and what it means to us and our future," it said. "But, be warned, democracy is not inherently good, for democracy is similar to freedom, and freedom itself is not inherently good. Why? Freedom is an avenue for both good and bad, because whenever there is free will, it creates an opportunity to choose evil. The same is true of democracy. A person can vote for a good leader, or a person can vote for a bad leader. True democracy makes no distinction, for democracy is only as good as its creators."

What is this? Bree mouthed to Kyber.

His frown was dark, and he shook his head.

" 'A democracy devoid of morals is chaos. Remember this! We have it in our power to begin the world anew.' " The voice rose in volume. " 'Many may cry peace, but as for me, give me liberty, or give me death!' "

Goose bumps tickled Bree's arms. *Give me liberty or give me death!* That was a direct quote of Patrick Henry's famous battle cry. She'd been guilty of not knowing as much American history as she should, guilty of taking for granted the sacrifices made by the founding fathers of the United States, guilty of seeing the Fourth of July as little more than a patriotic celebration with picnics and fireworks, but those words she remembered. Even after two—no, almost five centuries—Henry's words had the ability to inspire.

It took a few moments of silence for Bree to realize the voice had stopped. And yet it had been so hypnotic, so compelling, she remained standing there, stock-still, hungry for more.

Kyber, however, had a completely different reaction. "This is an act of war! They have invaded my palace, brazenly, used my communication system to spread their poison. Ax Armstrong dares to provoke me when I have his son in my hands? He will learn the consequences of his arrogance. Expansionist, imperialistic pigs!"

"Are you sure it was the UCE? That was Patrick Henry."

Kyber shook his head. "Do you know this man?"

She almost smiled. "Not personally. He died about five hundred years ago. He was a great statesman during the American Revolution. An advocate of democracy. But the UCE seems to be an autocracy, and so is your government. Someone's urging revolution, Kyber. And using the words of American patriots to communicate it. Knowing what little I do of your world, I don't think it's the UCE that's behind this."

"Bah! You do not know them as I do." Kyber started to walk away, stopped, and turned back to squeeze her arm. "My apologies for ending our evening so abruptly, but I must meet with my security adviser on this matter."

Exhaling, he escorted her to the door. "But do not worry, Banzai. All is well in my kingdom. This episode, like all others, will pass."

It probably would, she thought with regret. But silently, she cheered for whoever had the guts to transmit his or her beliefs on independence. And she wished the person luck. She didn't predict anyone taking chances like that anywhere in this world would enjoy a very long life.

Ty gripped the bars and listened to the speech blaring from the security screens imbedded in the ceiling of his cell. No image accompanied the sound. Only white. White light. " 'Many may cry peace—but as for me, give me liberty, or give me death!' "

Was this a new way for Kyber to feed propaganda to the prisoners? Hmm. The message of self-government didn't quite mesh with the Han prince's firm and absolute grip on his kingdom.

Ty waited for more, after the voice stopped broadcasting, but it seemed the show was over. Rocket-man, as Ty had come to call the rebel who'd been struck on the head, who'd shot the rocket at Kyber and Banzai, rushed to the front of his cell. He shouted down the corridor to Ty. "Did you hear it? That voice?"

Ty folded his hands over his chest and glared at the man. He'd since learned the agitator was harmless. An idiot, actually. A small-time crook. But even the most brainless of troublemakers could cook up stunts that could maim or kill.

Ty was glad there were bars between them. After having to go through seeing the pain in Banzai's eyes, knowing that he'd refused to help her, he was in a foul mood; he didn't trust his temper. "Yes. I heard it."

" 'We have it in our power to begin the world anew.' " The man threw his head back and laughed. "What do you think of that, UCE?"

"Do you really want to know?"

Rocket-man's head bobbed.

"It's a nice thought, but improbable. Starting the world over means unrest. Instability breeds more poverty, more pain. I've visited most of the world's cesspools of humanity. I see what it's like for those people. They haven't the power to begin anything anew, let alone being able to find a clean toilet to take a piss. Stability is the only fix. Stability produced by the UCE, the Euro-African Consortium, and, yes, even your Kingdom of Asia. But," he finished with a shrug, "that's only one man's opinion."

The outlook of a soldier paid to preserve that stability in key spots around the globe. The son of a man who had dedicated his life to keeping the peace.

Noises in the corridor grabbed Ty's attention. A couple of guards marched down the corridor. They rarely came around between the prisoners' meager meals, and now here they were, late at night. A guard unlocked Rocket-man's cell. "Come on," he said, and pulled the prisoner out of his cell.

"I . . . I have nothing more to tell you," Rocket-man yelled.

"Shut up. You're going home."

Rocket-man let out a whoop and pumped his fist at Ty. "I'm getting out!"

"I wish I were in your shoes, man," Ty admitted. Oddly, his full belly made imprisonment harder, not easier, to bear.

"I'll get you out."

Sure you will. "Thanks for the good thoughts."

"Look for the shadows!" Rocket-man called over his shoulder. "When they come, run!"

"Shut up." The guard shoved him on ahead. On his way past Ty's cell, he crashed his studded baton against the bars. "UCE scum! The prince isn't going to like your Shadow Voice disrupting the Interweb. I hope he lets me do the punishing."

Ty flipped him off, then walked to the back of his cell, his gaze fixed on the security panels above and outside. The guard thought that the UCE was somehow behind the broadcast. What the guard didn't know was that at home a message like that would get you arrested faster than you could say treason.

He retuned to the back of his cell and sat down. Leaning his back against the far wall, he shut his eyes. Shadows. "*When they come, run!*" What did the man mean?

Ty wondered if it had any connection with the graffiti on the cell wall. Obviously, Shadow Runners were protesters. But the guard had called the entity making the speech a "shadow voice," and attributed it to the UCE. Something didn't make sense.

Ty knew one thing, though. When you turned on the lights, shadows disappeared.

Chapter Twelve

In the chill hours after dawn two days later, the guards came once again for Ty. The nights had become progressively colder. Soon, autumn would arrive and Kyber would move to his wintertime digs in the state of central China, separating Ty from Banzai—maybe for good. The thought of it made Ty feel sick. Empty. He knew he could make her see the light, if only he could get her alone. Impossible, he was certain, but he longed for it all the same. Once, he'd considered his dream of finding her just as unattainable. And look—he had found her.

Only to have her stolen away.

The door of his cell rolled open. Ty squeezed blood into his numb fingers, but he remained on the floor. He wasn't getting up unless he had to. "Is it dinnertime already?" he asked with sarcasm. It had been almost a day since they last brought him a watery bowl of rice. And another whole day since the one before that.

"No dinner for you, UCE," the more squat of the two men growled. He was built like a badger, and his black eyes were as mean.

"Pity." There was nothing like a little food to remind you of what you were missing. Ever since the dinner in Kyber's quarters, he'd been starving for a meal. But Ty kept his misery to himself. No use letting the goons know that their tactics were beginning to wear on him.

With disdain, Ty climbed to his feet. The badger-like guard swiped for his sleeve to hurry him upright, but Ty jerked out of his grasp. He recognized the man as the guard who'd cracked Rocket-man over the head, knocking the rebel out for almost a day. Ty had no doubt the man would take pleasure in doing the same to him.

With fire in his dark eyes, the guard raised his rifle butt to smash Ty's skull with it.

The other guard grabbed the weapon and shook his head.

Badger hissed. "Another time, UCE scum," he promised. "You'll try to escape, but I won't stop you. Not right away. I'll give you a head start; then I'll kill you. At least then I'll have an excuse."

Ty turned to the other guard. "What the hell did he eat for breakfast?"

His answer was a sharp shove with a rifle butt between his shoulder blades, forcing him into the dank corridor.

The cold stone floor made no sound under his thin slippers. When the guards climbed a staircase and turned right, Ty realized that they were bringing him to the interrogation rooms. Beautiful. What did Kyber hope to get out of him now?

Information about the speechmaker, he realized suddenly. Maybe they thought he knew something about the transmission. " 'Give me liberty or give me death,' " he muttered loud enough for his escorts to hear, readying himself mentally for a long day of questions and possibly beatings.

They pushed him through one of the doors. The room was empty, and much larger than the one they'd used for his previous interrogations. There were no chairs, not even a stool. And it was spotless, the walls whitewashed, no bloodstains or crushed smokes anywhere. It even smelled clean. But then all he had with which to compare it was the dungeon.

The guards left him alone, locking him inside. Immediately, he searched for a way to escape, running his fingertips over the smooth surface, looking for telltale seams. A circuit of the room made one thing clear: the only way out was the way he'd come in—and it was locked.

Now to kill time waiting for whatever they had planned. Killing time—he'd done a fair share of that lately. One thing he'd learned about lengthy imprisonment was that it was boring as hell.

But this time he didn't have long to wait. Not five minutes passed before the door opened and a tall, grim, ascetic man strode inside. Kabul, Ty thought. The prince's security chief.

The man's elegant nostrils pinched closed at Ty's odor, but he said nothing. Crisply, he took up a parade-rest position in one rear corner, facing the door.

Ty rubbed his chin and pondered Kabul's appearance. Something big was going on. Maybe something good—as in the successful conclusion to his negotiated release. Yes, that was it. It was about time, too. He'd waited long enough for it.

Standing taller, he tidied his clothing—futile as the gesture was—half-expecting to see a representative of the UCE stride in next. When guards milling in the hallway separated to allow someone else through, Ty couldn't help smiling. *Here I am. Now, get me out of here.*

But no representative of his government walked through the door. Banzai Maguire did.

Ty's abdominal muscles went rigid, as if he'd taken a hit to the gut. In amazement, he watched her stride into the room. Her outfit was off-white and utilitarian—functional, with only a thick black belt, boots, and her hair hanging loose and shiny around her shoulders as adornment. Though she was small and feminine, the way she moved with her chin high and her shoulders squared demanded respect and notice. He would have noticed her no matter what.

She nodded curtly. "Hello, Commander."

He nodded back. Ran a hand through his shaggy hair before he dropped his arm. She was sleeping with the emperor; why would she care what he looked like? Hell, why should *he* care? If she wanted his company, she'd have to take him the way he was.

But, seeing how pale she was, almost careworn, he knew she'd made a liar out of him. He'd never leave the kingdom if it meant abandoning her.

A mix of emotions passed over her face when she made eye contact with him: dismay at his ragged appearance along with a good dose of empathy. And a flash of something else, gone before he could make sense of it. Ah, well, he supposed if she couldn't greet him with a hug and a kiss, feeling sorry for him was better than some other options he could think of, as in hatred or disgust. He'd given her a hard time the other night, and he was sure she remembered it, too. To her credit, she acted perfectly cool and in control.

He didn't like it. He'd thought of her all these years, had grown up with her picture hanging by his bed. The least she could do was show some sort of reaction to him. Something more than this, damn it.

Banzai turned her attention to the security chief. "Do you have to stand *there*, Kabul?"

"It is what His Highness wants."

She winced at the words "His Highness," as if she hadn't wanted Ty reminded of Kyber in any form. "I heard him. He said 'nearby,' not 'in the room.' Right there will work,"—she pointed to the door—"just outside."

"But, my lady—"

"Now, Kabul. Please."

With obvious reluctance, the thwarted chief complied. His glare in Ty's direction was hot with warning. Ty could guess the man's thoughts: *Touch her and die*. Or something like that.

The man had nothing to worry about. Ty could guarantee that if he ever had the chance to touch Banzai Maguire, it wouldn't be to hurt her.

Ty remained silent, waiting for her to take the initiative while he selfishly filled his eyes with her—the legendary Banzai Maguire, in the flesh. He thought of all the ways he'd attempted to forget his fascination with her, namely with other women. But the relationships never lasted; only a few had left even the barest of tracks across his heart. The affairs merely reinforced his loneliness, the tediousness of his solitary existence. Oh, he filled his time well, no one would argue that, but now that he saw what he'd been missing, he wanted no substitutes. Banzai Maguire would be good for the country, and good for him. Now all he had to do was convince her of it.

"I'm glad we were able to meet again," she said.

"As if I had a choice in the matter."

His sarcasm surprised her—he saw it in her eyes—but serenely she ignored it. Kudos for the lady, he thought. On the other hand, it meant if he wanted to unsettle her, he'd have to try harder.

He took a lazy few steps toward her. The scent of her warm skin came to him, aromatic with something exotic and expensive from the royal baths. He hoped Kyber wasn't the one who'd rubbed the oils over her body.

Her nose wrinkled. Not the reaction he was looking for, but it was a start. "Eau de Dungeon," he said. "Like it?"

"I've smelled worse."

He plucked at his grubby shirt. "Why didn't the prince order me cleaned up like last time, I wonder?"

"I hurried him into arranging this. There probably wasn't time."

"I don't think he wanted to risk you being attracted to another man."

Outrage and surprise flared in her eyes. "I hate to tell you this, Armstrong, but neither of you have anything to worry about."

"That's what you tell yourself."

She gave a soft but expressive snort. This time, the flash he'd seen earlier lingered long enough in her fiery green eyes for him to figure it out. It was awareness . . . of the male-female kind. Ah, yes. He'd gotten a reaction out of her, all right, with an added bonus.

She folded her arms over her chest and paused to study him. "You're right. I am interested."

She reached out and ran a finger from the hollow at the center of his collarbone down his chest before tapping that finger on his stomach. His muscles contracted involuntarily.

"Very interested," she said in a sultry whisper.

His body reacted to the change of attack even while his instincts told him to take cover.

Banzai lifted her chin to study his face, then paused. Did she know how badly he wanted to kiss her? No. "Interested in what you know about my wingman, Commander," she finished.

He hadn't realized how high he'd built his hopes until they came crashing down all around him. The woman had routed him! She'd correctly interpreted his desire to unnerve her and turned it back on him, letting him know as she did so exactly why she'd him brought here.

He made sure his embarrassment didn't reach his face. "I don't know anything," he said sharply. And he *wasn't* sure where to find the other cryopod. And if even if he were, he wouldn't tell her just to have her hand over the information to Kyber. These two fighter pilots belonged to the UCE.

And Banzai belongs to you.

She lowered her voice further to evade the pricked ears of any chaperones peering through the door. "Listen, we don't need to play games. You know why I arranged this meeting. You couldn't talk at dinner that night. But this time, it's just us."

"Just us"—he tipped his chin at the door—"a dozen trolls and their boss."

A depression formed between her brows. "It was the best I could do. Work with me, okay?"

He made no promises.

She exhaled. "Prince Kyber sent a rescue team back to the cave. They searched and couldn't locate Cam."

"Well, that's not surprising. They didn't know where to look."

"But you do." Hope flickered in her green eyes. He

found he had to look away. He was less successful at evading the desperation in her voice. "Please, Commander. I know you know where she is. Help me find her."

"And let you give her over to the Kingdom of Asia?" His tone was loaded with the disdain he felt toward the acting emperor. Little wonder she looked as if she wanted to leave the room. Or knee him in the balls. "Go back to Kyber and ask him to help," he said irritably.

"I did. He searched the cave. They found nothing."

"Well, then. I guess you're stuck."

Anger and frustration rolled off her in hot waves. "So that's what it comes down to. You against Kyber. Bad blood between your country and his." Her eyes blazed but her voice was remarkably calm. Under pressure, she'd fallen back on her combat training to act unemotional. He wondered if she'd be able to remain as unaffected if he ever had the chance to make love to her.

When he made love to her. He had to stay optimistic.

She lifted her chin another defiant notch. "That a soldier's life hangs in the balance makes no difference to you."

"Many soldiers' lives hang in the balance. That's why I'll resist all such efforts at interrogation. If you don't like it, have Kyber take over. But I warn you—I'll die before I give up anything of value to him."

He'd already given up the one thing that mattered. She stood within a meter of him, but it might as well have been a light year. He was as far from having her as he'd even been.

Banzai swallowed. "I was her commander." She made a soft sound of pain. Suddenly, the sport had drained out of the situation. He'd never meant to hurt her, but it seemed he was doing a damned thorough job of it.

"I was responsible for her. And I lost her." She lifted her eyes to his. "Do you have any idea what that means?"

He braced himself against the onslaught of memories of what he'd found in the Raft Cities. "Unfortunately, I do."

She regarded him with sudden curiosity. He could feel her body heat, magnified by his awareness of her. He smelled like sweat and filth, but he'd sell his soul to hold her close, to feel her in his arms. He'd gone to the ends of the earth to find her, and he'd do the same to find her wingman. But not at the risk of losing both of them to Kyber. "Tyler Armstrong," he recited. "Commander, eighty-twelve, one-one-seven-sixty-two-twenty-two. April third, twenty-one-forty-six . . ."

Banzai's hands opened wide, but she grabbed hold of the sides of her trousers and not his neck as he'd half-expected. She turned her back to him and walked away. Took three steps and stopped. He saw her fists unclench, her fingers flexing. Finally she spoke, a quiet admission. "I wouldn't have talked, either."

With that, she left him. Probably for good. Since he had no information forthcoming, she had no need of him now. And if she no longer needed him, then neither did Kyber.

Suddenly, Ty was awash in gloom. His living moments might very well be numbered.

* * *

After lunch, outside in Kyber's courtyard, the afternoon was cool, the sky heavy with rain clouds. The cold, damp wind was brisk, but Bree simmered with frustration.

She was alone. Kyber had disappeared into the palace to attend one of the innumerable meetings that cropped up unexpectedly throughout the day in addition to those that were scheduled. She'd long since learned that he was no decorative monarch, but a working king.

Arms folded in front of her, she watched plump, genetically engineered sapphire-and-gold fish wriggle in the clear water of Kyber's reflecting pond. Reflection was the last thing she wanted to do. Her meeting that morning with Armstrong couldn't have gone more wrong. She'd been sure he'd give her something, some tidbit, on Cam's whereabouts, especially with Kyber out of the picture. But Armstrong was a captive, bound by a code of honor not to give the enemy any information. And that's what she was to him, the enemy.

Or more accurately, Kyber was the enemy. The prince loomed over her shoulder, when not literally then symbolically. She was beginning to learn that it was more of a handicap than an advantage, being an extension of the prince, unless she wanted to intimidate people into coughing up what they knew about Cam and that cave. And she'd already learned that technique didn't work with a man like Tyler Armstrong.

More, Armstrong distracted her . . . in the very way she didn't want to be distracted. It was more than looks; she knew that much. He was cute, yes, but Kyber was more handsome. Yet, the prince didn't affect her in nearly the same way. Maybe Tyler Armstrong had her tied up in knots because he presented such a challenge; he refused to give her what she wanted. She admired his focus and his principles, frustrating as they were, and his determination in the face of adversity. Or . . . maybe it was the way he looked at her, seeing all the way inside, as if he'd known her forever. "Sleeping beauty," he'd called her, she remembered with a slight smile. He always knew just what to say to make her blush—and she wasn't the type to turn red. In the interrogation room, she'd had to call off her pretend seduction because she could see it was getting to her as much as it was to him. Yes, there was definitely something there—and she didn't want it.

"There's nothing wrong with seeing if there's more to it, you know." Cam's teasing so long ago in the locker room rushed back.

Bree gave her head a shake. No. There wasn't ever going to be anything "more" with Tyler Armstrong, a man whose father was the strong arm of the biggest imperial power the world had ever known. The idea of it was ludicrous. Not only that, the whole thing was technically impossible, pending his almost-certain conviction for trespassing.

"If you don't take the risk, you'll never find out."

She gave a silent snort. Either she was way overstressed or someone had put hallucinogens in the food she'd eaten for lunch.

Bree picked up a fallen leaf, red and delicate, and tossed it into the pond. The wind caught the edges and spun it around. Goldfish chased after the spinning leaf, pushing it across the water.

No matter how much Tyler Armstrong intrigued her, the fact remained that Kyber wouldn't let him go. And the commander wasn't talking as long as he remained under arrest. Two strong-willed men. It was obvious she wasn't going to be able to sweet-talk them into anything.

She needed a plan. It was going to take something devious and completely unexpected. But what? *Think, Maguire, think.*

Okay, ask Kyber to let her go on her own expedition to the cave. If he refused, well, she'd do it on her own—and take Armstrong with her. He'd know how to get there; plus he was experienced with this new world, if not the Asian Kingdom itself. Yep, she'd need him if she went. But how would she accomplish all this? Her mind dove so deeply into full-bore plan-making mode that Kyber startled her when he appeared at her side.

He smiled down at her, his gray eyes soft.

"Hi," she said. Guilt filtered through her. Her plans couldn't include him. Nor could she say anything about them. It would sabotage her efforts. "I didn't expect you back so soon." Desperately, she tried to keep her private thoughts from appearing on her face.

His hand was warm and dry as it slid over her cheek. "You're cold," he murmured.

She let him take her into his arms. He was warm, smelling of leather and sandalwood, and she felt soothed by the embrace. *Soothed, but not aroused*. It wasn't the same as touching Tyler Armstrong. . . .

She squeezed her eyes shut. *Stop*.

Kyber's palm rubbed over her back in expanding circles. The fabric of her outfit was so thin that she felt every contour of his strong hand. "You are thinking of those you've lost," he guessed correctly.

Well, sort of. "Yes."

He gave her a squeeze. "This is your life now. I know you still grieve, and that you have focused that grief on finding your pilot friend, but you must endeavor to put tragedy behind you."

Her eyes opened wide, and she stared into the garden. What if Kyber were right? What if she *was* dwelling too much on finding Cam? What if she'd become fixated on the rescue as a way of avoiding facing the loss of everything else that had been important to her, delaying acceptance of her new existence?

Kyber's hands stroked up and down her back. "You are here now—here with me. Forget about the rest. I am the only one who can make you happy."

That made her smile. "You are, huh?"

"Yes," he answered with certainty.

She tipped her head back to look at him. "And would I be the only one to make you happy?"

His eyes twinkled. He knew exactly what she meant. "You do not care for my courtesans."

"Competition energizes me. But not that kind."

"None would ever come close to competing with you, Banzai."

Her mouth gave a wry twist. "The perfect Kyber-answer."

"The answer is perfect only if it convinces you to think only of me." His fingers slipped into her hair, and he loosed it from her ponytail, spreading the strands over her shoulders. Then he kissed the side of her neck.

Her back tingled, and she gave an involuntary shiver. His lips were soft and warm. Her eyes closed as her head tipped back, exposing her throat to more kisses.

Her reaction to Kyber's touch was . . . nice, but somehow subdued. She tried to work up more of a response as his arms folded around her, molding her to his body. His kiss was firm, and her lips parted under the pressure. His tongue skillfully penetrated, enticing more than demanding.

She gripped his arms, trying to lose herself in his kiss, letting his hands go wherever they wanted, even though her thoughts were pinging off in a thousand different directions. When she felt his body tremble with pent-up desire, she wished she could feel the same.

But something was just . . . off. They were like two pieces that didn't fit together quite right. Should she let him make love to her anyway? To see if her feelings would change with intimacy, but the thought of that didn't feel right, either. She liked him too much to play with his feelings, if in fact he'd developed any for her. Come to think of it, she could never tell what he really thought of her, beyond being a challenge and a novelty.

She broke off the kiss. He mistook her restlessness for excitement. Nuzzling her throat, he asked, "Where would you like to make love? Here in the gardens? Or in the baths? Or maybe you would like the pleasurable conventionality of my bed. Perhaps all three, one after the other." He planted his hands on her hips, his expression one of lazy, sensual anticipation. "Well? Where shall we begin?"

She shook her head. It was hard to disappoint him. "I . . . can't make love with you. I'm not ready. I'm sorry."

Surprise and then displeasure flared in his face. Then he let out a heavy sigh. "Then we will wait," he said with forced cheer, as if straining to hide his disappointment. "But I must warn you—my patience will not last forever," he added in a joking way that hinted there was some truth there, too.

She wondered what would happen when his well of patience ran dry. Hugging her arms to her ribs to ward off the encroaching chill, she said, "It's not you, Kyber. It's me." What would Cam have advised in this situation? The thought of her missing friend almost brought tears to her eyes at the same time it conjured anger. She turned her head so he wouldn't see. "Maybe everything will fall into place when I have some closure."

" 'Closure.' What does it mean?"

"It's twenty-first century psychobabble for wishing I knew for sure what happened to Cam, so I can put it behind me."

Kyber walked away to stand by the reflecting pond. His

long shadow fell over the water, sending the fish bobbling away to cower under the broad leaves of the water lilies. More than ever, she sensed his loneliness. He was a physically imposing man, boisterous and giving, but there remained something defensive at the center of his personality. And it was that self-protectiveness that made him seem vulnerable. It was as if he used his exuberant charm as a shield to deflect anyone from noticing the sensitivity of his feelings, the hidden hurt. She hoped with all her heart that he found a woman someday who would love him the way he deserved.

Tiredly, he said, "Again, you're asking me to search for your missing friend."

She stood behind him, her hands squeezed together. "One last time. I'll go with the team myself—"

"No."

"I'm healed. I'm strong. I don't see a problem with it."

"I do."

"Please."

He turned around. His eyes were as cool and hard as granite. "No. I cannot allow you to leave."

"You can't or you won't."

"There are things you don't understand, Banzai."

"Like what? Tell me! I don't want to be kept in the dark."

He shook his head. "What you want can only lead to harm. You must stay here under my protection. Trust me in this. Let it go, this quest of yours."

Giving up meant surrendering. And Bree knew that was the one thing she couldn't do.

* * *

"Thirteen . . . fourteen . . . fifteen!"

At Joo-Eun's count, Bree dropped from her pull-up bar to the ground. Winded, she shook out her arms and walked in a little circle. Ever since she'd decided she was leaving the palace no matter what Kyber wanted, she'd been working out in earnest. Not only would it get her in shape for what hardships might come, it helped vent her frustration that came from not knowing exactly how she'd tackle her grand plan. A week had passed and still it hadn't left the drawing board, while autumn and colder weather were fast approaching. If she didn't figure out something soon, she'd have to wait until spring. More time wasted. And by then, maybe someone else would have gotten to Cam, someone not as generous and compassionate as Kyber—or as focused on duty as the soldier in the basement, who cared more about claiming a prize for his country than saving a soldier's life.

"Crunches next," Bree said, and sat down on the exercise mat. Ugh. She used to be in shape. So far, all she felt was sore.

Joo-Eun crouched down and grabbed hold of Bree's ankles. The embroidered tunic the girl wore fluttered over knee-length pants. Two long braids slipped over her shoulders, a hairstyle that made her look even younger than she was. Dutifully, she pressed Bree's bare feet to the mat.

"You don't need to do that." Bree patted the mat next to her. "Join me."

The girl's eyes widened. "Crunches?"

"That's right. You can do them, too. Building a little muscle is good for everyone."

Joo-Eun seemed to puzzle through that before she grinned. "I will join you!"

Her tunic swung as she bounced to the floor and got into position, hands behind her head. There was a flash of silver and black on her upper thigh, but by the time Bree processed what she'd glimpsed, the tunic had billowed back in place.

Joo-Eun stuck her elbows out to the sides as she'd seen Bree do. "I am ready."

"All right!" Bree put her hands behind her head and lowered her upper body to the mat. "On my count. One, two, three . . ."

Joo-Eun kept pace with her. Bree pushed herself, her abdominals burning, but her mind wouldn't step away from what she'd glimpsed strapped to Joo-Eun's thigh. What the hell was it? A knife? A gun?

Was Joo-Eun a bodyguard? If so, had Kyber assigned the girl for Bree's protection, or to keep her from running away?

Bree squeezed out one last crunch. Then she collapsed backward on the mat. Joo-Eun kept going, seemingly caught up with the enjoyment of the exercise and companionship.

Bree watched the teenager in awe. "Okay, Joo-Eun, I'm dog-tired and you're not even breathing hard."

The girl stopped immediately. She lay side by side with Bree and pretended to be out of breath.

"You can't fool me." Bree flipped over and raised her body on extended arms. "Ready for push-ups?"

Bree gutted out twenty-five push-ups before her arms turned to melted rubber, and, again, Joo-Eun stopped only because she did.

Bree narrowed her eyes at the girl. This equation didn't add up. One possible thigh holster plus one dose of incredible athletic conditioning didn't equal a housemaid. "How did you get in such great condition?"

Joo-Eun jumped to her feet. "I have many chores. They make me strong—"

Bree swung her leg out and hooked Joo-Eun behind the knees. The girl landed hard on her butt, her legs sprawled. Bree saw the holster again. It wasn't a gun but an industrial-sized blade strapped to her thigh.

"Is one of your chores me?" Bree grabbed for her wrist to put her in an arm-lock, but Joo-Eun evaded the move, jumping into a crouch. "A hard body, martial arts skills, and a weapon, too? I'm learning a lot about you today, Joo-Eun. You're not really a maid. Tell me the truth."

What little color remained in Joo-Eun's porcelain skin had pooled in her cheeks. Her shyness was gone, replaced by wary vigilance. Sweet? Slow-witted? That girl had vanished into thin air. Bree didn't know who had taken her place.

Sweat gleamed on Joo-Eun's forehead. She stepped backward, fear flickering in her eyes. The two women circled each other, the tension high.

"The others don't know about me," Joo-Eun said. "Will

you tell them?" She watched Bree carefully, as if gauging her reaction.

Bree thought of the blade and swallowed. The wrong answer could get her throat slit. "What is there to tell? You're carrying a knife. Is that a crime?"

Joo-Eun tugged on one of her braids. "I am not what I appear to be."

"Obviously." Her simpleminded companion was a street-smart knife-wielding karate champ. "Were you assigned to protect me, or spy on me?"

"Neither. I am your friend."

"Friends don't keep secrets from each other." But that wasn't true. Bree had plenty to hide. Joo-Eun wouldn't know of her plans to find Cam, because she hadn't confided in anyone, not even Kyber.

This time Joo-Eun's voice took on a pleading tone, sounding more like the girl Bree knew, the girl who looked up to her and wanted to be her friend. "Don't tell them."

The girl's reticence set off Bree's protective instincts. The king was upstairs in a back room, unable to hear, speak, or walk. She'd make damn sure Kyber didn't end up like his father. "On one condition. You give me your word that you're not undercover on behalf of some group that wants to kill the prince. Otherwise, no dice. And if you think you can kill me that easily with that knife you've got hidden under your dress, think again." Bree brought up her hands. "I won't go down easy."

Bree was ready for any movement that might indicate

Joo-Eun was going for her knife. She was mightily rusty with her self-defense training, but adrenaline would be her ally.

"I would never hurt you, Banzai Maguire."

"I wasn't talking about me."

"Hurting the prince would be hurting you."

Bree lowered her hands a fraction. She wanted to trust the girl, but some part of her held back, wisely reserving judgment. "I owe the prince my life. I won't let anything happen to him. If your group is involved in a plan to—"

"No. That is not what we do. We would never do such evil as was done to the king." Bree saw the truth in Joo-Eun's eyes. Whatever activities she was involved in didn't include assassinating the prince. "And, the shadows want you to succeed."

"Succeed in what?"

"In what destiny has brought you here to do."

Bree lifted her brows. "Destiny had nothing to do with it. A mad scientist did. You're looking at an experiment gone wrong."

Joo-Eun turned her hands palms up. "So are you."

Bree's defensive stance faltered. It felt as if someone had knocked the wind out of her. "Because you're a clone. . . ."

Joo-Eun's braids bobbed as she nodded. Her expression was wrenching and earnest. "Because my DNA will never allow me free travel in my own country. Because I will never be able to have children. Because one mention of what I am brings revulsion and fear."

Bree's heart went out to the girl. "Not to me," she whispered.

Joo-Eun bit her lower lip and glanced away. "I know."

The friction drained away. A truce had emerged between them. An understanding. Joo-Eun was involved in covert activities of some kind, but her loyalty to Bree wouldn't let her hurt Kyber. Bree believed her.

The girl had also mentioned destiny. Bree was less convinced of that. Unless that destiny included finding her best friend. If Joo-Eun was so much a believer in destiny, maybe Bree could convince her and her connections to lend a hand—not directly, but by giving her the one man who could.

Commander Tyler Armstrong.

Yet, to win his cooperation, Bree would need to give him something of value in exchange for the favor, something that would indebt him to her big time.

Joo-Eun might just be the path to that trade.

The clone took a shuddering breath and turned back to Bree. "I owe you much for keeping my secret."

"How much?" Bree winced at her shamelessness, but tragedy had made her an opportunist. If she let chances pass by, they might never come again.

"Anything, Banzai Maguire. Ask anything, and the shadows will fulfill your wishes."

Bree smiled. "Free Tyler Armstrong."

"Done," the girl said.

But the deal they struck came with caveats on both ends. Bree made sure the girl understood it mustn't be just any prison break. She herself must be the one to release Armstrong, so he'd know who gave him the gift of freedom. Then she'd tell him why.

As for Joo-Eun, she wouldn't tell Bree when the opportunity would come, assuring her only that it would.

"A day," Bree had asked. "Can you at least give me that?" She was a fighter pilot. Fighter pilots *prepared* for missions.

But all Joo-Eun gave her was: "Kingdom Day. Be ready when the shadows come."

Kingdom Day? It was a national holiday celebrating the anniversary of the Kingdom of Asia's declaration of independence, and it was only a few days away.

Chapter Thirteen

Bree planned and prepared for the celebration, but there was little she could get ready without arousing suspicion. All she put aside was a small survival pack with water, a little food that wouldn't go bad, a digital map, and a few tiny palace trinkets she knew had value but wouldn't be missed. She would have liked a couple of firearms to throw in, too, but where would she get them?

Now the day of shadows, Kingdom Day, had come. Joo-Eun told her to look for those shadows to make her move, but Bree didn't know what, where, or who. The sun was setting, and she hadn't seen any sign of *when,* either.

Bree pulled her hair out of her ponytail and shook it free, nervously jamming the loose ends behind her ears as she walked away from the window—and away from the inevitable fall of the sun behind the secluded wooded acres around the palace.

Kyber was off making appearances at the various festivals and fairs in the nearby vicinity—with his huge contingent of staffers, government officials, VIPs, and guards. Everyone except her. "You will be safer at the palace," he'd said, and for once she didn't argue.

She sat down at the desk in her room. Folding the note she'd written to him in half, she slipped it under the edge of the vase of roses he'd sent her. Did people handwrite notes anymore? She didn't know. Finding paper and an ink pen hadn't been easy. But saying "good-bye for now" via the palace computer and hitting SEND didn't seem to convey the message she wanted to get across.

Maybe she *was* an artifact.

She'd put her heart into that letter, hoping it blunted the hurt she knew she would cause him. It took away a little of the guilt she felt over abandoning the man who'd nursed her back to health. But only a little. Ignoring guilt was her specialty.

Of course, he didn't love her. She was a challenge to him, a novelty. Her leaving would be like the Hope Diamond sprouting legs and walking out of its display case. Traumatic, yes; psyche-bruising, no. *Kyber,* she'd written, *I hope you will see this as my duty, not my betrayal. I have to know what's beyond the palace gates. I don't have your permission, but I ask for your understanding. . . .*

She'd said nothing about looking for Cam. She'd left him thinking she'd gone off to search for her ancestors.

"You haven't touched your dinner." Dr. Park glided

over to the table wearing her all-business physician face. A server sister followed her and gathered up Bree's picked-at plates of food. "You've lost almost a kilogram this week. I will have to give you supplements."

Bree had lost all those grams from being too hyped-up to eat, but the doctor didn't need to know that. "I had a big lunch. And, I'm tired." Bree rubbed her eyes. "I think I may go to sleep early tonight."

"On Kingdom Eve? And miss seeing the fireworks and the parades from the balcony? No, you cannot. I know Prince Kyber will not let you sleep."

"He's out."

"He'll be back for you."

And that, Bree thought, would complicate things. Maybe she'd be gone by then. "I think I'll take a bath. Maybe it will wake me up." And deflect Dr. Park's overactive motherly worry. Then the woman would move on to other concerns. If she had any. Her life was seemingly dedicated to her work, and thus to Bree.

The doctor followed her to the bathing suite.

"Don't tell me you're going to work tonight," Bree said.

"I do have some tasks to attend to."

"If I'm going to stay up, then you have to do something fun, too." She practically pushed the woman out the door. "Go. I'll see you at the fireworks."

"I will look for you later, Banzai." The woman's expression went soft with tenderness. She smiled at Bree and left the suite of rooms.

Bree sighed as she watched the physician go. "Sorry,

Dae," she whispered. It would have been easier to leave if she was escaping a castle full of bad guys. Guilt, guilt, guilt. It sucked.

Joo-Eun would have accompanied her to the bathing suite, which was adjacent to Bree's quarters in the medical ward, but the girl was absent. If not for their strange encounter the other day, Bree would have assumed she was attending one of the holiday events. Now she couldn't help wondering what trouble the girl was getting into.

Yet, how often did she ever find herself alone? Not often. It was nice.

Bree stripped as she walked, leaving a trail of clothes, boots, and underwear behind her. Fragrant steam thickened the air, blurring the outer edges of the room so that she had a hard time telling how large it was. It was big, she knew that. Everything was always supersized in Kyber's palace. Supersized and luxurious.

She dove into an enormous bath rimmed with swirls of pale blue and gold glass mosaic tiles. The sound system played a recording of outdoor nature sounds that Bree preferred to music. As she paddled backward, the pool's rim of glass tiles glistened. Where would her next bath be?

Forget that, where would *she* be in the morning?

She was packed and ready to go, but so far, no shadows. The holiday was almost over. Time was running out, for Kingdom Day signaled the end of the summer season in Paekdusan and heralded the move to an even grander palace thousands of miles away in the city of Beijing. Had

Joo-Eun lied to her? She could have. Sure, Bree knew her secret, but it had no value if the girl had skipped town.

Bree dunked her head under water. Breaking through the surface, she flipped her hair out of her eyes. The wooded scene in the window-wall was gone, replaced by a floor-to-ceiling image of Prince Kyber.

She was in the bath, and Kyber was on the wall. Holo-communication was two-way. Didn't he know how to knock?

His eyes found her. "Ah. There you are, Banzai." He was decked out in full royal regalia: black clothes, topped by a black cape that flowed over his shoulders and swept the floor. Scraped back from his face, his hair poured from a platinum-and-sapphire tube, flowing in a shimmering ponytail over one shoulder.

Bree ducked low in the water. Her hair, dripping wet, hung around her shoulders. "I'm naked."

"I do not mind."

"I do!"

Kyber looked her up and down. "The water hides you."

"It does now. It didn't five seconds ago."

"Then I am five seconds too late."

He acted so matter-of-fact that Bree had to laugh. As usual, he didn't get it. He was a prince, used to going wherever he wanted, when he wanted, and, apparently, playing voyeur through two-way televisions when he wanted. "Next time warn me. Clothing may not be important to the other women in your palace, but it is to me."

He inclined his head in what appeared to be an apology. "As you are important to me, Banzai." He waved behind him, where she could see throngs of people celebrating the holiday. The dusk made it difficult to tell what they were doing, but they sounded happy. "I will be done here soon. Within the half hour. I invite you to watch the fireworks and parade from my balcony."

Damn. Dr. Park was right. "Sure, Kyber. I'll get dressed."

He waited.

"After you sign off," she hinted.

His mouth tipped roguishly. "Very well." He dipped his head in a small bow, and the screen went black.

Bree dressed quickly in her usual soft close-fitting outfit and boots. She donned a light jacket and fastened the travel pack to a belt, spinning it around to hide it behind her waist. It was time, she hoped, to meet the shadows. Unfortunately, it looked like she'd be doing it right under Prince Kyber's nose.

The noise from below the balcony sounded like thunder. Kyber greeted his people with fists pumping in the air. "Long live our kingdom!" he shouted, and Bree heard the answering calls from the crowd.

She watched him from the door to the balcony. Milky starlight edged his tall frame, turning Kyber into an ethereal being, a legendary prince from a fairy-tale kingdom. Toward the west, the light was almost gone from the sky. It would be a good night for fireworks.

And if that were all she witnessed tonight, if the night passed without shadows, then she would fall back on an alternate plan. That is, she would fall back on one as soon as she came up with it.

Bree alternated between disappointment and nervous anticipation as she watched palace staffers and society hangers-on flow in and out of Kyber's apartment and the balcony. Goblets of wine and other spirits made the rounds, passed out by servants dressed in outfits of every color in the rainbow, the clothing decorated with gems that Bree guessed were priceless if someone were to pluck, pool, and calculate them.

A hush momentarily came over the people crowded around her, and an entourage swept past, leaving behind trails of glitter dust and whiffs of exotic perfumes. On the balcony, Kyber turned around. "Mother," he said. His smile faltered a fraction. Bree wondered if anyone else noticed.

Queen Corrine of the Hans had arrived. Wrapped in a bejeweled sari and head-scarf, her slim frame looked fragile. But one glimpse of flawless skin told Bree that this was no old woman.

Bree had long wondered about the queen. She knew Kyber's parents lived in the palace, but she'd never seen either one leave the wing in which they existed in voluntary, virtual isolation. But tonight's events must be important enough for the queen to come out of seclusion.

A male escort supported the queen by the arm, but her gait was sure and strong. "Kyber," she said, her voice low and honeyed. Her smooth and slender hand grasped Kyber's, and he led her to the front of the balcony. The woman threw back her scarf, revealing the perfect profile of a goddess. Tendrils of long brown hair lifted and floated in the breeze as she laughed and waved to the adoring crowds. Gorgeous, graceful, and composed, the queen was obviously the source of a lion's share of the genes responsible for Kyber's good looks.

Bree stood in the background as the cheers rose to a crescendo. A hand came to rest on her shoulder. She jumped, startled, but it was only a server offering a glass of wine. She almost didn't take it, but changed her mind. It would make her look like everyone else. She didn't drink, though. If her chance to get Tyler Armstrong and leave with him came as Joo-Eun promised, she wanted all her wits about her.

There was a deep, muffled sound outside, like the slamming of a giant car door. Another boom followed, and Bree heard the crowd cheer. Sparkles in the colors of the kingdom's flag filled the night sky. The fireworks had begun.

Then, the lights in Kyber's apartment went out. For a moment, they flickered on again, as if a secondary source attempted to supply power, but the rooms plunged into darkness. Everyone gasped, but no one screamed. And then the guests laughed, as if it was part of the celebration. Bree knew better. The arrival of darkness meant only one thing: The shadows were finally here.

* * *

Eighteen slashes marred the wall above the filthy dungeon floor. Maybe his father had decided to abandon him here after all, Ty thought as he settled down to sleep propped up against the wall. The floor was wetter tonight than usual, perhaps because the days were cooling off outside, and after waking shivering and soaked the night before, he'd decided not to repeat the experience. He'd worked out as best he could over the past trying weeks, keeping his muscles strong, even when the lack of food sapped his energy. He lived in hope of release; and if not release, then escape. But so far, neither chance had come, which brought his thoughts back to his father.

Ty wouldn't blame the general for wanting to disown his only son. Ty's aborted treasure hunt would be an international embarrassment, and an expensive one at that. Kyber had made no secret of the fact that he'd found Ty's UV anchored to the rocks beneath the entrance to the cave. Yes, the UV had a security setting designed to destroy the cockpit should anyone without an access code decide to commandeer it, a feature added in response to the subs they'd lost during the Pirate Wars—but Kyber hadn't said anything about the *Sea Snake* blowing up. Either way, its loss was an expensive one—and humiliating. Ty's father would not be pleased.

All the more reason to steal Banzai from Kyber and bring her back to the UCE, where she belonged, Ty decided. His personal feelings for her aside, Banzai Maguire was a shining symbol of all that made the UCE great. Once home, she'd make appearances, motivate the population, inspire the United Colonies of Earth to aim for even more preeminence in the world. And then Ty's father would see that his son's actions were not as irresponsible as they appeared.

Ty rubbed his hands over his face and scratchy beard. Fantasies were fine and good, but dreaming of taking Banzai home with him? He might as well wish for Rocketman's "shadows."

"Look for the shadows! When they come, run!"

Sure, Ty thought, laying his head back against the wall. As his eyes closed, he decided to entertain himself with a fantasy that was even more far-fetched: his pretty little pearl, Banzai Maguire herself, showing up at his cell door to rescue him from Kyber's dungeon, a vision that certainly merited further reflection, if for the entertainment value alone.

Ty chuckled and let his chin fall to his chest. At least this night he'd fall asleep with a smile on his face.

Kabul, Kyber's security adviser, pushed through the throngs of people blocking the entrance to the balcony, his mouth drawn back in a snarl of a frown. Bree knew then that the blackout was more than an annoyance; it was a legitimate situation. Joo-Eun must have known it was coming, or she wouldn't have told her to wait for the shadows.

A hand landed on Bree's shoulder. "No, thanks," she said automatically, turning around, "I already have wine."

But it wasn't a wine server who'd tapped her. It was Joo-Eun. "It is time," the girl said softly.

Bree's heart did an aileron roll. She nodded and set her goblet on a nearby table. Joo-Eun walked away, and Bree followed. No one would think anything of her leaving with her lady's maid. And, in fact, no one looked at them at all. All eyes were on the fireworks, and those couples that weren't watching the show were in corners or against walls, stealing kisses in the amusement and confusion of the blackout. And Kyber, well, he was still sidetracked by his high-maintenance mama. For a fleeting moment, Bree felt sorry for him, trapped with no hope of escape in this odd world, composed of equal parts make-believe and mind-boggling responsibility.

Joo-Eun led Bree to the trapdoor in Kyber's floor, where he'd dropped her the first time she'd come to his room. His escape route. Joo-Eun lifted the door wide enough to allow her through. Bree dropped to the mat below. Hanging in an incredible feat of gymnastics, Joo-Eun shut the door behind her before falling to the mat next to Bree.

Joo-Eun pressed her finger to her mouth and took off running. Bree had to work to keep up in the darkness of the underground tunnels. She had the feeling that if she lost Joo-Eun, the girl wasn't coming back for her. If the blackout was a preplanned terrorist event, Joo-Eun had risked much by returning in the middle of it to take Bree to the dungeon so she could free Armstrong and escape the palace before the lights came back on. Of course, no one would have expected this of the shy and slow-witted little clone.

Bree saw a blue-silver glow ahead. The magcycle tracks. But the glow was soon lost when Joo-Eun veered away. The girl put her full weight into pushing open a heavy door, grunting with the effort.

"Let me help." Bree pressed her hands on the door and pushed.

"When the power went off, so did the computer assist on all the doors," Joo-Eun explained.

The door opened. A tidal wave of stench almost bowled Bree over. She slapped her hand over her nose and mouth. "Ugh! What is that?"

"Where your UCE man lives."

Joo-Eun disappeared down a staircase. Bree followed, her eyes watering from the smell. She didn't want to know what it was, but it was the worst thing she'd ever smelled.

If this was what dungeons smelled like, she was glad she'd never been imprisoned in one.

The air grew thicker and more humid as they rounded the second staircase and descended into hell. Their boots made sucking noises on the stone floor, covered in a coating of something wet and sticky. *Just . . . don't . . . fall.*

Joo-Eun stopped suddenly. Bree plowed into her back, almost putting them both on the floor. Joo-Eun steadied her and slid glasses over Bree's face. Suddenly, the features of the underground came into focus, outlined in soft green. Night-vision goggles. She could see in the dark!

"When you go, use the magtrack," Joo-Eun told her.

"But the power's out."

"The Halbach arrays still work."

The motion of the magcycle created inductive current, Kyber had said. No wonder it was his escape route.

"The shadows will await you at station eight. Do not be late. They will take you to New Seoul."

"Seoul? But I don't want to—"

Joo-Eun held up a finger. "Go to the Cheju Precinct. In the Celadon, shadows will find you." The clone threw a sack hanging from a strap around Bree's neck. "Do not lose this."

The girl took a step away, and then she was gone.

Bree heard nothing but her rapid breaths over the distant dripping of water and the squeaks of mice or rats. It was dark. And she was alone. Panic clutched at her chest. "Joo-Eun?" Her respiration doubled. Bree whispered louder. "*Joo-Eun.*"

No one answered. She was on her own.

Only sissies are afraid of the dark.

Bree felt like waving her hand and announcing, "Okay, I admit it. I'm a sissy. Now, someone turn on the lights, please."

But she pressed the goggles to her face, and convinced her eyes that she could indeed see in the dark. And if she could see, it wasn't really dark, was it?

With a shaky breath, Bree tore open the sack Joo-Eun had left her and reached inside. Her fingers closed around something cold and compact. She withdrew it and looked at the greenish object sitting in her palm. A pistol.

Finally, she had some real protection. Bree smiled. *Sorry, Cam. Joo-Eun's my new best friend.*

With the night-vision goggles lighting her way, and the pistol providing cover, she pressed her back against the wall and checked for guards before taking off for the dungeon. It wasn't hard to find the way. She just headed where the stink was the worst.

Chapter Fourteen

In his sleep, Ty felt something warm cover his mouth. Instantly, he was alert. He threw his hand over the fingers covering his lips, grabbed the wrist, and flung his attacker to the stone floor, falling over him. He'd barely registered the fact that the hand was slender and small and not the burly one of a guard when something hard thrust into his balls.

"Ooph!" His hips jerked upward as hot pain blossomed out from ground zero. His eyes watered. His attacker wriggled out from under his body. He grabbed for an arm, missed, and barely blocked the fist headed for his face. He used his assailant's arm to throw him onto his back—and came eye-to-eye with a very angry female in night-vision goggles.

"You idiot," she seethed. "I'm getting you out."

"Who are you?"

"Banzai." She gasped for air.

"Banzai?" He stared down at her in the dark. He couldn't see her eyes. But that mouth . . . he recognized the lips. "Banzai *Maguire?*"

"No. The other Banzai." She took one look at his expression of confusion and groaned. "Of course it's me! Who else would it be? And what's this stuff on the floor? Let me up!"

He felt her pelvis move under his aching groin. He lifted his buttocks, but not because the sensation was painful; he didn't want any more blood flowing into that sore spot than there needed to be.

She pushed him aside and sat up. An expression of revulsion crossed her face as she held out a sodden strand of hair and looked at it. "Gross. Tell me this isn't sewage."

"Whatever it is, I haven't died from it yet."

"Okay, let's save the mud-wrestling for later. We've got to get out of here before they get the power back on." She jumped to her feet.

"Wait. Slow down. Take two seconds to explain to me what's going on, and I promise you I'll listen."

"You used up your two seconds when you threw me into that shit." She appeared to struggle to control her temper before answering. "There's some kind of terrorist attack going on. The power's out. I'm not sure about the security systems, but I haven't seen a single guard."

"They're never around at night."

"Well, they might show up if they find out the cell doors are unlocked. I just pushed yours open and walked in."

And found me dead asleep, Ty thought. What kind of soldier was he? "Let's not give them the chance."

"Glad to see we're on the same page."

"Same page . . ." He shook his head. He was a devotee to old Americana and he still didn't understand half the phrases she used.

"It means we're on the same wavelength. Oh, just forget it. I have slang problems."

She ran off; he jogged after her. Banzai's night-vision goggles allowed her to navigate through the darkness; he had to concentrate to keep her in sight.

"We take a magcycle to station eight," she said. "There, the people helping us will be waiting. Supposedly, they'll be able to get us off the palace grounds."

"Supposedly? You mean you don't know?"

Banzai threw a scathing glance over her shoulder. "They got us this far, right?"

Ty wasn't inclined to argue.

She led him up the same stairs and along the same corridors that he'd traveled when the guards had escorted him for a shave and haircut.

"This way." She bolted toward a swath cut into the stone floor. Ty squinted along the track to where it disappeared around a curve. "There's no car."

"We'll have to call it." Banzai felt along the wall until she found a control panel. She pressed the icon and nothing happened. Her breaths were ragged as her head fell forward. "It's not coming. Maybe I need a code."

"All you need is power."

Her arm dropped. "And we don't have that." She thought for a moment. "If the magcycle won't come to us, we'll have to go to it. Kyber told me he has three. One's parked under his apartment."

"Hmm. Pick another one. You have the goggles. Which way?"

She looked right, then left. "With a fifty-fifty chance of getting it wrong, I say . . . *this way*." And off she went, Ty on her heels.

They ran along the tracks, glowing faintly with what Ty guessed was a residual charge, or perhaps an independent source of backup power.

They had been running for a good fifteen or twenty minutes when Ty started thinking of alternate plans. Find a door leading outside, and get through it before the power returned and locked them in. As he jogged, he noted the location's possible exits. He was about to suggest they try one when the tracks came to a loop. Tucked into a parking space against the wall was a vehicle.

Banzai bent over, her hands propped on her knees. Her hair hung dankly over her shoulders. Sweat made her pale skin shine. "There it is," she gasped. "The magcycle."

Ty was already walking around it, giving it a good look-over. The vehicle was a work of technological art, sleek and compact.

Banzai jumped into the driver's seat. "Somewhere there's a way to drive it using this handlebar. I watched Kyber do it."

"I'll drive," Ty volunteered.

"Good. You know how to handle these babies?"

"I know nothing about babies," he said to her apparent confusion. "But I can figure it out."

"So can I. At least I've seen it done." She bent over, searching for the starter.

"Fighter pilots," he said dryly. "They always have to be behind the wheel."

She spoke without looking at him. "Not always." He saw the mischievous little twist to her mouth. "It all depends who the driver is, and how good he is with the throttle."

He choked out a laugh, titillated. "I can teach you things about driving you never imagined, Banzai."

"Teach? What makes you so sure I'd be the student?"

Before he could come up with an appropriate response to her challenge, the magcycle vibrated and Banzai let out a small whoop. "We're good," she said. "Hop on." She twisted in her seat and tossed him the pistol.

"Good woman," he said. He released the safety on the pistol. "Making use of the available talents." She'd drive, and he'd shoot—*if* fired on. He liked to believe Kyber hadn't given the guards orders to kill him—*yet*—but in the dark and confusion, they probably wouldn't be able to distinguish him and Banzai from the terrorists who'd put out the lights. And then there was the matter of the guard who resembled a badger. The goon with the beady black eyes who would be looking for an excuse to shoot, and shoot to kill. Remembering the hatred in the man's face, Ty rechecked the weight and feel of the pistol in his grip.

He climbed on, saw no hand-rests, so he slid one hand around Banzai's waist. Her abdominal muscles contracted under his touch.

"We don't have helmets," she said. "At least put your straps on."

"I'll hold you."

She sighed. "I want you alive at the end of this, Armstrong."

"All right, then. That goes both ways." He fastened his safety straps. Then he wrapped an arm around her. Ah, his Banzai, his sweet little prize. She was his at last. "Take me for a ride, Banzai."

"Hang on." She twisted the handlebar and the vehicle moved forward. It went on that way for some time, slow and bumpy.

"Is this the fastest it—" In a whoosh of forward velocity, the magcycle roared off.

"Goes?" he finished. They'd achieved full levitation before he could finish the thought.

The magcycle raced into the darkness, soaring a few fingers' width above the track. He leaned forward. Banzai's hair whipped his face. He pushed the strands out of the way. "Do you know where you're going?" he shouted near her ear over the wind noise.

"That was station six." She hunched forward, the wind no doubt stinging her eyes. "We need eight."

He kept glancing back at their six o'clock position. No one was on their tail yet, but that could change.

Another station passed by. "There goes five," he shouted.

"We're going in the wrong direction."

The track curved. Banzai didn't let up on the speed. They leaned into the turn. "Here comes four." With the goggles, she had better vision. "Do you think it's an endless loop?"

"That's my guess. Let's see what we get after number one."

A light flared in the darkness, preceding the zing of a bullet. "Someone's shooting at us!" Banzai shouted.

No kidding. A hundred to one it was the badger, looking to bag Ty as his personal trophy.

His arm tight around her waist, he fired in the direction of the attack. Bullets whizzed past them like angry bees. One shot hit the magcycle, impacting with a metallic ping. "Faster," he shouted. They'd be out of range soon. Unless more shooters were stationed along the route. In that case, they might not escape so easily.

Banzai ducked down and sped up. He could see why wearing helmets had been a concern of hers. If they cracked up now, at this speed, it wouldn't be pretty. But then, neither would getting shot.

Station three passed by. And then two. Finally, one went flying past. Let the next one be eight, he thought.

"A station," Banzai yelled. He saw it a few breaths after she did. Number eight!

Banzai hit the brakes. Ty tightened his grip on her waist and pressed his thighs to the seat as if he were riding a newly broken horse. The magcycle decelerated and then bumped along the track before stopping. He and Banzai jumped off. "Where?" he asked.

"They didn't say. Do you see an exit?" She used her goggles to search out a door. "There!"

They ran for it. The last of Ty's newly issued prison slippers disintegrated before he reached the door. Now he was barefoot.

He used his shoulder as a battering ram. They spilled out of the stuffy basement into the cool, crisp night. Falling, they rolled down a grassy slope. He did all he could to keep her head from hitting a rock or log. Now that he had his treasure in hand, he didn't want a single scratch marring it.

They landed at the bottom of the hill, limbs tangled, Ty propped over her in a push-up. She tore off her goggles. "We have to stop meeting like this," she said, her eyes aglow with an incongruous mix of terror and mischief. But they seemed to have one thing in common: They didn't shrink from danger; it exhilarated them.

He grinned. "The atmosphere could use improvement, yes, but I have to say I like this."

She disentangled her legs from his. "If all goes well, Blue Eyes, we'll have plenty of time for atmosphere later. Where are our shadows?"

"Come on," he said. Together, they ran for the woods. Blue Eyes? He grinned. He had to say he liked that, too.

Ty threw a glance over his shoulder. No guards and no alarms, he noted—although the alarms would likely be silent. "Even if the entire palace security system was compromised, the system can come back up just as quickly. I don't want to be anywhere close by when it does."

"Neither do I."

"Who are the 'shadows'?" He remembered the graffiti in the cell, and what Rocket-man had told him. "Are they responsible for putting out the power?"

"That's my guess," Banzai answered, breathless. "I don't know what their goals are, but hurting Kyber isn't one of them."

He heard the protective edge to her voice. He also remembered the way Kyber had looked at her during their dinner. The possessiveness. The interest. That night, when Ty had returned to his cell, he knew it wouldn't be long before the prince charmed his way into Banzai's bed. When he saw her a few days later, he'd tried to tell if the deed had been done, but couldn't. And yet, here she was. With him! *Ha. Go to hell, Kyber.*

Ty decided not to waste anymore time wondering about his treasure's change of heart. Good fortune was like finding an unexploded grenade—if you analyzed it too closely, it could blow up in your face.

They stopped running a few meters past where the trees began so they could keep the palace in sight, and yet remain hidden from it. Pine needles stung the soles of his feet, but the cold turned the sting to a more palatable throbbing ache. In the silence, they listened to their harsh breaths. Then, footsteps crunched toward them in the woods.

"Well, well, UCE. I didn't have to listen for you. I could smell you!"

Ty squinted at the man walking toward them in the

dark. He waved with a thick cigarette pinched between his fingers. In the background, fireworks exploded in the sky. The flares lit the man's face in bursts of multicolored light. Rocket-man. Ty shook his head. "I don't believe it."

"I told you to look for the shadows, didn't I?"

Ty's goal of driving a fist through the man's face fizzled with the knowledge that the guy was involved somehow in springing him loose from the dungeon.

Rocket-man looked Banzai up and down. "I smelled you, too."

"Blame him," she said, throwing Ty a withering glance.

Ty shrugged. "What can I say? I wake up irritable."

Rocket-man had little to brag about, dressed in rags as he was. Looking around at the dark, palatial grounds, he smirked. "Worm," he explained, drawing deeply on his cigarette. Tobacco laced with some other substance, Ty guessed, probably nanoadditives for a cheap high, judging by the smell. "Shadows put it in the Interweb. Took out the palace. Temporarily. That Kabul, he'll get it fixed. Maybe soon." He took another long drag of his smoke-stick and threw it on the ground, grinding it out with his heel. "You ready?" He turned and walked away.

Ty flexed his hands and followed. Yeah, he was ready, ready to bring Banzai Maguire back to the UCE, where they'd welcome her as a returning hero.

Banzai caught up to Ty, her expression wary, her eyes questioning. "You know him?" she asked under her breath.

"We, ah, shared the dungeon for a time." He refrained

from telling her why the man had been there, and then figured, what the hell? "I call him Rocket-man. Any idea why?"

She shook her head.

"He fired the rockets at the balcony—at you and Prince Kyber."

Rocket-man overheard them. Without turning around, he raised his hand. "That would be me."

Banzai narrowed her eyes. "That was you?" Ty could tell that she, too, fluctuated between wanting to swear at the man for the rockets and thank him for showing up tonight. "What did you do that for?"

"To get inside," Rocket-man replied. "We wanted to see who the prince was hosting in his dungeon."

Ty regarded Rocket-man with new awe. He and his shadow people were willing to get arrested to accomplish recon? How long before Kyber realized they were outsmarting him?

In the starlight, a dirt path shone. Then, Ty heard the unmistakable moo of a cow. Many cows. But he couldn't discern the smell of manure from his own stink.

They broke through the trees. Ahead was a livestock-type vehicle, hybrid-fueled and not meant for travel on mag-roads. Cows filled the rear compartment. "I'll take you as far as Freedom City," said Rocket-man.

"That's only twenty-five kilometers from here."

Banzai touched Ty's arm. "Once there, we can get where we need to go. We just need to get away from here."

But Rocket-man reassured them. "Another driver will take my place. The shadows will bring you all the way to New Seoul. There, you must proceed to the rendezvous point. I will give you the location."

"Joo-Eun told me where to find shelter for the night," Banzai said. "Is that what you mean?"

"No. I am handing you the next bead."

She shook her head. "Say again?"

"Each of us holds only one bead in the necklace, you see. Joo-Eun, me, all the rest. None of us knows all—only our small part. As you pass from shadow to shadow, you will string these beads together. Go to the location Joo-Eun gave you, but the next morning, you must be on the southeast curve of the eighth radius of Bai-Yee Square at nine A.M. Don't be late."

Ty memorized the directions. "Bai-Yee Square is arranged in circles that radiate outward from a statue of the first Han Emperor," he explained quickly to ease Banzai's confusion. "Eighth radius means the eighth circle from the center. It's a street." He gave Rocket-man a frown. "And why is this necessary?"

"There, you will learn how to find the other one."

Banzai froze. "The 'other one.' Do you mean Cameron Tucker? You know where she is?"

Rocket-man's smile revealed nothing. "You will learn more then. Do not forget—the southeast curve of the eighth radius of Bai-Yee Square."

"Nine A.M.," Banzai said. "We'll be there."

As they climbed up into the livestock compartment,

Rocket-man issued more directions. "There are clothes. In the sack, there. You're a simple farm couple, returning home from Kingdom Day festivities at the summer capital—and too frugal to buy a mag-train ticket." He pinched his nose and took a few steps back. "When you get to New Seoul, the first thing I'd do is take a bath."

Rocket-man closed the gate, locking them in with the cows.

Banzai walked hunched over between the animals and found her way to the rear of the truck. She slumped onto a large platform of hay that stood above the cattle. It would keep them safe from stray hooves. Ty joined her.

Rocket-man started up the truck. Then they were off, bumping along the rutted dirt path until they veered onto the road proper. The truck accelerated with surprising efficiency.

Immediately, Banzai was up on her knees, opening a sack of clothing. "You . . . me . . . me . . . you . . ."

She sorted through the garments, separating them into two piles. The wind whipped her damp hair around her face. All Ty could see was her chin with its little cleft and her nose, smudged with dirt. More dirt rimmed her fingernails. One of her knuckles sported a bloody scrape. She was real. Real! He wanted to pull her into his arms and laugh out loud; he wanted to hold her up in front of Kyber's face and sneer. "You bastard, I've got her now," he muttered.

Banzai turned to look at him. "What?"

"I said I was thinking of you. In fact, you're all I've

thought about the past few weeks—how I could finish what I came here to do, how to take you back. And you fell right into my hands!"

She gave a soft snort. "Fell?"

He laughed with the relief of it all. "Yes!"

"Tyler—"

"Call me Ty."

"Ty. I didn't fall into your hands. I jumped. My wingman's alive somewhere. And you're going to help me find her."

Ty wasn't certain that he'd heard right. "Say again?"

"I need your help to find my wingman. Cameron Tucker. You couldn't talk at the palace, so I got you out. Now you can tell me everything you know!"

"That's why you helped me escape? Because you think I know where your wingman is?"

Fear flashed in her eyes. "Don't you?"

"I know where I found you," he hedged. He couldn't escape the disconcerting feeling that she'd return him to Kyber if she thought he wouldn't be of any use to her. If he wanted her to stay with him, he'd have to make sure she didn't stop believing she needed him, all while he kept both women out of Kyber's hands. "I assume Cameron Tucker is in the same location."

"She is. She has to be."

"The cave is in a shambles. Three-quarters of the walls are down. Part of the ceiling, too. I wouldn't have access to all the places her pod might be. I'd need extra men, explosives . . ." Before he realized what he was doing, the treasure hunter in him was pondering how to conduct such a complicated rescue on a shoestring budget while evading one of the world's most powerful rulers. But he caught himself in time. "No. It's impossible."

She tore off her travel pouch and threw it on the hay. "I'm 198 years old. Don't tell me about impossible."

Then she turned to him, her arms open, her hands upturned and pleading. "You're my last resort, Ty. I don't know this world, but you do. I need a guide, someone capable. I need . . . you."

It pained him to refuse her, but he had to. "I can't, Banzai. I can't risk your wingman falling into Kyber's hands."

"Yes, you can. A deal's a deal."

"A deal? What deal? I never agreed to anything."

"It was a tacit deal. I freed you. Now you owe me."

He coughed out a laugh. Her logic was incomprehensible. No, it was nonexistent.

"I read about you on the Interweb," she said angrily. "You're a SEAL. In my time that meant something. Never leave a man behind. Or don't you believe that anymore?"

Ty shoved a hand through his hair and turned his eyes to the dark countryside racing past. "I know what it's like to lose someone in my command."

He hadn't intended to say that out loud. He hadn't shared the experience with anyone. Maybe she hadn't heard him.

But she turned to face him in the dark, the wind blowing her hair over her face. "Did it happen in combat?"

He heard the careful respect in her tone. She knew what it meant, that loss. "The Pirate Wars," he began, with some reluctance. "It was our last major campaign, a crackdown on sea terrorism. We saw the loss of two military underwater vehicles—six men, all captured by the pirates. I led the mission to extract them. It was my first as a commander." He'd had Lopez with him, one of the best combat soldiers he'd ever worked with, and a great team to match. "Two of my men were killed. It's hard to accept, the first time men in your command die. And maybe that never changes." He swallowed.

"Did you find the captured crews?" she asked gently.

"I found them, found them all." He pushed aside the grotesque mental images burned into his psyche for all eternity. Jake, dismembered . . . Chance's head on a stake . . . Not all battle scars were visible, he knew. He'd relive the experience of finding those men for the rest of his days. "They were mutilated. Their body parts on public display."

Banzai made a sound of dismay.

"I blamed myself for not getting there in time. And I blamed myself for the deaths of my men. I did everything right. Logic says it wasn't my fault. But logic is not always the reality of our conscience."

"No," she whispered. "It's not." Her suddenly anguished gaze lingered on his face. She looked as if she was about to reveal a nightmare of her own, but changed her mind."

Her pain roused his curiosity. What did she hide beneath that tough exterior? It was strange to see his dream woman as flesh and blood . . . and pain.

"So, you see," he finished, watching her. "I know well the demons that drive a man to find those lost under his command. Or, her command."

"I admit I have demons, Ty. More than my share. But they won't hold me back from what I have to do."

"No," he said in a quiet voice. "Nor will mine."

Chapter Fifteen

Bree glared at Ty. He was as determined as she, she realized. Unfortunately, their goals were vastly different. "American Fighting Man's Code of Conduct, Article Three: 'If I am captured I will continue to resist by all means available. I will make every effort to escape and will aid others to escape.' *Aid others,* Ty. I'm bound by duty to look for her. Even if she weren't my friend."

A muscle in his jaw tightened. "It's too dangerous for you here."

"Kyber said it's too dangerous for me *there.*"

"Bah! He sees the UCE only from his own perspective. You know this."

"I also know that you see it only from yours. I'm reserving judgment until I see more of the world, especially after hearing you two argue politics and get nowhere. And see this world, I will."

He gave a clipped laugh. "Now that I finally have you, Banzai, I won't let you walk away without a fight."

The wind whipped both Bree's hair and the torn, billowing fabric of Ty's shirt, giving her a peek at his grime-streaked chest and hard abs. Sitting in the truck with his week-old beard and tattered clothes, he looked like a vagrant on a field trip. Not that she was much better off. She couldn't smell the manure anymore, which didn't say much for the odor coming off her body and his.

Then she noticed that he was watching her. It hit her that he'd seen her entire observation of his body. To her horror, she blushed, a reaction that he greeted with a slight, almost imperceptible curve of his lips.

She tried to grab back the fraying thread of their conversation. "Now that you *have* me? That sounds awfully possessive."

"We treasure hunters are like that about our booty," he drawled.

Great. So, he *was* a treasure hunter. A mercenary. She'd never fully believed Kyber, thinking he had exaggerated, as he was prone to do, to disparage the son of his enemy. Now Bree didn't know whether to laugh or cry. She'd been shot down, put in stasis, healed in a prince's palace, and now she was riding in a cattle car with Indiana Jones! A man who thought he'd salvaged her when in fact she had salvaged him.

Approaching headlights filled the cattle compartment with a white glare. Bree and Ty ducked down. When the truck was past, Bree snatched the old clothes she'd taken out of the sack. She wadded up Ty's outfit and boots and threw them at him. "I suggest we change clothes before anything else happens. I doubt Kyber will think to look for us in a truck full of cows, but you never know."

She crawled away, carrying an armful of clothing. Wobbling like a drunk in the moving truck, she used a couple of dozing cows as a privacy screen, turned her back to Ty, and pulled her shirt off over her head. Cool air hit her bare stomach. "So, you hunt treasure . . ."

"As a pastime," he said.

"What does a treasure hunter in this time do, exactly?"

"You could say I specialize in reclaiming what others allege are impossible finds. You and your wingman were the ultimate in impossible finds, considered lost for good. That was too much of a challenge to pass up."

She was eternally grateful he hadn't. "So, you do it for the sport, not the money."

"Oh, no. Not the money. Never that. I appreciate a good challenge. Treasure seeking gives me that." His battered prison pants landed hard in the corner of the truck.

Bree peeked over her shoulder as she buttoned a tunic shirt over a pair of baggy trousers. Ty, his back to her, thrust one arm into the sleeve of a faded blue long-sleeved shirt. He was broad-shouldered, but with an athlete's lean, efficient body. If he'd had any body fat before, it had evaporated in the past few weeks. Every sinew, every muscle on his naked back stood out. "How about being a playboy?" she asked. "Is that challenging, also?" There was something about him that made her want to keep flirting with him, even though she knew she shouldn't. It was like sneaking four more Oreos out of the box when you knew you should have stopped at two.

He sounded intentionally bored. "Ah, my status as a playboy. At times, the job can be high-maintenance—the social drinking, the dining out, the endless luxury hotel rooms. But mostly it's easy work."

She snorted. She knew he was teasing her, but he had self-confidence—lots of it. Well, he'd need it to get through what she expected of him. "I've never met a real-life playboy. Now I'm traveling with one. Should I be worried?"

His gaze slid over her simple outfit as he shoved his shirt into the waistband of his pants. Shadows hugged the hollows of his face. "Do you want to be?"

She knew better than to answer that question. But she persisted in her impromptu interview as she folded up her old outfit and draped her travel pack over the new one.

This outlaw son of the world's most famous army officer half scared and half fascinated her. And now she'd broken him out of jail. Had she opened Pandora's box? "You said you don't hunt treasure for the money, yet you came all the way around the world to find out if Cam and I were still alive."

"Actually, it was mummies I thought I'd find. I was going to bring you back and put you in the Smithsonian Museum. But then"—his eyes glinted—"I found you alive."

His features were as rawboned as the elder Armstrong's were: defined cheekbones, an angular jaw, square chin, and those vivid blue eyes contrasted with thick, dark brown hair. But while General Armstrong looked mean and hard, Ty lacked his father's stark severity and purpose, although Bree knew better than to fall for that. Ty Armstrong was a hardened combat veteran, and he'd come halfway around the world, risking death, to find her. "So, you're rich and bored. That's what I see."

"I'm a military man. I don't have time to be bored."

"But you're rich."

"My family is. I live by my own means."

"Except for having access to an army's worth of equipment for your treasure-hunting trips."

Ty's body went rigid, and his expression sharpened. "The underwater vehicle. You know about it?"

"Kyber mentioned it."

"Did he say where it is? The UV?"

She winced. "He said he destroyed it."

"It destroyed itself. It's set to explode if anyone attempts unauthorized use."

"Too bad. We could have used the transportation."

"Yes. And I wouldn't have had to pay the bill when I arrive home."

"That would be millions, Ty."

"Two hundred and seventeen million UCE dollars, to be exact."

This time she had the feeling he wasn't joking. "Where would you get the money?"

"I can't, of course. And that's my dilemma. I'll have to repay my father in a different way." As he contemplated her, something intense and speculative sparked in his eyes.

"Uh-uh. No way, Ty." She raised her hands. "I'm not the answer."

"But you are. Don't you see? Your connection to the past will revitalize what's at risk of becoming stale at home. It will inspire."

"And you called my plan to rescue Cam impossible? Listen to you! Revitalize the UCE? How would I do that?"

"You are a shining symbol of all that makes the UCE great. You'd make appearances, motivate the population."

"Nothing I say or do could help. I saw the tax revolts, the boycotts. Excuse my saying so, but the UCE needs a better government. Not an artifact."

"The UCE needs *you*."

"Are you listening to yourself? Starvation has eaten away at your brain, Tyler Armstrong! I'm not the answer to your debt. Or your country's problems. I'm afraid you'll have to think of another way to pay back your dad. You should have bought submarine insurance."

She sat on a bale of hay and pulled on her boots. "Just don't forget how you lost your UV, Ty. It exploded, from unauthorized use. I can blow up just as easily."

His brows lifted. "Shall I consider that a warning?"

"Consider it a reminder. I'm not a prize. I'm not your little challenge. I'm an air force pilot on a mission."

"To find your wingman."

"Yes."

"In an underwater cave in the middle of the Kingdom of Asia on one of the most rugged stretches of coastline I've seen."

"Yep."

"That's not a challenge?"

"Well . . ."

"Yet, I'm required to assist you because you released me from prison. How did you put it? A deal's a deal."

She grinned with wry amazement. "Wow, Ty. You catch on fast."

She made her way to the rear of the raised bed of hay and fell onto her back. "I've slept on better, but this will do." She draped one forearm over her eyes. "I don't think I've ever been this exhausted in my life."

Ty lay down next to her. "I don't think I've ever been this hungry."

She reached over and gave his hand a quick squeeze. His callused fingers were warm and strong. Surprise at the contact flickered in his eyes. It was a spontaneous move, a gesture of friendship, but it was with unexpected reluctance that she pulled her hand away. "You need to eat, Ty. We'll tell the driver when he stops."

"What we need is water. I can live without the food." He chuckled. "I'm not happy about it, but I can. But I'm going to make up for lost time—and lost meals—when we get to New Seoul."

"And then we're supposed to find the Cheju Precinct and the Celadon. Whatever that is."

"It's likely an inn. Or I hope it is. When Kyber mobilizes his security forces, we won't want to be caught out in the open."

She frowned at the stars overhead. "New Seoul is so far from the cave. Too far south. But the shadow people . . . they might have information about Cam. Otherwise, I'd have suggested we get off halfway, not even go all the way to Seoul, and hide where no one would think to look for us."

"Suggested? To put it mildly. Likely it would have been more like you dragging me out of this truck."

"Hey. The sooner we would have stopped, the sooner you'd have eaten."

"Eat? With what money?"

"In that sack I was given, I found digital credits, but not a lot. When those run out I have some jeweled trinkets I took from my room. They're small but look expensive. Though I'm worried we'll be caught if we try to sell them."

"If it comes to that, we can find someone to buy them who'll send the pieces on to the black market in Macao. They can launder anything there, trinkets to humans."

"I thought Macao was part of Kyber's kingdom."

"Technically, it is. But controlling the lawlessness and chaos would cost too much in time and money, and lives, so Kyber leaves it mostly alone. The only thing he insists on is Macao's loyalty to the crown, which they give happily to keep him off their backs. Sometimes I think the UCE could take a lesson or two from the man about some of our colonies."

Bree came up on her elbow. "Did you just give Kyber a compliment?" she teased.

Ty's mouth gave a wry twist, and he laced his hands behind his head. "For a domineering, autocratic despot, he's doing something right. For over a century, they've surpassed us in all areas, including technology."

The world had changed, she thought. "There was a time, my time, when the U.S.A. was the innovator."

"Innovation." Ty looked grim. "A lost art."

"Find it," she said. "Get it back."

"Our national focus is on stability. Keeping the peace."

"You mean keeping the colonies in line."

A parade of emotions crossed Ty's face, doubt, anger, and despair among them. She remembered the doubts she'd seen in him at the dinner with Kyber, and wondered again what opinions he kept hidden. "The UCE brought stability to the world. Look at history. There hasn't been a major war since the late twenty-first century." His voice dropped lower, as if he were worried about others listening in on their conversation. She'd bet Ty had been walking on political eggshells all his life, never able to trust anyone fully with his private, political thoughts. "Of course . . . some wonder if we created peace at the expense of something more precious."

Some? Bree wondered whom he meant. Probably himself. Maybe others he knew. Other officers? Could be. Discontent in the ranks of its officers could bring a government down. Bree had seen examples of that in her own time. Grandfather Vitale had told her that the military was like an intelligent, intensely loyal guard dog. If mistreated, it turned vicious. And like a highly valued watchdog, the military worked best as a supporting player. Its role was to support a government, to protect a government, not to be the government. General George Washington himself had recognized that when he shocked the entire world by resigning his commission in the Continental Army before taking over the presidency of his newborn nation.

"And you?" she ventured carefully. "Do you think something precious was lost to have peace in the world?"

His answer was totally unexpected. "I don't know that we can say anymore that the world is at 'peace.' It's not just the UCE that's experiencing unrest. The Euro-African Consortium has seen a number of attempts at revolt. Everywhere but in this kingdom. But then what of the 'shadows' who are helping us? What role do they play? Are they revolutionaries? Or only troublemakers? They certainly aren't loyalists. I think we're seeing a world at the threshold of change."

She watched his expression twist. It was as if he feared that change as much as he longed for it.

"And you're not sure if the UCE will get through it," she finished for him.

Ty rolled onto his back. His body language told her that he wanted the conversation to be over. "That was not what I said, Banzai. I merely stated the facts of the world political situation."

Don't take me farther down that road. She could hear

the warning without him voicing it. Bree knew then that he agreed with her but didn't want to admit it. How could he? His father was the most powerful military man in the Western world. On top of that, he himself was a military officer, which required him to appear loyal in public and use private avenues to convey his concerns no matter who his father was. As a fellow officer, Bree understood. She had represented her country, defended it with loyalty and honor, though there were times when certain policies she had been obligated to support seemed . . . well, not the courses of action she'd have chosen, though she would have upheld them all the same.

But for Ty, the UCE's colony problems weren't just a particular campaign but the entire national focus, and the virtual underpinning of the current government's powerbase. It put Ty and any other like-minded officers in a real quandary. To refuse to defend the policy of mistreating the UCE colonies would be treason. And yet supporting a flawed directive, as he was under oath to do, was to go against his principles.

And he had them. Principles. Somewhere.

Or so she hoped.

She went back to thinking of her immediate situation and not the grander scope of world politics. A treasure hunter playboy would make her search interesting. An unprincipled treasure hunter playboy would make it a disaster.

She'd pray for his principles.

The truck drove on through the night. The cows drowsed, quietly chewing their cuds.

On their backs, Bree and Ty watched a black sky full of stars. Then, out of the blue, Ty spoke. He sounded more like himself. "I was thinking . . . you informed me a little while ago that you're equipped with defense measures similar to my UV, and you'd explode with unauthorized use. Tell me, Banzai, what sort of use constitutes 'unauthorized'?"

Holding back a smile, she rolled her head to look at him. "Forcing me to change my mind about finding Cam, for one."

"There's more?"

"Treating me like I'm booty."

The little scar on his upper lip compressed, and she knew Ty was fighting a smile. "That's two. More?"

"I guess you'll have to learn the rest as you go."

"So be it. Unlike you, Banzai, I don't mind being taught." Fatigue made his voice deep and raspy. He lowered it further and murmured, "Particularly when the lesson's one I enjoy."

She could hear his body shift positions on the hay. She remembered what he looked like without a shirt, and the heat of sexual attraction blossomed in her belly and spread to the four corners of her tired body. It made her feel languid and warm. Spontaneously, she slid her hand over the hay. When she felt the warmth of his wrist, she circled her fingers around it.

He said nothing. She said nothing. In the silence, they let their fingers twine together. The more she touched him, the more she wanted.

Her hand slid up his arm, pushing up his sleeve. His biceps was rounded and firm under her palm. She rolled onto her side, facing him. His body was so close . . . so warm. She ached for more. But then she remembered how badly she smelled. How dirty they both were.

She took back her hand and rolled onto her back. She could feel Ty's frustration rolling off him. It joined hers and created a tidal wave of dissatisfaction.

Unlike with Kyber, she could easily imagine making love with Ty: him, lean and strong, and her, needy as she lost herself in the sensations he conjured.

She hadn't stopped to ponder it, but now that she took the time to do so, she saw how ragged she was, emotionally. The past few hellish weeks had taken their toll. It would be nice to be able to lose herself in something—or *someone*—if only for a few hours. She'd tried with Kyber, but hadn't been able to do it. But what about Ty? She sure thought of him enough, whether it was with anger, annoyance, or desire.

Bree stared at the stars overhead, her pulse racing. It had been a long time since she'd let a man get under her skin. Hell, it had been a long time since a man had gotten anywhere at all with her. Again, she thought of the conversation she'd had in Life Support with Cam as they'd dressed for their last mission, when Cam had accused her of being afraid to let a man get too close.

Fear wasn't a factor when you hooked up with the right guy. Ty felt more "right" than anyone had in a long while. Or maybe ever. But as Cam always said, finding out for sure would require taking risks with her personal life—something Bree had been averse to before.

And that, she decided, was a long time ago. She was in a new world now, with new rules. It was time to let the old game plan go and see what happened next.

It was well after noon the next day of traveling when the truck pulled off the road. The change in motion startled Bree out of a deep sleep. She'd slept most of the day napping, curled up in a ball in the hay, her head pillowed by Ty's shoulder.

But he'd rolled to his knees, his pistol drawn, before she could blink the sleep out of her eyes. She was a fighter pilot, not a special-ops type; she readied for action at a briefing with a paper cup of java warming her hand, while soldiers like Ty were combat-ready twenty-four/seven.

"What is it?" she whispered, trying to clear her brain of fog.

Ty flattened his hand on her head and pushed her down. "Driver's gone," he said in a low voice. "He went into that farmhouse, there."

Across the road, a small house sat in front of a few acres of unsown fields. It looked deserted. There was nothing else around but woods, thick trees broken only by the farm.

All was silent except for the gentle mooing of the cows in the truck and the rustling hay. Ty crouched in the hay and waited for the driver's return. They'd changed drivers once already in Freedom City, stopping only long enough to say farewell to Rocket-man and get a quick-charge of the fuel cell, which, unfortunately, hadn't given them time to find food. They were hungry and dehydrated.

A light breeze moved the air. "Lord, we stink," she whispered, wrinkling her nose.

"It's not us. It's them."

"The cows? I don't know, Ty. I can't smell them anymore." They exchanged wry glances.

Two gunshots rang out from the direction of the farmhouse. Startled birds squawked into the sky. The cows bellowed. Ty grabbed Bree by the hand. She'd barely gotten her hand around her travel sack before he dragged her out of the truck.

She knew why. In the truck, they were too exposed—and trapped. Taking cover behind the vehicle, he pushed her down into a crouch and peered around the cab, his pistol ready to fire.

Bree's heart thundered in her ears, and she tried to work moisture into her mouth, which proved impossible. She wished they had two guns. She felt naked without one.

Then she heard the crunching of gravel on the shoulder across the road. The gait was irregular, and then it slowed to a shuffle.

Ty disappeared around the front of the cab. A moment later he skipped backward, dragging a man with him. Bright red blood made a gruesome trail as Ty pulled the driver to safety behind the truck. He attended the injured man with a paramedic's expertise. Tearing open the shirt,

Ty exposed an open chest wound, a horrific mess of broken ribs and torn flesh.

Bree fought her gag reflex. It was an exit wound, she realized. Someone had shot the driver in the back. There was more blood than she'd ever imagined, and it kept coming, a vast and expanding pool under the driver's quivering body. Ty wore a good deal of it on his hands and clothes. But the smells were what struck her: sweat and a sharp, pungent metallic scent mixed with the faint odor of feces.

Until now, the escape from prison, while nerve-racking, had seemed more of a prank than a deadly venture. In a few seconds, everything had changed. Now she felt the pressing urgency of a life-or-death situation. Evil forces were at work here, "loyalists" who might or might not actually give loyalty to their ruler, rather using the label to sanction their violence. Yes, she wanted to find Cam. But at the risk of leading these people to her? She prayed she'd learn more at the rendezvous with the shadows. Now more than ever she knew she mustn't be late.

The wounded man pushed at Ty. "Go," he gurgled. Blood welled up in his mouth and spilled to each side. His eyes rolled back in his head, but with what looked to be a great effort, he spoke again. "Loy . . . loyalists. Drive—drive away. Take Banzai . . ." The man convulsed, and a fresh gush of bright blood spurted from his mouth. His struggles to breathe made a horrible sucking sound. Ty did what he could, but Bree knew nothing would help. He was drowning in his own gore.

Bree pressed a fist to her stomach. She was an air warrior. She'd trained to do her killing from the sky, too far removed to see actual casualties. But here was death up close and personal, the way Ty and his brethren faced it in every battle, in every war.

"He's dead," Ty said. She didn't realize she'd been staring, morbidly transfixed, until he took her by the chin and turned her head. His eyes were the color of the sky. "Are you all right?"

She yanked herself out of her stupor. "Yes, yes. I'm good. I'm fine. You heard him—he said drive away. I say we do that right now."

"I couldn't agree more." Ty pulled open the passenger-side door, and she jumped in while he covered her with the pistol. "Keep your head down, Banzai!" He yanked hard on her sleeve, pushing downward.

She was face-to-face with the steering wheel. "Where are the keys?"

"They stopped using keys a hundred years ago." He reached across the seat and used his thumb to punch an icon on a touch-activated computer that put anything she'd used in fighter aircraft to shame. The engine hummed to life.

"Gears?" she asked, fastening her seat belt harness.

"None. Just step on the accelerator. Go!"

She jammed her feet onto what looked comfortingly familiar to a gas pedal, which was next to something that was reassuring in its similarity to a brake. The truck squealed on the asphalt and lurched forward, which sent Ty scrambling to find his seat belt.

He turned in his seat. "They see us."

Her stomach dropped. "What do you mean?"

"Drive faster!"

"Ty! What? Why?"

"A man and a woman came out of the house."

And . . . ? She gritted her teeth. "Will you stop feeding me the juicy parts in tiny pieces? This is a getaway, not *Mystery Theater*!"

He glanced at her, his expression one of utter male bewilderment.

"Give me a clearer picture of what's happening," she pleaded. "Spoilers welcome. The couple. Where'd they go?"

"They took the body away from the road, dragged it back to the house."

Was this the way SEALs communicated in battle? They fired bullets and they spoke in them, too?

She inched higher in the seat to see the road and pressed the accelerator to the floor. The digital speed readout crept higher as Bree sped up to pass a vehicle, another truck. Vibrations she hadn't felt before made the steering wheel buzz. Instability made the tires dance. It appeared she'd reached max speed in the cattle truck.

Yet thoughts of the dead driver and the smell of death kept her foot pressed to the accelerator. Another thing she hadn't considered—and hadn't wanted to consider—was if the so-called loyalists had acted on Kyber's orders, and not according to their own agenda. She may have made a vast miscalculation in estimating Kyber's reaction to her defiance. As friendly as he was to her, he hadn't survived as monarch all these years because of his congeniality. She'd damn well better look at the situation from all angles now, or she and Ty wouldn't survive the day.

"There's another road coming up," she yelled.

The smaller path they traveled was about to merge with a larger, wider one. To the right, a magcar highway paralleled their track. Levitated cars whipped past a variety of old-fashioned fuel-cell-propelled vehicles not capable of traveling on the magroads, everything from motorcycle-looking modes of transport to ramshackle trucks that looked as if their sole use was to serve the local farms.

A display on the dashboard showed the upcoming merge. The roads appeared as arteries: the one they were on in white, the upcoming highway in pulsing red. "We need South, right? To New Seoul!"

Ty was already scanning a glowing map-screen he'd unrolled on his thigh. His finger remained pressed over their pistol's trigger. Dried blood covered the back of his hand. "Yes. We'll be there by nightfall."

Their grave situation made New Seoul an even better destination, despite its distance from the cave. It was in the same spot as the original city, but now, thanks to higher sea levels, it was a busy port, and a big enough city to allow them to disappear into oblivion once they ditched the truck. There, they could hole up and wait for the storm to pass. If the storm passed.

Thunder exploded from behind. "Incoming!" Ty shouted.

Bree jerked her attention to the rearview mirror. Ho, baby! He wasn't kidding! A low-flying aircraft hurtled toward the truck.

Ice dumped into her veins as her combat instincts kicked in. She half expected the truck's radar to warn her of the threat. But the truck had no antiaircraft radar.

The jet roared overhead so low that it kicked up a storm of pebbles and leaves. Dust hissed against the windshield, and rocks bounced off the hood. She heard the cows, but didn't dare look back there, in case the stampede was already under way. Then a splat of something liquid hit the windshield, bubbling where it had dribbled. "They sprayed something at us!"

Ty flashed a look at the front of the vehicle. "Nanoenhanced acid. It'll melt right through metal."

Humans, too, she thought. But he didn't need to spell it out. She got the picture.

"If you see it coming, steer around it."

"Sure." The truck burst through the cloud of debris. Ahead, she faced a picture she didn't want to see. "It's coming back for more!"

The acid-shooting jet banked sharply as it reversed course. It looked similar to the one she'd seen taking off vertically when she was on the balcony with Kyber. A civilian craft if she had to guess, not military. The driver had called them loyalists. But were they? The further she got into this, the more certain she was that the people who had killed the driver hadn't acted under Kyber's orders. Likely, they might be rogues with their own issues with the shadow people, and these might not have anything to do with her escape or Ty's. After all Kyber had said and done, she couldn't imagine him wanting to kill her to save himself from the embarrassment of the world knowing Ty had escaped. Or so she hoped. Either way, having rogues on their butts was much more potentially dangerous.

The dark silver craft whooshed over the truck again. More acid hit its mark. The hood was sizzling and so was the far left corner of the windshield. A section had melted and was buckling under the pressure of the wind. A hissing glob fell through the roof and boiled its way through the cushion on the seat. The acrid stench of melted plastic burned her nose as the substance bored straight through the chassis. Through the new hole in the seat, she could see the road racing by underneath the vehicle.

The dust kicked up was thicker this time. Bree couldn't see the road ahead, and eased off the accelerator. The tires bounced over the shoulder, and she pulled back toward center. Then she was in the clear again.

Ty tried to lower the passenger window but it was stuck. He smashed out the glass with the butt of his pistol, making room for his shoulder and arm. Shattered glass snagged the fabric.

"Careful," she yelled over the noise. "The glass!"

He glanced down, seemed to deem it okay, and aimed his weapon out the window.

Bree couldn't stand the sight of him hanging out of the truck. *Please, please, don't get killed, Ty.* "What are you doing? You can't shoot a plane down with that!"

"I would if I could. But maybe a few pings on the fuselage will send them home."

Not only was he a treasure hunter and playboy, he was a *cocky* treasure hunter and playboy. "I'm going where there are more cars," she said with determination. Traffic would make the truck a harder target to hit, if that's what the pilot decided to do. An F-16, radar, and some guns sure would go a long way in helping her feel less inadequate. But she had a pistol-toting SEAL hanging out the car door. That had to count for something.

Bree turned hard, racing up the ramp to the bigger highway. The truck skidded on its right-hand-side tires before settling back on all four.

The cows protested loudly. She could feel the shifting of their weight, and it was playing havoc with her driving. She chanced a peek. Some had froth spilling out of their noses. Others stomped around with the whites of their eyes showing. She didn't know what the cows liked less, the noisy airplane or her driving.

Bree checked the rearview mirror. "Here she comes again!" The aircraft roared toward them, even lower this time. Instinctively, Bree ducked down, felt the vibration of the jet's engines in her stomach.

Ty took aim. As the craft passed overhead, he fired——once, twice. Bree's ears rang from the bangs.

The jet's wings rocked. Hydraulic fluid or similar stuff

streamed out the belly of the craft. "You got a hit!" Bree yelled. "Woo-hoo!"

As the craft banked away from the road, gaining altitude, Ty pulled his body back in the cab.

"You're a wild man," Bree praised.

"I've been called worse." His smile was anything but humble.

She almost expected him to blow smoke off the tip of his gun, like the victorious cowboy after an old-fashioned shoot-out. "You do this type of thing much?"

"Not from a cattle truck," he admitted.

"That makes two of us."

"Ah, hell." Bree followed his disbelieving gaze to the wounded craft. It was descending, coming down fast, its wings rocking, as if the plane had become difficult to control.

"It's making an emergency landing," she shouted. "And it's going to use the road as a runway!"

She scanned the highway, and the display in the truck, looking for exits. But there were none. The plane was coming down. Other drivers saw it, too. All began pulling off the road. Bree jerked the wheel to the right. The truck bounced over the shoulder. She smelled dirt, hot tires, and cow manure.

The jet hit the road, hard. The wheels ejected smoke and flames. Sliding sideways, it careened toward the truck.

"Get out!" Ty grabbed Bree by the hand and pulled her from the cab.

Screeching over the asphalt, the jet slid past. A sharp burning odor filled Bree's nostrils and made her eyes water. She ran with Ty through clouds of powder. In a tornado of dirt and noise, the feel of his hand was welcome.

"Go, go, go!" He propelled her in front of him where he could keep her in sight, though it slowed his pace. His legs were longer; he could outrun her. Yet Ty Armstrong would die saving her. That, she knew in her gut. He remained staunchly at her side, pushing her ahead of him as they veered into the woods. They broke through trees into farmland. Cabbages grew in neat rows. Puffy clouds dotted the sky above. The scene was bucolic and peaceful, an illusion destroyed by the sound of an explosion.

"Oh, my God. You did it. It blew up," Bree said between gasping breaths.

"It was a lucky shot."

"I'll say."

"It'll draw attention away from us—for a while, anyway."

"And I think it'd be a stretch to relate us to the accident in the first place."

Ty made a sound of agreement. He sounded more winded than she was. But exertion was a bitch when your stomach was empty. "Eighth radius, Bai-Yee Square. All we have to do is make that rendezvous. Focus on that, Banzai. Getting there in time."

At nine straight up. She squeezed her eyes shut. They had to make it, no matter what.

They reached a farmyard. Another large truck sat behind a barn, its engine idling, its covered bed full of cabbages and cool shadows. It was market-bound.

Ty's big hands curved around Bree's waist. He threw her into the back of the truck and jumped in after her. The cabbage smelled wretched, but it was head-and-shoulders above the cow manure. They buried themselves in hay and cabbages and hunkered down.

Sweat dribbled down Bree's temples. She swiped it from her eyes and yanked the pieces of hay poking her out of her pants. She felt heat and exhaustion radiating off Ty. His eyes were bright blue in his grimy, bearded face.

Footsteps approached. Ty pressed his finger to his lips. Bree nodded, her heart thumping so loudly she was sure the farmer outside could hear it.

But the truck only jerked and began to roll forward. For a long time it bumped along what felt like narrow side roads. Then the ride smoothed out and the truck accelerated. Apparently, the farmer had used back roads to circumvent the airplane accident.

Once they were under way, Ty took the map from Bree's travel sack. Direct signals from satellites provided a simple map with instantly updated positions. Who had said she'd had her fill of tech? Now Bree was singing its praises. "Where do you think we're headed?"

"To the south." Ty's relief was visible. "Let's hope it's the nonmanufactured-food market in New Seoul."

He exchanged the map for a head of cabbage. No . . . he wasn't. He couldn't. But he did. With the kind of eagerness a man like him might devote to a steak dinner, he thrust his thumbs into the cabbage and tore it apart. Ravenously, he bit into one half. Then he glanced up. "Don't look so shocked," he mumbled between mouthfuls. "It's good." He offered her a bite.

She swallowed. "No, thanks."

The more Ty ate, the more color left his face. With a great effort, at last he swallowed what he'd chewed and threw the rest of the cabbage into the pile, wiping his mouth with the back of his hand. "Good intentions," he said. "Bad idea."

Bree grabbed a fistful of hay and offered it to him.

He laughed. "Thanks, but I'll wait for dinner."

Exhausted, Bree turned away to stare out the back of the truck until the adrenaline drained from her system. *Scarlet, I'm coming for you. It might take a little longer than I thought. Don't give up on me, Cam.*

But instead of bringing her closer to her friend, every mile Bree traveled took her farther away.

When the cabbage truck finally stopped, it was dark. Bree smelled the sea and tasted salt in the air. Shivering from the cold, hunger, and exhaustion, she crouched next to Ty and peered outside through a gap in the tarp. They'd pulled into a port. Shouts and activity from all sides told her that it was a dock where farmers unloaded their produce. Their driver left the cab of the truck. Without checking the back, he walked away and disappeared into the crowd.

"Do you remember what we briefed?" Ty asked.

"We drop and run like hell."

"We walk like hell. It won't draw as much notice." He squeezed her shoulder. "And you don't let go of my hand." He checked the pistol and its futuristic version of an ammo clip before giving her one curt nod.

Ty shimmied on his butt to the rear opening, as if he were preparing for a low-altitude parachute drop out the back of a C-130. She heard his borrowed boots hit the asphalt. And she jumped out after him, her heart dancing like crazy.

She'd barely gotten her balance when he snatched her hand and lugged her forward. A wall of crates led to the front gate where the truck had entered the dock area a short time ago.

Bree tried to look normal. She shivered, but sweat still formed on her forehead. She wiped it off, but the evidence of her tension kept coming back. Ty put his arm over her shoulders and drew her close, as if she were a fragile, ailing wife. She wished she could feel his body heat, but what little he had seemed to roll off her. He felt her shivering, drew her even closer, but it didn't help. She recognized her symptoms as the beginnings of hypothermia. But there was nothing more she could do than what she was already: walking at a pace just under a run.

Ty limped, but she could tell he tried to hide it. She

remembered his bloodied feet, and now they were crushed into ill-fitting boots.

The dock was a makeshift produce market, where farmers sold food directly from the backs of their trucks—a little side profit before the produce had to be packaged and shipped elsewhere. The area was small, but crowded with nighttime shoppers. The bounty of the early fall was displayed with pride; the smell of freshly picked fruits, vegetables, and cooking food filled the air, making Bree's stomach demand sustenance.

Having survived the past few weeks on bowls of rice with an occasional sliver of boiled meat, Ty was surely reeling with hunger, but his concentration centered on getting them to a safe haven for the night. "Not here," he said under his breath. "We'll eat after we find lodging."

Except for the countless electronics accompanying the hundred or so shoppers and a few helper-robots like Pip, the scene was remarkably twenty-first century. Unlike Kyber's palace, Bree didn't feel as much of a stranger here. Both shoppers and sellers looked healthy and well fed. There was a noticeable absence of poverty—in any form.

That is, there was an absence of poverty in any form except for her and Ty, if anyone had tried to take a closer look at them. They were grubby and dressed like poor vegetable pickers. The shadows had chosen their clothing well. But nothing would have helped if Kyber had launched an all-out search. But if he had, wouldn't there be police at every dock and every station, looking for them?

So far, Bree saw no signs a search was under way. Their only hope was that Kyber wouldn't expect them to be in New Seoul, and so quickly. The gruesome scene at the farmhouse lingered in her mind. Bree could still hear the driver's last gasps for air. It reminded her that the people in the violent group who'd killed him and attacked them with acid were the ones to fear—not Kyber's police. The loyalists had appeared out of nowhere before. Just as likely, they could do it again.

Heads down, she and Ty made their way through the crowds. As they neared the front gate of the dock area, they drew a few curious glances but that was all.

The exit loomed. Beyond was freedom.

Ty's grip on Bree's hand tightened. Those last few feet were the worst.

She fought the urge to break into a run. As she and Ty passed by the bored-looking gate guard, she imagined everyone within five miles could hear her heart beating.

Then they were out of the dock and on the street proper. Her held-in breath rushed out. But the flight to safety was just beginning.

Ty took her hand again. She didn't ask again how he knew where to go. She'd asked the question earlier, and he'd explained mysteriously that he knew the layout of many cities, although he'd never visited them. She understood. As a fighter pilot, she knew every airplane and helicopter in the world from memory without having flown most of them.

They walked through a warren of dark, narrow streets.

The air reeked of overcrowded humanity: smoke, garlic, sweat. Stores hawked items using digital price displays and flashy holographic ads. Ty searched the signs, looking for a promising place to stay.

Here, the buildings clustered so tightly together that they blocked the starry sky. Walls of brick or stone transformed to laser-bright ads or exploded into three-dimensional, holographic images before morphing into other, decorative textures. Ty didn't seem to notice, but the barrage made Bree feel as if she'd stayed too long at a carnival midway. Her nerves were raw after a while. She felt jumpy, overstimulated. She supposed that's how someone from the Civil War might have felt, if brought to the twentieth or twenty-first centuries and face-to-face with billboards and televised entertainment.

A few locals had set up temporary cookeries outside their shops, open late at night the way Bree remembered from the Korea she once knew. One woman dipped a ladle into a tub of batter and poured it onto the red-hot top of a metal drum. Working quickly, she swirled the batter around until it simmered. As it cooked, she threw in a handful of prepared meat and vegetables. With a spatula, she deftly folded it into a tube with closed ends, wrapped it in paper, and handed the bundle to a waiting customer. Then she started all over again.

Bree planted her boots, forcing Ty to stop. "Cover me. I'm buying us some of that."

Ty glanced up one side of the street and down the other, and gave her a nod. She paid for three of the stuffed pancakes—one for her, two for Ty—and a couple of bottles of juice. They huddled close to the building and began to eat.

While Ty wasn't as desperately hungry as he was the night he'd come to dinner in Kyber's apartment, Bree could tell he wanted to shove the food into his mouth but held back for fear of offending her. "You're starving, Ty," she mumbled, her mouth full. "Eat as fast as you want. Who cares about manners!"

He glanced up. "Mmm?"

"No! Don't stop. Eat." She chuckled. "Listen to me now. I sound just like my grandmother Vitale."

Ty wolfed down his food, but never fully lost his veneer of manners. The Ax and his wife had been taskmaster parents, apparently.

Bree couldn't eat fast enough. Gravy dripped from the wrapper onto her wrists. Only the scalding center of the pancake slowed her down. But she'd eaten less than half of hers when Ty wiped his hands on his shirt and swallowed his last bite. "Good," he grunted in true caveman fashion, and lifted the juice drink to his mouth.

Her attention was still on Ty's face when she saw his expression change abruptly. He lowered the bottle, his gaze tracking upward. "It's back. . . ."

Bree spun around. The billboard across the street was white. Bright white. Then a voice erupted, rumbling like thunder: " 'These are the times that try men's souls. The summer soldier and the sunshine patriot will in this crisis shrink from the service of his country; but he that stands now deserves the love and thanks of men and woman. Tyranny, like hell, is not easily conquered.' "

"Holy Christmas," Bree whispered.

" 'Yet, we have this consolation with us: The harder the conflict, the more glorious the triumph. What we obtain too cheap, we esteem too lightly; it is dearness only that gives everything its value.' That, my friends, is what Thomas Paine told his fellow revolutionaries more than five hundred years ago. And I bring his words to you now. Rise up! Rise up! Let this be the shot heard around the world!"

"It's like a telemarketer calling during dinner," she said, her mouth full.

"Tele . . . marketer?" Ty asked. "What's that?"

"Thank you," she said to his puzzlement. "You have just made the future a better place."

"Some will tell you to ignore my call to arms," the voice declared, rising in volume. "If you do, remember this: Those who give up essential liberty to preserve a little temporary safety deserve neither liberty nor safety; those who expect to reap the blessings of freedom must undergo the fatigue of supporting it. Now that you have won your liberty, Banzai Maguire, you must win freedom for us all!"

What the hell?

Bree's pancake fell to the sidewalk with a soggy thump.

"Let's go," Ty said, grabbing her. He strode away from the pancake stand at a near run, his arm tight over her shoulders.

"Did you hear that? It said my name."

He tucked her face against his chest, shielding her, but that made it hard to walk without tripping over her feet.

"I don't want to be involved with this," she mumbled, her mouth crushed against his shirt.

The voice continued to echo all around them. Some of the vendors had shut off their billboards, but many were still on. She cast a furtive glance at the people milling around her. She would have thought any calls to rise up would cause alarm in a foreign state, but most of the pedestrians appeared to treat the voice exactly like that telemarketer who called at dinnertime—an annoying entity they tried to ignore. Or, maybe they recognized it as she did: a message meant for UCE, and not them.

"Banzai Maguire!" She cringed at the sound of her name booming in the crowded streets. "I am well aware of the toil and blood it will cost you to come to me, but come to me you must. Hear my words; heed my call. I will be waiting for you, Banzai Maguire."

Bree exchanged a panicked glance up at Ty. "All I di
was sleep through two centuries. Now this person thi
I'm a hero."

"I did my duty, that's all," she remembered telli
ber at the palace. *"I'm nothing special."*

"You are the stuff of legends, Banzai," he'd

And Joo-Eun had insisted, *"The shadows*
succeed."

Succeed in what? Shivering, Bree swea
time, her stomach filled with butterflies

"In what destiny has brought you here to do."

She cringed at Joo-Eun's conviction. This wasn't Bree's fight. She wasn't from this world. She was Bree Ann Maguire, the daughter of an auto mechanic and a stay-at-home mom, a small-town tomboy with a keen sense of competition and a heart full of patriotism. Give her a mission plan and she'd fight courageously to the death, because that's what she'd pledged the day she received the gold lieutenant's bars on her shoulders. But lead a revolution? Was that what the owner of the voice wanted? She wasn't qualified to lead a campaign of that magnitude, let alone to inspire anyone to fight a revolution—and she didn't want to be.

Those who give up essential liberty to preserve a little temporary safety deserve neither liberty nor safety; those who expect to reap the blessings of freedom must undergo the fatigue of supporting it. Bree shrank from the voice's

ation. The American flag waved behind her eyes . . .

her. *The summer soldier and the sunshine pa-*

crisis shrink from the service of his coun-

ds now deserves the love and thanks

he white screens returned

strians who had been

n several imperial

ced a storefront. Trying

nded to look at the window display of holographically enhanced clothing. Ty's face was shadowed, but she knew a mask of indifference hid his fear of recapture. It would not go well for Ty, if that happened. And who knew what would happen to her?

But the guards strode past, talking and laughing.

"Come on." Ty took her by the arm and urged her across the street. "We've got to get out of the open."

"The Celadon," she whispered.

"Yes."

On a small television sitting on the ground next to a man stirring a boiling pot of noodles, the news showed a scene of jubilation. Ty slowed to watch the crowd cheering a screen of solid white.

Hanging from a tall flagpole over the crowd was a huge flag Bree recognized as the UCE banner—a white globe on a blue square in a field of solid red. "It's coming from the UCE," Ty confirmed. His shock melted into acute dismay and then reluctant acknowledgment. "The central colony, where the boycotts started. What you knew as the United States."

A narrator said, "For a fourth consecutive day, a broadcast has interrupted communication across a broad area. President Beauchamp today called the speeches 'a revolting example of Interweb terrorism.' "

So many people, Bree thought. The camera panned over streets and streets of them. Those close to the camera yelled; some shook their fists; others cheered; a few even cried. So many emotions. She could feel the passion rising off them like steam from boiling water. And in the midst of it all, she saw someone in the crowd of protestors lift a flag, an American flag, and wave it slowly back and forth.

The sight hit Bree like a fist in the stomach. It was something from the past—her past. It didn't belong in this turbulent demonstration in a futuristic city. And yet, somehow, it did. "Old Glory" was a symbol all at once incongruous and poignantly familiar waving above the protestors. Did these people understand what those stars and stripes meant? Did they know how many had bled to keep that flag waving?

She did!

That's why the voice wants you.

Averting her eyes, she winced and turned her head. That's when it hit her that Ty stood at her side, her hands crushed in his. On opposite sides, she and Ty were in this together.

Something very close to real emotion pressed behind her eyes, but she caught herself before the ache could turn into tears. She'd spent the past few weeks entombed in blessed numbness. But that protective cocoon had just ripped wide open.

The narrator droned on in a tone that was an oddly subdued counterpoint to her boiling emotions and the crowd's vehemence. "Listening to the speeches will only encourage its organizers, the president warned. All suspected agitators will be tried for treason."

Treason? Bree turned to Ty and said, "He means me."

Chapter Sixteen

Autumn in northern Asia brought chilly nights. Tonight was no exception. It didn't help that the so-called Cheju Precinct was on the opposite end of town. And so they'd walked on through the night, the air growing damper and chillier with each passing hour. Bree had completed a number of intense survival courses as a cadet and later as a pilot, but never did she remember feeling so low. Hunger and exhaustion had allowed the cold to burrow deep inside her. By the time she and Ty reached Cheju, located on the fringes of the city proper, it was on the dawn side of midnight and shivers wracked Bree's body.

Here, inns were few and far between. When at last Bree read the green lettering on one humble and slightly shabby edifice called the Celadon Inn, she thought her knees would give way with relief. That is, if her legs weren't too stiff with cold to buckle.

All we have to do is get safe for the night, so we can make the rendezvous in the morning.

Ty scouted out the immediate area with keen soldier's eyes before pushing open the door and following her inside. The place was part bar, part eatery, chaotic with noisy patrons. The air was damp, and scented thickly with garlic and white pepper. Bree tried to soak up the warmth, but her shaking wouldn't stop. Her cold seemed to go much deeper, settling in a place where warmth couldn't reach.

Music played, more of a synthesized throb than a melody. It was a young crowd. She couldn't help wondering about them. Were they shadow people or regular locals? Bree's instincts told her they were normal citizens, but then she'd been wrong about Joo-Eun.

Those patrons not eating were engaged in loud conversations; others interacted with screens flickering with a variety of 3-D images. As her eyes adjusted to the dim light, she noticed that the game players wore hats with glasses and headsets, and had covered their hands with thin gloves. Wireless virtual reality.

It was just another late night in New Seoul. And while she and Ty looked disheveled, no one seemed to care.

An ancient-looking woman appeared out of the crowd. Her skin was seamed and leathery. Where the flesh covered the tops of her hands and neck, it was almost transparent, revealing a network of blue, coiled veins. Life expectancies reached to the mid-100s now. Bree clocked this woman at no less than 130.

Yet the old woman's eyes were discerning and bright as she scanned Bree and Ty's ragged appearance. Her nostrils flared—with recognition or at the odor, Bree didn't know, but sagging lids masked her eyes and what hints they held.

"A room if you have one," Ty told the proprietor.

To Bree's joy, she nodded. "You want food, too?"

"Yes," Bree answered, maybe a little too eagerly.

"But you clean up first, or I won't serve you. Come." The old woman turned and walked away.

Bree and Ty followed. "How much?" he asked when she handed them something the size of a memory stick that Bree assumed was a room key.

"Twenty-five. Includes both of you."

One hundred credits were all Bree had. Total. Twenty-five was a lot to spend the first night out, but they needed shelter. Teeth chattering, she paid for the room.

They tromped up a narrow, dark staircase. It was cold in the building, too, she was dismayed to discover. Ty unlocked the door. They spilled into the room and he locked the door behind them. The lights came on automatically.

Bree stood there, shivering. Cold had settled so deeply inside her that she wondered if she'd ever feel warm again.

Ty pulled their pistol from his pocket and laid it on the bed. "So we'll be ready no matter who stops by to welcome you to town."

"G-good." She tossed her travel pack on the bed next

to the pistol. "I've got to get warm. Wh-where's the shower?"

In the harsh, halogen-bright light, Ty looked down at her face. At the sight of his shock, she coughed out a weak laugh. "By the expression on your face, I must look pretty bad."

"Your lips are blue. Why didn't you say something?"

"The chattering teeth weren't a c-clue?"

Ignoring her, Ty crouched in front of her. "Boots," he said. She gave him her feet, one at a time. He threw the boots in a corner. Then he shoved a chair against the door, followed by a table, wedging the furniture together. Finally, he strode to the bathroom, and then she heard the hiss of water. He came out and pointed. "Go."

He was so serious that it was almost scary: Commander Armstrong ordering his troops into action. She hoped she'd never end up on the shooting end of his rifle. Teeth clattering, she gave him a stiff salute. "Y-yes, sir," she said and followed him into the bathroom.

She'd learned something else about him. When he was worried, he became cold and businesslike. Strangely, she remembered the image she'd watched of his father, striding to a waiting car. Was that man's icy demeanor due to his worry about his son? Did even the "Ax" fret about his babies?

That "baby" was a tall, dripping-wet SEAL now hunched over a bathroom sink in a third-rate inn in the wrong part of town. Ty scooped water into his mouth, rinsed, and spat, and then splashed handful after handful of soapy water onto his face, scrubbing it into his hair until he was soaked from the shoulders up.

He straightened, tossing back his head as he expelled a gust of air. Then he lifted the hem of his shirt to his face and dried off, exposing the whipcord-lean, tightly muscled body of a professional soldier.

Steam billowed in the small space. Bree's clumsy fingers hadn't made much progress with the buttons on her overtunic. She was shaking too severely to focus on one button at a time. Since it was her only outfit, ripping it off was out of the question. "Screw it," she muttered, and stepped into the shower fully dressed.

Warm water gushed down onto her. She lifted her face, closed her eyes, and backed against the tiled wall. She didn't know if it was from the relief of finally being inside and out of imminent danger, or the sheer pleasure of the water, but her legs felt like rubber, and she almost sagged to the floor.

Two strong hands grabbed her upper arms. "Don't pass out on me."

"I wouldn't care." Her speech was slurred. She sounded drunk. "I'd be warm. . . ."

Eyes closed, she heard him tap the icon that controlled the water temperature. The spray got hotter. "Take off your clothes," he said in a no-nonsense tone.

She opened her eyes. Ty stood under the deluge with her. Mist enveloped them in a sheltering fog, and moisture glittered on his hard, stubbly jaw. He was exactly what she needed to get her mind off everything that had happened tonight. If she were in luck, he'd feel the same about her.

"You first," she said.

Ty's expression softened with apology. "Hey . . . I didn't mean while I was in here."

"I did."

It went very silent in the shower chamber. His eyes sharpened with a different kind of hunger. She pulled his hands to her sodden collar. "Help me with these buttons."

His throat moved. For the first time, she saw his confidence waver. She'd thought he was a playboy. A bachelor stud. He didn't act like a playboy; he acted like a choirboy. She hoped it wasn't because he thought of her as something apart from a living, breathing woman. If so, she hoped he'd soon see how wrong he was.

But her condition forced him to comply: Borderline hypothermic, she needed hot water on her skin to get warm.

His strong hands undid her tunic, one button at a time. But his expression remained dead serious, as if she'd asked him to defuse a bomb.

When her top was undone, his hands spread the fabric wider, smoothing around to her ribs and down to her hips, where he hooked his fingers under her waistband and lowered the baggy trousers.

She let the shirt slide off her shoulders. Then, she undid her bra, letting it fall. Water ran over her face, streaming down her exposed body. Her nipples pinched tight from arousal and the cold. Between her legs, her pulse throbbed in a steady drumbeat, but her shivering wouldn't go away. "Hold me, Ty," she said quietly.

He drew her close to his wet body, a layer of sodden clothes between her skin and his. She burrowed closer, and a soft groan rumbled deep in his throat, his hands smoothing over her back and then cupping her butt. Her thigh grazed over a huge bulge straining his fly. So, he wasn't immune to her after all. She wrapped her arms around his hips, her cheek pressed to his drenched shirt as she greedily absorbed his body heat.

As they stood there, clinging to each other in the shower, each for maybe very different reasons, something let go in Ty. The crook of his index finger nestled under her chin, lifting her head. She saw only his parted lips as he bent his head to kiss her.

A shock of pure pleasure shot through her when their mouths touched—and surprise. Kissing Ty Armstrong was far more powerful than she'd ever imagined.

Desire scorched through her as his fingers tangled in her hair. Water thrummed against her upturned face and the back of Ty's head, streaming past their locked mouths. Ty slid his hand slid up her rib cage to cup her breast.

His rough thumb tracked back and forth over the center of her breast, and she felt the answering heat down below. The kiss turned forceful and hot, a sexy, reckless mix of growing need on her part and fading restraint on his.

Tyler Armstrong felt right in a world that felt so wrong. Period. Did she really need a better reason to make love?

She reached for his belt buckle. But he took over, throwing off his clothes with amazing speed and kicking the sodden mess out of the way. Vaguely, she wondered how they were going to make it to dinner—or even breakfast—dressed in soaking wet clothes, but she took the practical side of her and quashed it. Nothing she'd done so far since checking into this hotel had been anything close to practical.

As serious as a commando preparing to head out for a mission, he squeezed liquid soap into his hands and just as thoroughly proceeded to spread that lather over her naked body. She wasn't as cautious. With a palm full of soap, she closed her hand around his swollen member and stroked. His breath hissed in, and his body went rigid. Then he found her mouth again, kissing her hard as she stroked him. Once, twice he pushed into her hand. Then, with what seemed like a tremendous effort, he took her by the wrist and guided her away. An instant later, his soapy hand slid between her thighs. And those fingers knew exactly where to go.

Convulsively, she grabbed his wrist, her hips jerking; but not because she wanted to stop him.

She didn't want that hand to leave.

Ty responded with a throaty rumble of satisfaction, and she glimpsed his treasure hunter's grin before he brought his mouth down to kiss her. But her attention was diverted far lower, where he slipped one of his fingers, thick and hot, inside her. Her inner walls contracted, squeezing him. Immediately, he withdrew his hand; he sensed how close she was, how close they both were.

He scooped her into his arms. Water battered them, hissing and spraying. Shutting off the water with his shoulder, he walked quickly to the bed and laid her on the cool sheets. That's when she discovered she was no longer shivering.

He lay down next to her, kissing her neck as his hand tracked south. "Banzai," he whispered in her ear.

"Bree," she murmured back.

He lifted his head.

"Bree," she explained breathlessly. "That's my real name. Call me Bree."

"Bree . . ." He kissed her throat. "Mmm. A feminine name. Delicate . . ."

"And nothing like me, right?"

"No." His eyes were dark as he stroked her wet hair off her forehead. "Everything like you, sweetheart."

His warm hand smoothed up her ribs to her breast. She gave in to the pleasure of his caress, her eyes half closed. Smiling, she sighed. "You really know how to make a pilot feel like a woman. It's that playboy thing, huh?"

He groaned against her neck. "Playboy? That, Banzai, is an example of fabrication by a bored press corps. The only thing that makes me a target is my father's position as supreme military commander. Where would I find the time for that kind of socializing, even if it were true?"

Bree lifted her leg over his hip and rubbed the back of his leg with her toes. "I like that you're not a playboy. Though it does take away some of your mystique."

He gave a muffled bark of laughter.

"And since we're busting first impressions, I'm not the kind of girl who sleeps around."

"I knew that, Banzai," he replied low in her ear, slipping his hand between her legs to caress her.

"So, if you're not a playboy . . . and I'm not a loose woman, then what are we doing in bed?"

He rose up on his knees. "You'll see . . . " His voice held such carnal promise, such honest desire, that her breath caught and her toes curled.

She waited impatiently for the thrust that would carry him deep inside her. It didn't come.

Instead, Ty pushed up on his arms and gazed down at her, his face shadowed. She went still with the raw intensity in his gaze. When she'd made eye contact with him at the dinner with Kyber, and when he refused her pleas for help in finding Cam, she'd thought there was more to his hunger than the greed of a treasure hunter or the appraising study of a collector, but she wasn't sure. Now she was certain. What she saw was passion, pure and frank, radiating from the heart of a man who had real feelings for her as a person. As a woman. All of a sudden, she found it very hard to breathe.

Ty cupped her face in his hand, his eyes dark, his voice quiet. "I used to say that my job was too dangerous for me to get too involved with a woman. It served me well as an excuse. But the truth of it, Bree, is that I could never shake the feeling I was destined for something big . . . something different and wonderful." He slid one arm under the small of her back, lifting her hips. "I think I've been waiting for you."

In one firm push, he thrust all the way home.

Her fingers grasped his wet hair as he seated himself deeply inside her. Before she could decide whether to moan or sigh, his mouth found hers. Her eyes closed and her lips opened under the soft, warm pressure. As he moved inside her intimately, his tongue lovingly stroked hers, setting up two disparate erotic sensations.

She couldn't remember anyone making love to her and it feeling like this. It was more than a matter of skill; it was the tender awe he brought to the act. She willed her body to remember it all, in case life intervened and they never got another chance to repeat this.

"I've wanted you since I was ten," he whispered in her ear, bringing her thigh over his back.

"Since you were *ten?*" Her question sounded more like a gasp, but Ty was moving inside her even as he'd spoke. And the *way* he moved . . . well, what woman wouldn't lose her verbal skills?

"In a different way than this, I promise you." There was a hitch in his voice with every determined push of his hips. "I saw your biography in a war textbook. Then I found a photo on the Interweb—you, posed in front of your F-16 fighter. At Kunsan Air Base."

"You know about Kunsan?" she asked breathlessly. "About the F-16?"

His broad hand cupped her buttocks and he lifted her

toward him, deepening their contact. It was all she could do to keep her eyes from rolling back in her head.

"I know about it all." Arousal had thickened his voice, making it deeper, sexier. "Your picture remained in a place of honor for all the years I lived at home. I went to Harvard and then to medical school for a year. When the war started, I joined up. But I never forgot you."

It was the most amazing story. It made her feel even more displaced in time, but for once she didn't mind. She reached up and rubbed her thumb over the outline of his lips. The bristles of his beard pricked the pad of her finger. "Why?" she dared ask.

"Why didn't I forget you?" His mouth spread in a smile. "You're beautiful. And you can kick ass."

She grinned back at him. "Is that it?"

With a bark of laughter, he rolled her atop him. Balancing herself with hands flat on his stomach, she pressed her pelvis down, taking him inside her, as deep as he could go. Her inner muscles clamped down around him.

He made a deep growl in his throat, arching his body upward, his fingers sinking into her hips, grinding her against him. "But in person, you're much, much more," he said on a gasp of pleasure.

Bree trembled, but not from the cold. Her decision to go to bed with Ty and somehow remain unaffected had been shattered. But he wasn't having sex with her; he was making love to her. She knew enough of the former to recognize the latter.

"I never forgot you. . . ."

And she had never known him. But she'd been dreaming of someone like him, only that dream-lover had never taken on form until now.

"I've wanted you since I was ten. . . ."

With a sudden swell of emotion, she lowered her upper body, winding her arms over his shoulders to hold him close. They undulated as one, his damp beard pressed to her cheek, her lips pressed to his jaw.

"You're beautiful. . . ."

Warmth pooled in her belly, deep and low. She threw her head back and moaned. "Ah, Ty . . ."

His strong body arched between her thighs. He seemed barely in control, and when she breathed his name, he gave a short, strained hiss that told her his willpower was on the brink of splintering. Grasping her hips, he flipped her again, onto her back this time, and pressed her into the sheets. His kiss was greedy; he demanded everything she had, even what she held in reserve, both physical and emotional.

There was no talking now. Only the expression of physical need. The sensation low in her belly intensified, turning liquid. Her breaths came faster, and a low moan began deep in her throat. The pleasure reached a heart-stopping peak . . . and hovered there.

At the very moment that she came apart, he slanted his mouth over hers, stealing her cry as his thrusting hips bore her down into the sheets. His entire body went rigid for one . . . two heartbeats. He shuddered, arching his back, and then his body went slack. But they continued to rock together, slowly, until their fatigue grew so overpowering that it swamped them both.

They collapsed like two dead people. Bree felt so lightheaded, so weak, that she wondered if in fact she *was* about to die. Not a bad way to go, she reasoned, dazedly running her fingers up and down Ty's damp back.

Ty lowered the lights. "Don't shut them off all the way," she said sheepishly.

"Why? Are you afraid of the dark?" he teased.

She didn't say anything as she pulled the sheet over their legs.

Leaning on his elbow, he propped his head on his hand and scrutinized her. "Incredible. You *are*. My kick-ass girl is—"

She shoved him. "Shut up." She rolled onto her back. He was still watching her. Groaning, she flopped onto her side. "I don't like it. Being in the dark."

"The past few days that's all we've been doing, running around in the dark. You should have said something."

She sniffed. "The mission came first."

He shook his head in amazement.

"So I dealt with it, okay?" Her eyes were adjusting to the dim light in the room. Details were coming into view. It was darker than she liked, but in Ty's company she hoped it wouldn't matter. "It's . . . left over from something that happened to me when I was a kid. I'll tell you about it, but not now. Not tonight."

He drew her close. In his arms, the darkness wasn't so bad. "We all have something," he reasoned.

"What do you have?"

"You."

She lifted her head and smiled down at him in disbelief. "Me."

"Yeah. You."

"Good or bad?"

"Good," he assured her. "It's very good. But complicated."

"Hmm." She could only imagine. One of the world's most eligible bachelors secretly infatuated with a woman who existed in legend only, and then getting thrown in jail for finding her in the flesh.

"Hold me tight," she whispered. And he did.

In the dimness, they cuddled. A good sign, that. Despite what he'd revealed about his feelings, they hardly knew each other; the whole "after" business could have been awkward, but there was none of that.

Ty's fingertips wandered over the contours of her back. "In the heat of the moment, I didn't ask if you had protection," he said.

"You mean birth control."

"Yes, that. I assumed . . . I mean, I'm used to—"

"Don't worry about it." But she liked that he'd asked. That he cared. "They gave me something at the palace, along with all the other meds. It's supposed to work for six months. They said in my condition, getting pregnant wouldn't be a good idea. I didn't pay much attention to the whole explanation, really, because I didn't think I'd be doing anything with anyone that would warrant me worrying about it."

"So, you and Kyber didn't . . ."

She could tell by his pained expression and the way he braced himself that he really believed she'd slept with Kyber. "No," she said. "There was never anything between us like that." She left out the rest. She owed Kyber that.

Ty seemed inordinately relieved. Smiling, she wound her arms around his neck and angled her mouth over his. His lips were warm, his mouth moist and hot as his tongue slipped firmly between her lips. The kiss was long, slow, and tender.

"Are you warm enough now?" he murmured when she pulled away.

"Yeah. It almost makes me want to get cold again, just so you can warm me up."

She felt the rumble of laughter in his chest. "They say that man can't live on sex alone. After tonight, I'm not sure. I haven't thought about food in an hour. But if memory returns, I may have to resort to cannibalism, Banzai." He bit her neck, pretending to devour her.

They laughed, kissing. Then he pushed off the bed. "One last thing," he said, disappearing into the bathroom then returning a moment later. "I threw the clothes onto the DM rack along with the towels. They'll be ready in the morning."

"DM rack?"

"De-moisturizing rack," he explained. "It'll dry the clothes in about a minute."

"Wow. A super high-tech clothes dryer. Too bad we don't have a food maker, too." Her grin faded as he laid his pistol between their pillows, easily reached by both of them, and climbed back into bed.

"Get some rest, Bree." He tugged the blanket higher. "Don't get too comfortable, though. We're not in the UCE yet."

"*Yet*?" She came up on her elbow. " 'Now that you have won your liberty, Banzai Maguire, you must win freedom for us all.' You heard it, Tyler. You were there. This person, or group, whatever it is, is using me as inspiration to overthrow your government. And you think I'll be safe in the UCE?"

"I do."

"Argh."

"Do you think you'll be safe *here*?" he asked. "Do you think Kyber will allow you to saunter into that cave and just look under rocks for Cameron Tucker? After you escaped him? He'll have his entire army waiting for you—if they're not already camped outside this door."

"That's a comforting thought."

"It's reality, Bree."

Pride kept her from admitting that Ty was right. She was no freer outside the palace than she'd been within its luxurious walls. Prince Kyber, acting Han emperor, still controlled her—and everyone else within the borders of his kingdom. Everyone but the people who called themselves the shadows.

Battles changed minute to minute—often second to

second. She had to learn to be as adaptable on the ground as she was in the air, especially if she wanted to achieve her goal of ultimately finding out the fate of her friend. To do that, she had to shift her focus from risking all to reach the cave to doing whatever it took to make the meeting with the shadows in the morning.

Ty pulled her into his arms and kissed her to cut off any protests. Stroking her hair, he held her close. The feel of his strong, warm body was something she didn't want to argue. "I'll make sure you get to the rendezvous point," he murmured into her hair.

A peace offering, she thought; he wouldn't be biased and pig-headed about the rendezvous, at least. What happened after that, heaven only knew. "Eighth radius," she murmured wearily. "At nine."

She closed her eyes, trying not to dwell on the mysterious person summoning her, the driver who died before her eyes, and the terrifying dash across town to the Celadon Inn in the cold. But the images haunted her—and would, she knew, for a long time to come. She liked combat a lot more from behind the controls of an F-16.

Slowly, her mind shut down. As her energy dwindled to nothing, the deepest of sleep claimed her.

Bree started into heart-thumping alertness. No sound had jarred her awake; rather it was awareness that something had changed, the way a shift in the wind direction sometimes woke her when she slept with the windows open.

Ty's slow breaths rustled her still-damp hair. So

tired . . . But the feeling of change wouldn't let her close her eyes. Maybe a storm was brewing. She hoped not. Bad weather would present yet another obstacle to making the rendezvous on time.

Too weary to get out of bed, Bree peered out the window. Tall buildings blocked the sky. Then, in her peripheral vision, she glimpsed movement. To the right. Inside the room.

Something dropped silently from the ceiling and crouched down in the shadows pooling at the far wall.

Her blood ran cold. *Danger,* her senses cried.

Bree shoved Ty's arm from around her waist, pushing him away. Her fingers landed on the pistol, and she swung it around to intimidate whoever had invaded the room. But a flash of light burst from the direction of the intruder. Something thumped into the mattress. A hole of scorched cotton marred the spot where Ty's body had been seconds before.

"I owe you for that," Ty said with wild-eyed awe. He obviously had been awakened by her shove. "Now—get down!" Snatching the pistol from her hand, he lunged off the bed on one side, and she on the other.

Ty had disarmed her, Bree thought, outraged. Now, how was she supposed to help fight?

The attacker raised his weapon to fire at Ty's head. Bree grabbed a pillow, flinging it across the room before his silencer-equipped gun flashed again. If she didn't have bullets, she had bedding. As she'd hoped, the man's shot went wild. But not wild enough. Ty stumbled backward with a grunt of surprise and pain.

Ty! His name—a silent plea—pushed its way up her throat. Then he proved himself unneedful of fear, deftly shooting the weapon out of their assailant's hand.

"Lights!" Ty shouted. Illumination revealed a man wearing a mask fleeing, hoisting himself up a rope dangling from an air vent in the ceiling.

Instantly, Bree knew this was no ordinary intruder. He had "paid assassin" written all over his muscular, black-clad body. Someone must want them dead pretty badly if they'd hired a professional to do it.

Chapter Seventeen

Ty dove for the assassin's legs before the man could escape back through the ceiling. The bastard swung his legs, trying to dislodge him. Ty hung on. Razor-sharp agony shredded his upper right side. With an experienced combat soldier's detachment, he figured the bullet had entered below his collarbone, with an exit somewhere in his upper back. But his lungs felt clear, and his right arm still worked. It was his lucky day.

The assassin kicked and whipped himself around, trying to dislodge his captor. Lips peeled back with exertion and pain, Ty slammed his pistol viciously against the man's pumping legs. He heard the snap of a cracking shinbone. With a hoarse howl of pain, the killer released his handhold.

He and Ty fell to the floor and rolled.

A fist caught Ty in the chin, but he was too high on

pain and adrenaline to feel the blow. He rammed his knee into his opponent's broken leg. A cry of pain told him he'd hit his target. Then Ty brought the pistol across the assassin's face, breaking his nose.

"I don't want to kill you," he gasped. "I just want to hear who sent you to murder Bree in her sleep!" He slammed his weapon again across the bastard's face, and then a third time—bone-crushing blows. Only the black mask worn by the assassin kept Ty from a shower of blood. "Who do you work for? Tell me!"

He flipped the man onto his stomach. Straddling the assassin, he jerked an arm into a brutal lock that would keep the guy still if by some chance the broken leg and shattered nose didn't do the trick. His harsh breaths rivaled the downed assassin's in volume. Fighting naked, Ty was lucky he hadn't crushed his own balls in the process.

"Are you Kyber's vermin? Did he send you here?" Ty tore off the mask. Covered in blood, the other man's features were almost unrecognizable.

Almost.

Ty fought down a rush of bile. "Lopez. . . ." As SEALs, he and this man had spent weeks in deep cover in the Raft Cities. Later in the war, Lopez had been on Ty's team to find the mutilated UV crews. Lopez was one of the most brilliant and brutal soldiers he'd ever worked with. And, he'd thought, a friend. "Jesus. What the fuck is going on?"

Lopez gave a drawn-out moan.

"Who sent you here?" Ty's heart hammered. Pain

gripped his chest and made it hard to breathe. He blinked away the telltale black spots of blood loss and gave Lopez a vicious shake. "Who gave you a coward's orders to shoot me in the back?"

That's where the bullet would have impacted if Bree hadn't shoved him out of the way. He knew all about assassination missions. If Lopez had struck true, the next bullet would have found Banzai's head. It was the classic one-two punch: first, you got rid of my obstacles; then you hit your target. "Who was it, Lopez? Tell me! I'm your goddamned friend. Not the enemy."

"Use . . ." Lopez whispered. "Use . . ."

"Who? Speak up, soldier." He was losing Lopez to unconsciousness. He shook him hard. "Use what?"

"Use . . . UCE."

"The *UCE* sent you?" Ty reared back in shock. Everything he'd believed, everything he'd taken for granted, came crashing down around him. Yet, it all made sense. Murdering Banzai Maguire would keep that Voice of Freedom from using her for any gain. They must be scared of her. But why? And to enter the Kingdom of Asia to do this? Only one man could have given the order for such a mission. "Was it General Armstrong? Did *my father* send you?"

He thought he heard a groan in the affirmative, but when he bent down to listen, there was only silence. Lopez stared unseeing at the foot of the bed. Ty checked for a pulse. There was none.

Holy Mother of God. He'd beaten the man to death.

Beaten him out of rage. A fellow soldier. A friend.

Ty stared at the blood on his hands—his own mixed with that of a man he'd once trusted. *He tried to kill you. He tried to kill Bree,* he told himself.

But only one man could have given such orders—"Ax" Armstrong himself.

A worse and more surprising thought occurred to Ty: If his father had acted on intelligence that Banzai Maguire had escaped, he would have known that Ty was with her. And if that were true, the general would have understood that in order to take out Bree, he might have to kill Ty. Collateral damage: every mission carried the risk.

Was that all he was to his father? A calculated risk?

Revulsion and a soul-deep sense of betrayal squeezed his gut. He loved his father. But his father, it was clear, loved the UCE.

The roar in his head swelled in volume and blackness rolled over him like a tidal wave.

"Thank God." Bree leaned over him. "You're back."

It took Ty a moment to realize that he'd passed out. How long he'd been out, he didn't know. A pillow cushioned his head, but he didn't remember her putting it there—or that she'd donned her clothes and had somehow gotten him into his pants. A field dressing made of sheets and towels constricted his chest. Bree had done that. Good girl, he thought. A true soldier. Worthy of all he felt for her. Probably more.

He swallowed, panting in an effort to control the pain.

He had to stay awake. He had too much to tell her yet.

She squeezed his shoulders. He couldn't tell if her face was wet from sweat or tears. "Don't die," she whispered. "I need you."

He managed a smile. "Yeah?"

"To help me locate Cam," she replied—a little too quickly.

"That's all?" He gave a pain-filled laugh.

Her shoulders sagged. Then a slight, almost self-deprecating smile curved her lips. "Well, the old me would like to think that," she admitted in a quiet voice and brought a warm hand to his cheek. "But, okay, there's more to it than that." Her throat moved and tenderness filled her eyes. "I want you to stick around," she whispered. "And by God, you will if I have anything to do with it, Tyler Armstrong." Abruptly, she bent her head to tightening the dressing around his chest. "How did the UCE know I was here?"

"Oh, the UCE will have known about you for some time." He paused for a spasm of pain to pass. "Especially if Kyber mentioned it to them. And he would have, I think. He'd gloat over you like he did me. And when the voice started using your name, you became a real threat to them. To the UCE."

"The voice? That was tonight! How could they react so fast?"

"The broadcasts have been going all week. I doubt tonight was the first time it mentioned your name."

"Mentioned?" She shook with uncertainty and anger. "It summoned me. You heard it."

"Yes. And so did everyone else. Special Ops has probably been in the kingdom for weeks, working on getting me out, covertly, while the aboveboard negotiations took place."

"Even so. How would they find us so fast? I thought we got out under cover."

"They could be working with the shadows. Or have informants in the group."

"Check Lopez," he said, his breathing labored. "See if he brought the usual supplies."

"I already frisked him for weapons." She showed Ty a pistol she'd shoved in her waistband, one that had evidently belonged to Lopez.

"Find his meds, Bree. He'll have something I can take." He licked his dry lips. "It'll slow the bleeding. It'll keep me alive until we rendezvous with the Shadows."

"What's this?" She held up a small, chunky weapon.

"His fryer. Take it."

"His . . . what?"

"Fryer. His neuron fryer." He panted as she stowed the fryer in her pants pocket. *Stay with her, Armstrong. Stay conscious,* he told himself. "Doesn't kill. Knocks out an assailant. Erases short-term memory." He stopped to take a breath, fighting off the encroaching blackness. "Look under the belt for the med kit—inside his uniform."

"Eureka," she cried, tearing open the pouch. "What do you need? What do I give you first?"

"The patch. Unseal it, then press it under my chin. Make sure the spikes puncture my skin. It'll release nanomeds. Slow the internal bleeding."

The room spun, and he felt lighter than air, as if he were floating. And he was cold . . . so cold. The tremors that had so far remained in his abdomen had spread to his limbs.

"You're shivering," she said. "You're losing too much blood. But then you know that. You're the one who was premed. You know how serious this injury is. Why aren't the meds helping?"

"Takes time." He lifted a leaden arm and brushed his knuckles across her cheek. "It's okay, sweetheart. It's okay."

"My guts are twisting, Ty. Will we be able to stop the bleeding? Will I lose you before I can get you to a doctor? Where will I ever find a doctor who won't turn us over to Kyber? And you tell me it'll be okay?" She looked sick to her stomach with worry. Her dread-filled gaze shifted to the door. "I'll go find a doctor. I'll get you care. The Shadows will help us."

"Will they? The shadows facilitated your escape, but maybe we should question that. Who can we trust? What if they're undercover operatives of the UCE and not rebels? Lopez found us here . . ."

She appeared to struggle with that. "We have to put our trust in someone. They've done nothing so far to indicate they're trying to hurt us. Do you think they would have brought us all the way to New Seoul just to be in this hotel room for their man to come through the ceiling?"

Ty shook his head. "I don't know what my father

is capable of anymore," he said wearily. "And yet, I can't blame him."

Bree's cheeks reddened with anger. She seemed surprised. "How could a man pay someone to kill his only child?"

"He stands to lose far more than a son if this call to revolution takes hold." The sights and sounds of the demonstration roared back into his skull. "It's haunted me, Bree, that scene we watched on the news. And, to my alarm, it stirred me."

Bree paused. Then, "Me, too," she whispered.

In thirty years spent as the son of a powerful man, and as an officer serving his country, he'd never seen anything like what he'd witnessed last night. Lopez's appearance confirmed what he already knew in his gut: He and Banzai were witnessing the birth of something that would change the world.

And Bree Maguire was the rallying point.

"I can't help thinking I'm committing treason to even think this way. Treachery is not in my blood," he said, almost as if compelled to convince himself of it. "I'm a loyal soldier."

"You *are*," she said, her eyes filling. "That you were moved by what you saw doesn't mean you're a traitor."

"Then what am I, Bree? What am I if not a soldier of the UCE?" He felt lost, truly lost, for the first time in his life.

She rested her hands on his. "Now you know how I feel. When I realized I could no longer be a USAF pilot,

I didn't know what I would do that would give any meaning to my life. Maybe . . . maybe this is it. Maybe it is for you, too."

He grimaced, both from the pain of his wound and the turbulence of his emotion. "I took an oath. I swore to defend the laws of my country."

"Ty, tell me the truth. Do you think the men you serve are representative of the people you protect? They're not elected, from what I understand. They're appointed. Including your president."

"Appointed, yes. By other appointees."

"Exactly." She used a towel to wipe her hands clean of blood. "While you were unconscious, I started thinking of my great-grandmother. I admired her greatly. She was a true patriot, and I learned a lot from her. She'd been imprisoned once, like me—though they didn't call it that—but she never let her love for her country die. Just because I'm a hundred-and-seventy years from where I started out, doesn't mean I should, either. It's twenty-one seventy-six. Like *seventeen*-seventy-six. I don't think it's a coincidence. Fate brought me here for a reason." Bree's gaze softened. "My great-grandmother used to tell me a favorite quote of hers—'don't be afraid of death. Be afraid of the unlived life.' Maybe that's what I was—afraid. I wanted nothing to do with the voice or its call to arms because I was sure I wasn't up to the task. That I couldn't possibly influence things on such a grand scale. But I must be capable of helping, Ty, in a bigger way than I ever wanted to admit, or the powers that be wouldn't be trying so hard to kill me."

Her chin lifted. " 'I serve in the forces which guard my country and our way of life. I am prepared to give my life in their defense.' I am, Ty. If the voice is calling me, I want to go to it. Its preaching is a return to the country my great-grandmother loved. I want that country back."

"I think the people in the UCE do, too," he said. He'd known from the start that her reappearance would inspire and motivate—it was the excuse he'd given himself when he decided to go in search of her—but never had he imagined this. The attempt on her life had just demonstrated quite graphically that she wasn't only his to have anymore; she belonged to the world. For the first time, he grasped the awesome responsibility that lay in his hands. And he knew what he had to do.

He stroked his fingertip down her cheek. He was sluggish. It was getting harder to move. He began to have his doubts about the nanomeds and their effectiveness. "I will stay with you in whatever you decide to do."

She bent down and kissed him, drawing away slowly.

He'd go with her as her protector, wherever that duty would ultimately bring him. *Treason!?* Perhaps. But after what he'd witnessed tonight on the news, what right did he have to change the momentum of world events before he had all the facts? The winds of change were upon them all, and he was in the eye of the storm. "You have to live, Bree. I'll stay with you to make sure you do."

He heard the overwhelming weakness in his voice, and it made a mockery of his vow. Why hadn't the nanomeds helped? Was he too far gone for them to work? "Bree, listen to me. If . . . if I don't make it, we need a contingency plan."

"Stop that. You're going to make it, you big dumb SEAL." Her joke was at odds with the alarm in her eyes.

"Bree, if I don't," he began again. "Don't go to the UCE for any reason. You won't be safe there."

She nodded. "I can only imagine what it cost you to say that," she said gently.

"Keep yourself alive, even if it means going to Kyber for help."

Her mouth dropped open. "Kyber? You're delirious."

There was a crash at the door. Bree whirled around, drawing Lopez's weapon as a gunman burst into the room, scattering the furniture blocking the door. Unarmed and almost unconscious, Ty could do nothing but watch.

Chapter Eighteen

Bree felt a whoosh of cold wind as a man dressed all in black strode in, a hood drawn low over his face. He was tall, powerfully built. *Another assassin*.

A thin stream of laser-sharp light burst out of the folds in his billowing cloak. Bree's finger depressed her weapon's trigger at the same time the beam impacted it. Her weapon became instantly molten hot. But she so badly didn't want to fail Ty, to be disarmed so quickly, she gripped the pistol a few seconds longer than she should have.

She stifled a yelp, dropped the pistol. She knew martial arts, but the assassin was armed. Muscles and bone didn't fare well against superheated atoms. Her right hand throbbed, angry welts preceding the blisters she knew second-degree burns would bring. But she wasn't going to lie down and surrender, no matter how bad the odds.

I will never surrender of my own free will. If in command, I will never surrender my men while they still have the means to resist.

No, she hadn't wanted this kind of attention. She'd wanted to find out Cam's fate, and either find her, or if that was impossible, go on with her life. But she now saw that there were bigger things in the world than her own little goals. As a military officer, she'd already grasped that fact. Only now did she truly understand the concept of selfless duty.

The intruder closed the door behind him, smearing something around the entry keypad—to keep others out?

Suddenly, above Bree's head, there was a noise in the air vent, from where the first assassin had come. The black-clad man at the door fired—not at her, but at the newest intruder.

A heavy body fell from the ceiling and landed in a heap at her feet. "More UCE scum," the man at the door said. "It seems I was just in time, Banzai."

She recognized the voice. She bit back her shock. "In time for what, Kyber?"

He threw off his hood, his nostrils flaring as he took in the carnage in the room. "Aren't you going to thank me?"

"Thank you." She swallowed. "For all you've done for me," she said. Her voice sounded thick with an odd mix of gratitude and panic. "But, I'm not going with you."

"Aren't you?" Dressed simply in black, dark gray tattoo patterns swirling from the outer corner of one eye down to his jaw, he didn't look like the king he was. "See this?"

he said, waving a hand at the bodies all around. "This is what you can expect in the UCE."

She said nothing. He'd come here undercover—alone, apparently; no entourage and no guards; nothing but advanced weaponry, the best money could buy in a land known for its innovative technology—and tracked her all the way to where the Shadows said she'd be safe. He had a better grip on his kingdom than she'd ever dreamed. In that instant, she both hated and admired him for it.

"I had to put down the proprietor and her security guard. No, not permanently, Banzai. Don't look at me like that. When they wake up, they won't remember that they were on their way to your room—or why."

A neuron fryer! Her heart leaped. She had one of those hidden in her pocket, thanks to Lopez.

"The noise," Kyber went on, explaining. "You did not make good guests."

"Too bad," Bree said with a frown. "If her security was better, we wouldn't have had to make all the noise."

"I doubt a simple inn's security could have stopped the powers behind this plan." He aimed the sleek gun at Ty.

Ty glared back at him, half-unconscious but his expression firm. Bree's heart twisted with his heroism. Wounded, he'd killed the assassin. Now he faced his nemesis, ready to fight despite pain and blood loss. The SEALs of her day would have been proud to have this man in their ranks.

Kyber strode past her, headed for him. "Don't touch Ty," she warned.

The prince's mouth tightened. "So, she has feelings for you, Armstrong. Feel blessed."

"I never hated you, Kyber," she blurted. "I considered you a friend."

"A friend." He made a face. "How sweet." Then he aimed his pistol at Ty. "This will cook your brain before you have the chance to say ouch. So don't try anything." He glanced at Bree. "Sit on the bed where I can keep an eye on you. Move!" he growled when she was slow to respond.

She walked, sullenly, where he directed. As she passed Kyber, she thought she saw a flicker of remorse, of regret. "I'm not going back with you," she told him again.

"You both are. You and Armstrong. If you think you'll be safe anywhere else, then perhaps you're too stupid to go through the trouble of saving. But you aren't, Banzai. I know you are an intelligent woman. I know you'll make the right choice."

The right choice was risking all to get to the Shadow Voice. Somehow she knew that. She met Ty's gaze. She was surprised by what she saw there. *Maybe you will be safer with Kyber*, she read in his eyes.

Frowning, she shook her head. Safety wasn't everything. And in this situation, it meant nothing. *Don't be afraid of death; be afraid of the unlived life.*

But she had to do something quick. She didn't know what time it was, but already it was growing light outside. Any more delay, and they'd miss the morning rendezvous. She began to sweat.

Kyber crouched by Ty. The emotions passing from one man to the other almost set the air on fire. They were competitors on every level. "I'm not going to kill you," the prince said with disgust. "But you'll surely do it to yourself if you don't do as I say. Convince her to come back to the palace and stay there. Anywhere else, she'll be in danger. I'm sure you appreciate that." Kyber's gray eyes turned smoky and shifted to her. He added, "I'm going to treat him in order to stabilize him for transport to my physician."

No. When he turned his attention back to Ty, Bree slowly sank her hand into her pocket and pulled out the neuron fryer. She swallowed, aimed. "So sorry," she whispered. Then she fired. Kyber stiffened and fell over.

Bree pressed her hand to her stomach, her breaths short gulps. Then she got hold of herself. "We've got to go. Now!" she said to Ty.

To her amazement, Ty staggered to his feet. "The nanomeds," he whispered. "I do believe they'll keep me alive until we reach the Shadows." He limped toward her, and she grabbed him by the arm.

"Let's hope they know a good doctor, because before we go anywhere or do anything, we're getting that hole in you patched up.

She gave him a hug, a long and tight squeeze that she knew made all his injuries cry out in misery. But she needed it and so did he, so she held him close for a few precious seconds longer. Then they hurried from the room, bound for their meeting with the Shadows, and armed with the most coveted gift of all: freedom.

Chapter Nineteen

The warm Indian Ocean swelled in front of the small borrowed ship, a speck on a seemingly endless expanse. Bree lifted her hand to shade her eyes from the setting sun. The familiar tug of the machine gun slung over her shoulder and the knife strapped to her thigh reassured her that for this night at least, she'd be safe.

Their craft might be small, but their arsenal was enviable. And Ty had proved to be a memorable instructor—in this era's high-tech weaponry, and many other things.

Aside from some soreness and stiffness, the only visible sign of Ty's gunshot wound was a protective bandage-like patch and a temporary sling. And her? A patch of puckered skin on her palm marked the place where Kyber's pistol had burned her. A small battle scar, she thought. Perhaps the first of many. She had the feeling the months ahead would be loaded with danger—of all kinds.

"We'll go to the Raft Cities," Ty had told her, and that's what they were doing. "It's not a country. It's the lawless stronghold of the pirate lords. We beat them back in the war, but their kind survives."

"If you fought them, I can't see them being too happy to see you."

One corner of his mouth had quirked, and she had almost seen the string of memories in his ice-blue eyes. "I have a friend there. A pirate. And he owes me."

So that's where they were headed. After they'd met the Shadows and been tended by their physicians. After they'd learned more of the Shadows' plans.

Ty joined her at the rail, his hands sliding around her waist from behind. Both he and Bree stood gazing out at the sea, the two of them lovers of open spaces—she of the sky, he of the water.

"Now that you have won your liberty, you must win freedom for us all."

Bree opened the floodgates that held back the images of the forlorn but proud flag waving in the crowd. Her country. Her way of life. She was Banzai Maguire, the shot heard around the world. A revolution was brewing, and she was now ready to play her role in it. But it had come at the expense of a friend. Kyber had not been evil; he had just wanted more than Bree could give him. And he had wanted something that wasn't right for her.

Ty's finger landed on her lips and traced her pout. "You'll find Cam. Put away the guilt. And whatever happened in your past will have to stay in the past. I speak from experience. We have too much to deal with now. But we won't forget her."

The past? The guilt? He meant her little brother's death.

Ty so startled her with his insight that Bree almost jumped out of her skin. No one but Cam had ever talked like that to her. And she'd never expected it from a guy. The men she'd known before were always all too grateful that she'd never pushed them into long, touchy-feely discussions on "feelings." Only Cam, whose recognition of Bree's reluctance to let others see her inner feelings had started them down the path to becoming best friends, had.

Cam. Cam, who'd been able to draw her out, and to whom confidences had finally become easier. That was one reason Bree missed Cam so damn much. That, and because they both shared the code of warriors.

Had she found a similar kind of friend in Ty?

Had she found more?

Only time would tell.

She leaned back into Ty's arms. "You can still change your mind, you know. You don't have to do this." She knew it challenged everything he'd once stood for, joining her in this quest. There was so much they still didn't know.

"I'm a treasure hunter," he replied as heartily as always. "I love a good challenge. And this is going to be much too interesting a voyage to stand missing. Imagine, being the first to see the face behind that voice."

The Shadow Voice. The Voice of Freedom. The man or woman who'd begun a revolution and wanted Banzai at the forefront. That was a lot to ask. But now she had help. Ty had pledged himself, and Bree began to feel hope. Things would turn out okay. It was just going to be a long road to get there.

Ty's words trailed off as rafts owned by his pirate friend appeared on the horizon. A steady breeze stirred Bree's hair as the ship sped toward an immense floating city. From there, in safety, they'd follow the plan they'd determined. They'd reach the Shadow Voice and, maybe, change the world.

Epilogue

And thus I obtained my freedom from Kyber's kingdom and seemed to have met my soulmate. Everything seemed all right. I was on my way to the Raft Cities, where a pirate owed Ty a favor. But ahead I still had a world to conquer and a heart to lose.

Finding the Shadow Voice would not be easy, nor would my navigation of the many twists and turns of a new love. Although I didn't recognize it then, I had much yet to learn. My incredible journey was only half over. . . .

Turn the page for a sneak preview of
the next installment in the *2176* series. . . .

Day of Fire

by

Kathleen Nance

Coming in May!

Prologue

Canada
Year of our Lord 2176
Post Epidemic Year 106

"Tyranny, like hell, is not easily conquered."

The ancient quote blasted across the Saskatchewan prairie, slicing the predawn vastness like an icy javelin. Settling her hat firmly on her head, Day Daniels studied the source through her sight goggles, then gave an irritated huff.

She was out here at three A.M. following a lead to the No-Borders. She'd expected to infiltrate a clandestine meeting of armed men.

This, she had not expected.

She lowered the goggles, then blinked to warm her eyeballs. Her breath formed a steady white mist in the teeth-numbing cold, while she assessed the situation.

An enormous, concrete moose stood in the fallow wheat field near the TransConnect train station. Mac the Moose, enduring symbol of Moose Jaw, Saskatchewan, all ten meters, nine tons of him. His nose was pressed against a green wooden grain elevator, another historical relic. The elevator, newly restored before the first Viral Epidemic, now showed the gaps of neglect. Not so Mac.

Tied to the moose was a sign, a single scarlet word: Revolution. Two teen-aged boys, their down jackets aflap in the freshening wind, balanced on the moose's back. Probably aiming their message to the TransCanada Connect trains, Day decided. The boys' handhelds hung from the moose's antlers, blaring their message into the gray stillness.

"The days of our deliverance draw nigh."

Scraping a nail across the comm patch behind her ear, she signaled to her backup, Luc Robichaux. Her body went on hold for a second, until at last Luc returned the signal, sending a faint vibration to the patch.

"I'm a kilom from the Connect station," he said, sounding breathless. Good thing he was retiring next week. "Coming up the rails. What's your situation?"

"I'm looking at Mac the Moose. Couple of lads on his back, maybe hopped up on something, since they don't seem to be feeling the cold."

"A prank and not the No-Borders? We're out in this hibernating cold because of a stupid prank?"

She took another look at the painted sign. "Maybe."

They were definitely out here because of youthful rashness, but the purpose seemed more earnest than prankish. Still, this was definitely not the work of the vicious No-Borders.

"The oppressions of the colonizers have planted the seeds of revolt."

"What's that?" Luc asked.

"Some broadcast from their computers." The broadcast voice was strange—sexless, but impassioned; human, but disguised. Compelling and persuasive. Dangerous.

She frowned. Faceless, mechanized messages—especially a lawless message of revolt—meant brewing trouble. Time to find out a little more what prompted this display of teen-aged stupidity.

"Wait for me, Day." Luc's cautionary words came before she took a step.

"Sure," she responded.

"I'll have your hat if you do this alone."

"Just reconnoitering." Annoyed, she signaled an end to the communication. That's what happened when you worked with a guy for three years: He got to thinking he could predict you.

Annoying as hell when he was right.

Her boots crunched on the remnants of wheat stalks as she strolled closer to the moose. Reaching its base, she placed one boot on a cloven hoof, then tilted her head back, her braid swinging free. "Hey, boys, what are you doing up there?"

A mix of curses—both English and French—came in response, ending with a fear-filled, "Vic, it's a Mountie!"

"She's puck-sized," came the scornful reply from the bigger of the two. "And a chick."

"I don't care if she's short or a woman, look at the hat. She's a *Mountie*."

She got tired of the chatter. "Yep, I'm a Mountie, boys. You didn't really think we weren't going to be called in, now, did you? A moose this big gets noticed."

"That's why we took it," shouted down Vic. He was the one who'd called her a chick. "Nobody can ignore us."

"Out here?" she asked, gesturing to the open prairie.

"We Canadians don't gather anymore, but everyone on the Connect trains will see our cause."

"What cause would that be?" Day crossed her arms.

"Freedom! For the world! The Voice of Freedom spoke last night!"

"The Voice of Freedom? I assume that's what I'm hearing on your handhelds."

"We burnt it into a chip, so we could play it over and over."

Oh, fabulous. Day rubbed her neck, stiff from looking upward. "You got your message there. Now, time for you two to come down." She glanced around. Except, how had they gotten up there?

The explanation came swiftly. "Our mates took away the ladders. We're not leaving 'til we have our say." They stood, feet spread and defiant, scowling down at her.

From the corner of her eye, Day could see the first tinges of light in the east. Along the horizon, dust spun in a miniature tornado. Wind bit at her cheeks. She frowned and activated her comm. "I'm going up the grain elevator, Luc. See what I can find out." She needed to be closer. See if she could persuade them off that damn moose.

"I'm almost there. Wait—oh, why do I bother?"

"*Join the revolution.*" The pair kept broadcasting their messenger of sedition, oblivious to the rising of the wind.

"Like hell," Day muttered back to the impassioned voice as she scrambled inside the dilapidated grain elevator. Anarchy, even when spouted to the ghosts of an empty prairie, was still anarchy.

Not waiting for her eyes to adjust to the gloom, Day balanced on the first bucket of the elevator leg, the central shaft that had once conveyed grain from wagons up to the storage bins. She hefted herself upward, arms dragging her half the distance to the next bucket, then her feet scrambling to balance on the swaying rim. Steadily, she climbed, shifting from one bucket to the next. Her breath led the way in white puffs of effort. At least it was still in here, dry and cold and motionless as the inside of a crypt.

Except for that damned voice.

Grain dust—not even the centuries could rid the elevator of it all—tickled her throat, and she swallowed against the irritation. Her fingers and shoulders ached from gripping the elevator, pulling between the gaps of missing or broken buckets, and catching herself from a fall when one shattered beneath her boots. The ache turned to burning, as her arms and legs protested the strain, but she kept moving. Her heart drummed against her ears—damn, but she was getting to sound like Luc.

Still, the image of the two boys on the back of a moose, with no way down except a three-floor fall, propelled her up. Once at the top, she dragged air into her lungs. *Be it All, Do it All, Day.*

Steadying herself, she perched in the tiny door of the grain elevator, where once the chute reached out to the trains stopping for their load of grain. The end of her braid whipped around her neck. The wind was getting worse.

The lads were still standing on the moose. Dear Lord, they were younger than she'd realized. Barely into secondary level.

Vic spied her. "Get away!" he shouted, scrambling wildly backward. "We're not leaving."

"Not leaving!" echoed the other, shivering in the dropping temperature.

Demanding they get off the moose wasn't going to work. Keep them calm. Gain a measure of their trust. Day forced herself to relax against the window frame, even as adrenaline revitalized her muscles, and she mouthed to her comm, "Get air rescue here, Luc. And a bounce pad."

"Understood."

Nonthreatening and conversational was the way to start. "Just thought it would be easier to chat up here. What are you revolting against?"

"Why should we tell you?" Vic asked.

"Because with a two-meter-square sign announcing revolution, I'm assuming you want people to know. You might as well start with me; I'm the only one listening."

"Oppression," answered the smaller one. "We're fighting oppression."

She turned her attention to him. "What's your name?"

"Don't tell her," said Vic with a tremble in his voice. "Don't tell her anything. Mounties get the evidence, and they convict you then and there."

She gestured to the moose. "I'd say you two already provided the evidence, ten meters of it. All I want is to know who I'm talking to. First name's okay. Mine's Day." She'd already scanned their images and sent them to Depot. She'd have more info than just names momentarily. "So, what's yours?" she asked again.

"André."

"*Bonjour*, André." She nodded acknowledgment, then bent her knee and propped one foot on the moose's nose. The wooden window sill where she perched bit into her rear as she bent forward. Out of the protection from the elevator, the wind drove the cold against her cheeks and tugged apart her tight braid. She let none of her discomfort show. "Tell me about this Voice of Freedom. Who is it?"

The boys exchanged glances. "We don't know, but the message is exciting."

"I'd have a tough time trusting anyone who distorted their voice and hid from folks," she suggested.

"It's for safety," insisted André loyally. "Until the strength of the oppressors can be met."

"Who's oppressing you?"

A moment's silence followed.

"It's not *us*. It's the world. The UCE. We can't ignore the suffering," André explained.

Day nodded as if the logic made sense, and she gestured to the sign. "So, you're leading a revolt against the Dominion of Tri-Canada?

Vic snorted. "Canadians don't revolt."

"Then why the sign?"

"To support those who *will* revolt. Listen to the Voice."

She'd had enough listening. Maybe a revolution was coming, but it was none of Tri-Canada's affair. The world had turned its back on Canada during the Epidemics; now Canada had no need of the world. The border laws Day upheld reaffirmed her own beliefs.

Still, she kept her opinions to herself. They wouldn't help get the boys off the moose and safe from their misguided idealism.

Jamming her hat on her head, she slid down onto the moose, straddling its nose, and signaled Luc. "Where's air rescue? This williwaw is turning lethal, and the dew slick isn't helping."

"They're almost here. I'm right below you."

She spared a glance down, where Luc paced fussily on the ground. The whir of an approaching chopper sounded.

"You stay right there, Luc."

"And do what? Block their fall with my body?"

"No, direct the chopper. Do you hear that, boys?" She pointed at the now visible aircraft. "It's someone to help you get off here."

"We won't go." The boys each grabbed for an antler, the wind catching their sudden movement. The gust sent André slipping, but he caught his fall. Day's heart skipped two beats, while her stomach tied a square knot.

"Eventually you'll have to." She forced calm to her voice. "You'll have to eat. Or pee."

"If we leave now, you'll take our sign down before the trains come through."

She pondered the complaint. "If you agree to come off, I'll leave the sign on for twenty-four hours."

"You gonna arrest us?"

"Yes. You broke the law." She ignored their twin scowls. "But, I also have the authority to assess your fine."

André paled. "We don't have any money."

"Not that kind of fine. You'll pay off your debt in information. Record everything you know about this shadowy 'voice of freedom,' anything you've heard about it, and give it to me."

"That's it?" asked André.

Vic stuck out his chin. "How do we know you're telling the truth?"

Anger coursed through her. They might be young, but they should know better. "The word of a Mountie is not questioned." She curbed her ire. "You knew the law, you knew there'd be consequences. But, you also should know I'll do what I say."

Again a moment's silence fell. The boys exchanged a glance, then nodded and let go of their respective antlers. They both started edging across the moose toward her.

"No! Wait for the air rescue—"

A polar wind swept across the prairie, carrying the frigid power of a thousand kilometers of unhindered passage. A premature harbinger of winter's gales, the gust staggered her. André slipped, his arms flailing. Day's heart skipped two beats again before he caught himself. Another gust sucked out her breath. Vic plastered down against the moose's neck, hanging on as though his life depended upon it.

Day slid across thick nose and over the head. Her jacket caught on a gigantic antler, and she heard it tear as she stretched down the neck toward Vic. She locked her ankles around the antlers for support.

The chopper finally reached them. It hovered above, its jets of directional air along the side adding to the fury of the williwaw. A ladder came down from the belly of the chopper, and another Mountie came down it, but the currents of wind were too erratic for him to be able to get off and onto the moose next to the boys. Instead, he shouted to the chopper, and they threw down a bucket and rope. He shouted at Vic to get in.

Vic was too frightened to do anything but cling to his perilous perch, shaking his head in denial.

"Get in the bucket," Day shouted to him. "I'll help you."

Keeping her gaze locked with Vic's, keeping one hand

on him for reassurance, she helped him slide over until his feet rested safely inside. She squeezed his shoulder, forcing him to look at her. "You're inside. You can't fall. Let go of the antlers and stand in the bucket. They'll pull you to safety."

Vic stared at her, the whites of his eyes huge. He clutched the antlers.

"Vic, take my hand," Day commanded firmly, and he obeyed. "Now the other."

When she had both of his hands in hers, she signaled the chopper. Gradually it moved forward, catching more of the boy; then she let go of Vic. There was a moment's panic in his face, a desperate clutch for her as he realized he was swinging up. Then the air-rescue Mountie had him in hand.

That left André. Day unwrapped her ankles from the antlers, then slid down the neck and across the back of the moose. André must have caught the movement, for he started to come toward her.

"No, André, stay there! Do not let go until—"

André slipped, scrabbling furiously and futilely against the moose, trying to stop the inevitable. Day lunged, blood raging, and threw herself forward, grabbing André's wrists as he slid down the side. His weight yanked her arms with a blazing shaft of pain. She gasped, blinded by the intense agony, and nearly lost her grip. *Be it All, Do it All*. Sheer determination kept her fingers closed around the boy.

The world narrowed. Pain in her shoulders. Straining.

André's white face. Fire down her spine. Digging in her toes and moving backward. The fury of the north battering her. Pain. André back on the moose at last. Air rescue taking advantage of a lull in the wind to close in.

Dimly, Day saw air rescue give her the thumbs-up, indicating they had André secured. One finger at a time, each tiny movement screaming, she let the boy go, then watched him swing up to the chopper.

"We're full up, Day." The air rescue team sounded in her comm. "But the bucket can swing you to the ground."

"I'd appreciate the lift." She forced herself to sit upright.

"Join in the revolution, my sons and daughters who crave liberty!" The Voice of Freedom—a voice of shadows, Day couldn't help thinking—raged on from the boys' abandoned broadcasters. As Day slid into the waiting bucket and was deposited to the wheat field, she shook her head.

Where was Luc? She opened her comm. "Luc, where'd you go?"

"I heard something at the station," he whispered. "The No-Border meeting we were expecting, I think. I'm at the container hold building."

"Luc, wait for me!"

"Unlike you, I will. Going silent."

Cradling her abused arms against her waist, she ran forward, comming Depot for more backup. Arms like this, she was virtually useless.

No lights shone in the empty station. The only sound

was the Voice of Freedom, still ranting outside. She circled the container hold building, and her feet hit something solid in the shadows. Dropping to her knees, stomach churning, she fumbled for her light.

Luc! Her partner was sprawled on his back, hat fallen to the side, his throat slashed. Choked on his own blood.

Oh, God. The pain in her shoulders was nothing compared to this.

Outside, the disguised, sexless Shadow Voice continued. *"We shall have our freedom, but beware: We shall lose good men these days."*